Isaac Asimov has been one of the most prolific and widely read authors in the field of popular science for the last twenty years. Over a hundred of his books have been published, ranging from science fiction and pure science to history, religion and geography. His work is received with equal enthusiasm by sf fans, academics and students. Dr. Asimov currently lives in New York City, devoting the greater part of his time to writing.

*Also by Isaac Asimov and available
from Sphere Books*

PEBBLE IN THE SKY
A WHIFF OF DEATH
THE BEST OF ISAAC ASIMOV
THE HUGO WINNERS Books 1 and 2 (Ed.)
WHERE DO WE GO FROM HERE? Book 1 (Ed.)

Where Do We Go From Here?

Book 2

Edited by ISAAC ASIMOV

SPHERE BOOKS LIMITED
30/32 Gray's Inn Road, London WC1X 8JL

First published in Great Britain
by Michael Joseph Limited 1973
Copyright © Isaac Asimov 1971
Published by Sphere Books (in
two volumes) 1974

Dedication

To Judy-Lynn Benjamin who is full of surprises,
birthday and otherwise

Set in Linotype Baskerville

Printed in Great Britain by
Hazell Watson & Viney Ltd
Aylesbury, Bucks

ISBN 0 7221 1251 3

Publisher's Note

In order to produce this excellent collection at a reasonable length and price, it was necessary to divide the original publication into two books. Isaac Asimov's introduction and the appendix are printed in both.

Grateful acknowledgement is made to the following for permission to reprint the articles included in this book:

'Pâté de Fois Gras' by Isaac Asimov, first published in *Astounding Science Fiction*, September 1956. Copyright © 1956 by Street
& Smith Publications, Inc. Reprinted by permission of the author.

'The Holes Around Mars' by Jerome Bixby, first published in
Galaxy Magazine, January 1954. Copyright © 1970 by Jerome
Bixby. Reprinted by permission of the author;

'The Deep Range' by Arthur C. Clarke, first published in *Stars
Science Fiction* no. 3, edited by Fredrik Pohl. Copyright © 1954
by Ballantine Books, Inc. Reprinted by permission of the author
and the author's agents, Scott Meredith Literary Agency, Inc.;

'Dust Rag' by Hal Clement, first published in *Astounding
Science Fiction*, September 1956. Copyright © 1956 by Street &
Smith Publications, Inc. Reprinted by arrangement with the
author.

'The Cave of Night' by James E. Gunn, first published in
Galaxy Magazine, February 1955. Copyright 1954 by Galaxy
Publishing Corporation. Reprinted by permission of the author
and his agents, Scott Meredith Literary Agency, Inc.;

'Omnilingual' by H. Beam Piper, first published in *Astounding
Science Fiction*, February 1957. Copyright © 1957 by Street &
Smith Publications, Inc. Reprinted by permission of the estate of
the late H. Beam Piper;

'Country Doctor' by William Morrison from *Stars Science
Fiction* no. 1, edited by Fredrik Pohl. Copyright © 1953 by
Ballantine Books, Inc. Reprinted by permission of the author;

'Neutron Star' by Larry Niven, first published in *Worlds of IF*,
October 1966. Copyright © 1966 by Galaxy Publishing Corporation. Published in *Neutron Star* by Larry Niven. Reprinted by
permission of the author and Ballantine Books, Inc.;

'The Big Bounce' by Walter S. Tevis, first published in *Galaxy
Magazine*, February 1958. Copyright © 1958 by Galaxy Publishing Corporation.

CONTENTS

Introduction   9

1. Country Doctor, by William Morrison   11

2. The Holes Around Mars, by Jerome Bixby   34

3. The Deep Range, by Arthur C. Clarke   52

4. The Cave of Night, by James E. Gunn   63

5. Dust Rag, by Hal Clement   81

6. Pâté de Foie Gras, by Isaac Asimov   102

7. Omnilingual, by H. Beam Piper   121

8. The Big Bounce, by Walter S. Tevis   166

9. Neutron Star, by Larry Niven   178

   Appendix   199

INTRODUCTION

I have long maintained that science fiction has potential as an inspiring and useful teaching device. For this anthology, therefore, I have selected seventeen stories which, I think, can inspire curiosity and can lead the student into lines of questioning of his own that may interest and excite him, and may even help determine the future direction of his career.

This is not to say that the stories are all scientifically accurate though some, of course, are indeed accurate by the standards of their times. After all, a science fiction story cannot be (except by inspired guessing) more accurate than the scientific knowledge of the time makes possible. A story written in 1925 can only by accident deal accurately with Pluto, the ninth planet; and the situation is similar in stories about the atomic bomb written in 1935; artificial satellites written in 1945; quasars written in 1955, and so on.

In many science fiction stories, a scientific principle is deliberately bent for the sake of making a particular plot possible. This can be done skilfully by an author knowledgeable in science or clumsily by another who is less well versed in the matter. In either case, even in the latter, the story can be useful. A law of nature ignored or distorted can rouse more interest, sometimes, than a law of nature explained. Are the events in the story possible. If not, why not? And in tracking that down, the student may sometimes learn more about science than from any number of correct classroom demonstrations.

This anthology is prepared, then, on several different levels.

In the first place, the seventeen stories included are all good ones, all clever and exciting in their own right. Anyone who wishes can read them for themselves alone, need make no conscious effort to learn from them, and may totally ignore my own comments after each story.

For those who would probe a little deeper, I have placed after each story a few hundred words of commentary in which I talk about the scientific points made in the story, pointing out their validity or, sometimes, explaining their errors.

Finally, after each comment, I have appended a series of suggestions and questions designed to direct the reader's curiosity in possibly fruitful directions. These are not simple, nor are they intended to be simple; sometimes indeed I ask questions that have no known answers. Nevertheless, I give no hints and there are no answers in the back of the book. I have, however, in an appendix at the end of the book, listed two items for each story that might interest anyone who found himself gripped by the science involved. The further reading may not give the answers to the questions I posed but they will answer other questions which I did not ask and they will very likely lure the reader onward.

Even this appendix, rough and non-specific though it is, I present reluctantly. I want the reader completely on his own. I don't want to give answers but to stimulate thought; I don't want to point out solutions but to rouse the kind of curiosity that may begin a self-directed drive.

There is, after all, no requirement that any reader follow up all or even any of the lines of inquiry I suggest, but a few might, out of a desire nurtured by the stories in this anthology, or even by just one particular story.

If that happens, then for each reader that finds even one thread of suggestion exciting and proceeds to lose himself in the search for knowledge, I win immensely more than I would have won by merely providing an interesting anthology.

And the involved readers win immensely more as well.

1. COUNTRY DOCTOR

William Morrison

He had long resigned himself to thinking that opportunity had passed him by for life. Now, when it struck
so unexpectedly and so belatedly, he wasn't sure that it
was welcome.

He had gone to sleep early, after an unusually hectic
day. As if the need for immunizing against the threat of
an epidemic hadn't been enough, he had also had to
treat the usual aches and pains, and to deliver one baby,
plus two premature Marsopolis calves. Even as he pulled
the covers over himself, the phone was ringing, but he
let Maida answer it. Nothing short of a genuine first-
class emergency was going to drag him out of the house
again before morning if he could help it. Evidently the
call wasn't that important, for Maida hadn't come in to
bother him about it, and his last feeling, before dropping off to sleep, was one of gratitude for her common
sense.

He wasn't feeling grateful when the phone rang
again. He awoke with a start. The dark of night still
lay around the house, and from alongside him came the
sound of his wife's slow breathing. In the next room,
one of the kids, he couldn't tell which, said drowsily.
'Turn off the alarm.' Evidently the sound of the ringing
hadn't produced complete wakefulness.

While he lay there, feeling too heavy to move, Maida
moaned slightly in her sleep, and he said to himself, 'If
that's old Bender calling about his constipation again,
I'll feed him dynamite pills.' Then he reached over to
the night table and forced himself to pick up the phone.
'Who is it?'

'Doctor Meltzer?' He recognized the hoarse and excited tones of Tom Linton, the city peace officer. 'You
better get over here right away!'

'What is it, Tom? And where am I supposed to get?'

'Over at the space port. Ship out of control – almost
ran into Phobos coming down – and it landed with a
crash. They need you fast.'

'I'm coming.'

The sleep was out of his eyes now. He grabbed his emergency equipment, taking along a plentiful supply of antibiotics and adjustable bandages. There was no way of knowing how many men had been hurt, and he had better be ready to treat an entire crew.

Outside the house, his bicar was waiting for him. He tossed in his equipment and hopped in after it. A throw of the switch brought in full broadcast power, and a fraction of a second later he had begun to skim over the smooth path that led over the farmland reclaimed from the desert.

The space port was less than twenty miles away, and it took him no more than ten minutes to get there. As he approached the light blinked green at an intersection. Ah, he thought, one advantage of being a country doctor with a privileged road is that you always have the right of way. Are there any other advantages? None that you can think of offhand. You go through college with a brilliant record, you dream of helping humanity, of doing research in medicine, of making discoveries that will lengthen human life and lend it a little added happiness. And then, somehow, you find yourself trapped. The frontier outpost that's supposed to be the steppingstone to bigger things turns out to be a lifetime job. You find that your most important patients are not people, but food-animals. On Mars there are plenty of men and women, but few cows and sheep. Learn to treat *them*, and you really amount to something. Save a cow, and the news gets around faster than if you saved a man. And so, gradually, the animals begin to take more and more of your time, and you become known and liked in the community. You marry, you have children, you slip into a routine that dulls the meaning of the fast-hurrying days. You reach fifty – and you realize suddenly that life has passed you by. Half your alloted hundred years are gone, you can't tell where. The opportunities that once beckoned so brightly have faded in the distance.

What do you have to show for what the years have taken? One wife, one boy, one girl—

A surge of braking-power caught him from the direction of the space port. The sudden deceleration brought him out of his musings to realize that the entire area

12

was brightly lit up. A huge ship lay across the middle of the field. Its length was at least a thousand feet, and he knew that there must be more than two dozen men in its crew. He hoped that none had been killed.

'Doc!'

Tom was rushing over to him. 'How many hurt, Tom?'

'Our injuries are all minor, Doctor,' said a sharp voice. 'Nothing that I can't handle well enough myself.'

As he stared at the man in the gold-trimmed uniform who was standing alongside Tom, he had a feeling of disappointment. If there were no serious injuries, what was the rush all about? Why hadn't they telephoned him while he was riding over, told him there was no need for him, let him get back to bed?

'I thought there was a serious crash.'

'The crash was nothing, Doctor. Linton, here, was excited by our near-miss of Phobos. But we've no time to waste discussing that. I understand, Doctor Meltzer, that you're a first-class vet.'

He flushed. 'I hope you didn't drag me out of bed to treat a sick dog. I'm not sentimental about ship's pets—'

'This is no pet. Come along, and I'll show you.'

He followed silently as the Captain led the way up the ramp and into the ship. Inside the vessel, there were no indications of any disorder caused by the crash. One or two of the men were bandaged around the head, but they seemed perfectly capable of getting around and doing their work.

He and the Captain were on a moving walkway now, and for three hundred feet they rode swiftly along it together, towards the back of the ship. Then the Captain stepped off, and Dr. Meltzer followed suit. When he caught sight of the thing that was waiting for him, his jaw dropped.

Almost the entire stern of the ship, about one third its length, was occupied by a great reddish creature that lay there quietly like an overgrown lump of flesh taken from some giant's butcher shop. A transparent panel walled it off from the rest of the ship. Through the panel Dr. Meltzer could see the thirty-foot-wide slit that marked the mouth. Above that was a cluster of breathing pores, looking like gopher holes, and above these

13

was a semi-circle of six great eyes, half closed and dulled as if with pain.

He had never seen anything like it before. 'My God, what is it?'

'For lack of a better name, we call it a space-cow. Actually, it doesn't inhabit free space – we picked it up on Ganymede as a matter of fact – and as you can see, it doesn't resemble a cow in the least.'

'Is that supposed to be my patient?'

'That's it, Doctor.'

He laughed, with more anger than amusement. 'I haven't the slightest idea what that behemoth is like and what's wrong with it. How do you expect me to treat it?'

'That's up to you. Now, wait a minute, Doctor, before you blow up. This thing is sick. It isn't eating. It hardly moves. And it's been getting worse almost from the time we left Ganymede. We meant to land at Marsopolis and have it treated there, but we overshot the place and then something went wrong with our drive so we had no choice but to come down here.'

'Don't they have any doctors to spare from town?'

'They're no better than you are. I mean that, Doctor. The vets they have in Marsopolis are used to treating pets for a standard series of diseases, and they don't handle animals as big as the ones you do. And they don't meet the kind of emergencies you do, either. You're as good a man as we can get.'

'And I tell you, I don't know a thing about this over-grown hunk of protein.'

'Then you'll just have to find out about it. We've radioed Earth, and hope to be getting some information soon from some of their zoo directors. Meanwhile—'

The crewmen were bringing over what appeared to be a diver's uniform. 'What's this?' he asked suspiciously.

'Something for you to wear. You're going to go down into this animal.'

'Into that mass of flesh?' For a moment horror left him with his mouth open. Then anger took over. 'Like hell I am.'

'Look, Doctor. It's necessary. We want to keep this beast alive – for scientific purposes, as well as possible

14

value as a food animal. And how can we keep it alive unless we learn something about it?'

'There's plenty we can learn without going into it. Plenty of tests we can make first. Plenty of—'

He caught himself abruptly because he was talking nonsense and he knew it. You could take the thing's temperature – but what would the figure you got tell you? What was normal temperature – but what would the figure you got tell you? What was normal temperature for a space-cow? What was normal blood pressure – provided the creature had blood? What was normal heartbeat – assuming there was a heart? Presumably the thing had teeth, a bony skelton – but how to learn where and what they were? You couldn't X-ray a mass of flesh like this – not with any equipment he had ever seen, even in the best-equipped office.

There were other, even more disquieting ways in which he was ignorant. What kind of digestive juices did the thing have? Suppose he did go down in a diver's uniform – would the juices dissolve it? Would they dissolve the oxygen lines, the instruments he used to look around and probe the vast inside of the beast?

He expressed his doubts to the Captain, and the latter said, 'These suits have been tested, and so have the lines. We know that they can stand a half hour inside without being dissolved away. If they start to go, you'll radio up to us, and we'll pull you up.'

'Thanks. How do I know that once the suit starts to go, it won't rip? How do I know that the juices simply won't eat my skin away?'

There was no answer to that. You just didn't know, and you had to accept your ignorance.

Even while he was objecting, Dr. Meltzer began putting on the suit. It was thin and light, strong enough to withstand several atmospheres of pressure, and at the some time not so clumsy as to hamper his movements considerably. Sealed pockets carried an assortment of instruments and supplies. Perfect two-way communication would make the exchange of ideas – such as they might be – as easy as if the person he was talking to were face to face with him. With the suit came a pair of fragile-looking gloves that left his hands almost as free as if they were bare. But the apparent fragility was misleading. Mechanical strength was there.

15

But what about resistance to biological action? The question kept nagging him. You can't know, he told himself. About things like that you take a chance. You take a chance and hope that if anything goes wrong, they'll pull you up before the juices have time to get working on you.

They had everything in readiness. Two of the other men were also wearing uniforms like his own, and when he had put his on, and tested it, the Captain gave the signal, and they all went into a small airlock. They were in the chamber where the great beast lay and quivered dully as if in giant pain.

They tied strong thin plastic cords around Doctor Meltzer's waist, tested the oxygen lines. Then they put a ladder up in front of the beast's face. Doctor Meltzer had a little trouble breathing, but it was not because of anything wrong with the oxygen supply. That was at the right pressure and humidity, and it was mixed with the correct amount of inert gases. It was merely the thought of going down into the creature's belly that constricted his throat, the idea of going into a strange and terrible world so different from his own, of submitting to unimaginable dangers.

He said hoarsely into the radio speaker, 'How do I get in anyway, knock? The mouth's at least forty feet off the ground. And it's closed. You've got to open it, Captain. Or do you expect me to pry it open myself?'

The two men with him stretched out a plastic ladder. In the low gravity of Mars, climbing forty feet was no problem. Dr. Meltzer began to pull his way up. As he went higher, he noticed that the great mouth was slowly opening. One of the men had poked the creature with an electric prod.

Dr. Meltzer reached the level of the lower jaw, and with the fascinated fear of a bird staring at a snake, gazed at the great opening that was going to devour him. Inside there was a grey and slippery surface which caught the beam of his flashlight and reflected it back and forth until the rays faded away. Fifty feet beyond the opening, the passage made a slow turn to one side. What lay ahead, he couldn't guess.

The sensible thing was to go in at once, but he couldn't help hesitating. Suppose the jaws closed just as he got between them? He'd be crushed like an egg-

16

shell. Suppose the throat constricted with the irritation he caused it? That would crush him too. He recalled suddenly an ancient fable about a man who had gone down into a whale's belly. What was the man's name, now? Daniel – no, he had only gone into a den of lions. Job – wrong again. Job had been afflicted with boils, the victim of staphylococci at the other end of the scale of size. Jonah, that was it. Jonah, the man whose name was a symbol among the superstitious for bad luck.

But a scientist had no time for superstition. A scientist just thrust himself forward—

He stepped off the ladder into the great mouth. Beneath him, the jaw was slippery. His feet slid out from under him, and then his momentum carried him forward, and he glided smoothly down the yawning gullet. It was like going down a Martian hillside on a greased sled, the low gravity making the descent nice and easy. He noticed that the cords around his waist, as well as the oxygen lines, were descending smoothly after him. He reached the turn, threw his body away from the grey wall, and continued sliding. Another fifty feet, and he landed with a small splash in a pool of liquid.

The stomach? Never mind what you called it, this was probably the beginning of a digestive tract. He'd have a chance now to see how resistant his suit was.

He was immersed in the liquid now, and he sank slowly until his feet touched more solid flesh again. By the beam from his flashlight, he saw that the liquid around him was a light green. The portion of the digestive tract on which he stood was slate grey, with bright emerald streaks.

A voice spoke anxiously in his ears. 'Doctor Meltzer! Are you safe?'

'Fine, Captain. Having a wonderful time. Wish you were here.'

'What's it like in there?'

'I'm standing at the bottom of a pool of greenish liquid. I'm fascinated, but not greatly instructed.'

'See anything that might be wrong?'

'How the devil would I tell right from wrong in here? I've never been in one of these beasts before. I've got sample bottles, and I'm going to fill them in various places. This is going to be sample one. You can analyse it later.'

'Fine, Doctor. You just keep on going.'

He flashed the beam around him. The liquid was churning gently, possibly because of the splash he himself had made. The grey-green walls themselves were quiet, and the portion underfoot yielded slightly as he put his weight upon it, but was otherwise apparently undisturbed by his presence.

He moved ahead. The liquid grew shallower, came to an end. He climbed out and stepped cautiously forward.

'Doctor, what's happening?'

'Nothing's happening. I'm just looking around.'

'Keep us informed. I don't think there's any danger, but—'

'But in case there is, you want the next man to know what to watch out for? All right, Captain.'

'Lines all right?'

'They're fine.' He took another step forward. 'The ground – I suppose I can call it the ground – is getting less slippery. Easier to walk on. Walls about twenty feet apart here. No sign of macroscopic flora or fauna. No artifacts to indicate intelligent life.'

The Captain's voice sounded pained. 'Don't let your sense of humour carry you away, Doctor. This is important. Maybe you don't realize exactly how important, but—'

He interrupted. 'Hold it, Captain, here's something interesting. A big reddish bump, about three feet across, in the grey-green wall.'

'What is it?'

'Might be a tumour. I'll slice some tissue from the wall itself. That's sample number two. Tissue from the tumour, sample number three.'

The wall quivered almost imperceptibly as he sliced into it. The fresh-cut surface was purple, but it slowly turned red again as the internal atmosphere of the beast got at it.

'Here's another tumour, like the first, this time on the other side of the wall. And here are a couple more. I'm leaving them alone. The walls are getting narrower. There's plenty of room to walk, but – wait a minute, I take that back. There's some kind of valve ahead of me. It's opening and closing spasmodically.'

'Can you get through?'

'I'd hate to take a chance. And even if I did make it

18

while it was open, it could crush the oxygen lines when it closed.'

'Then that's the end of the road?'

'I don't know. Let me think.'

He stared at the great valve. It moved rapidly, opening and closing in a two-second rhythm. Probably a valve separating one part of the digestive system from another, he thought, like the human pylorus. The green-streaked grey flesh seemed totally unlike human muscle, but all the same it appeared to serve a similar function. Maybe the right kind of drug would cause muscular relaxation.

He pulled a large hypodermic syringe from one of the sealed pockets of his diver's uniform. He plunged the needle quickly into the edge of the valve as it paused for a fraction of a second before closing, shot a pint of drug solution into the flesh, and ripped the needle out again. The valve closed once more, but more slowly. It opened, closed again, opened once more – and stayed open.

How long before it recovered, and shut off his retreat? He didn't know. But if he wanted to find out what was on the other side, he'd have to work fast. He plunged forward, almost slipping in his eagerness, and leaped through the motionless valve.

Then he called up to tell the Captain what he had done.

The Captain's voice was anxious. 'I don't know whether you ought to risk it, Doctor.'

'I'm down here to learn things. I haven't learned much yet. By the way, the walls are widening out again. And there's another pool of liquid ahead. Blue liquid, this time.'

'Are you taking a sample?'

'I'm a sampler from way back, Captain.'

He waded into the blue pond, filled his sample bottle, and put it into one of his pockets. Suddenly, in front of him something broke the surface of the pond, then dived down again.

He came to a full stop. 'Hold it, Captain. There seems to be fauna.'

'What? Something alive?'

'Very much alive.'

19

'Be careful, Doctor. I think there's a gun in one of the pockets of that uniform. Use it if necessary.'

'A gun? Don't be cruel, Captain. How'd you like to have somebody shooting off guns inside you?'

'Be careful, man!'

'I'll use my hypodermic as a weapon.'

But the creature, whatever it was, did not approach him again, and he waded further into the blue pond. When his eyes were below the surface of the liquid, he saw the thing moving again.

'Looks like an overgrown tadpole, about two feet long.'

'Is it coming close?'

'No, it's darting away from me. And there's another one. I think the light bothers it.'

'Any signs that the thing is dangerous?'

'I can't tell. It may be a parasite of the big creature, or it may be something that lives in symbiosis with it.'

'Stay away from it, Doctor. No use risking your life for nothing.'

A trembling voice said, 'Larry! Are you all right?'

'Maida! What are you doing here?'

'I woke up when you left. And then I had trouble going to sleep again.'

'But why did you come to the space port?'

'Ships began to flash by overhead, and I began to wonder what had happened. So I called up – and they told me.'

'Ships overhead?'

The Captain's voice cut in again. 'The news services, Doctor. This case has aroused great interest. I didn't want to tell you before, but don't be surprised if you come up to find yourself famous.'

'Never mind the news services. Have you heard from Earth yet?'

'No message from Earth. We did hear from the curator of the Marsopolis Zoo.'

'What did he say?'

'He never even heard of a space-cow, and he has no suggestions to make.'

'That's fine. By the way, Captain, are there any photographers around from those news services?'

'Half a dozen. Still, motion picture, television—'

'How about sending them down inside to take a few pictures?'

There was a moment of silence. Then the Captain's voice again: 'I don't think they can go down for a while yet. Maybe later?'

'Why can't they go down now? I'd like to have some company. If the beast's mouth is open—' A disquieting thought struck him. 'Say, it is open, isn't it?'

The Captain's voice sounded tense. 'Now, don't get upset, Doctor, we're doing all we can!'

'You mean it's closed?'

'Yes, it's closed. I didn't want to tell you this, but the mouth closed unexpectedly, and then, when we did have the idea of sending a photographer down inside, we couldn't get it open again. Apparently the creature has adapted to the effects of the electric shock.'

'There must be some way of getting it open again.'

'Of course there's a way. There's always a way. Don't worry, Doctor, we're working on it. We'll find it.'

'But the oxygen—'

'The lines are strong, and the mouth isn't closed tight enough to pinch them off. You can breathe all right, can't you?'

'Now that I think of it, I can. Thanks for telling me.'

'You see, Doctor, it isn't so bad.'

'It's perfectly lovely. But what happens if my uniform or the oxygen lines start to dissolve?'

'We'll pull you out. We'll do something to open the mouth. Just don't get caught behind that valve, Doctor.'

'Thanks for the advice. I don't know what I'd do without it, Captain.'

He felt a sudden surge of anger. If there was one thing he hated, it was good advice, given smugly when the giver could stand off to one side, without sharing the danger of the person he was helping. Don't let this happen, don't get caught here, take care of yourself. But you were down here to do a job, and so far you hadn't done it. You hadn't learned a thing about what made this monstrous creature tick.

And the chances were that you wouldn't learn either. The way to examine a beast was from the outside, not from within. You watched it eat, you studied the transfer of the food from one part of the body to another, you checked on the circulation of the body fluids, using radioactive tracers if no other methods offered, you dissected specimens of typical individuals. The Captain should have had a few scientists aboard, and they should have done a few of these things instead of just sitting there staring at the beast. But that would have made things too easy. No, they had to wait for you to come aboard, and then send you deliberately sliding down into the guts of an animal you didn't know anything about, in the hope of having a miracle happen to you. Maybe they thought a loop of intestine or some gland of internal secretion would come over to you and say. 'I'm not working right. Fix me, and everything will be fine.'

Another of the tadpole-like creatures was swimming over towards him, approaching slowly, the forepart twitching like the nose of a curious dog. Then, like the others, the creature turned and darted away. 'Maybe that's the parasite that's causing the trouble.'

Only – it might just as well be a creature necessary to the larger creature's health. Again and again you were faced with the same problem. Down here you were in a world you knew nothing about. And when everything was so strange to you – what was normal, and what wasn't?

When in doubt, he decided, move on. He moved.

The blue pool was shallow, and once more he came up on what he decided to call dry ground. Once more the walls grew narrow again. After a time he could reach out and touch the walls on either side of him at the same time.

He flashed his light into the narrow passage, and saw that a dozen yards ahead of him it seemed to come to an end. 'Blind alley,' he thought. 'Time to turn back.'

The Captain's voice came to him again. 'Doctor, is everything all right?'

'Beautiful. I've had a most interesting tour. By the way, did you get the creature's mouth open yet?

'We're still working on it.'

'I wish you luck. Maybe when those reports from Earth come in—'

'They've come. None of the curators knows anything about space-cows. For some reason, the electric-shock method doesn't work any more. and we're trying all sorts of other stimuli.'

'I take it that nothing is effective.'

'Not yet. One of the photo service men suggested we use a powerful mechanical clamp to pull the jaws open. We're having one flown over.'

'Use anything,' he said fervently. 'But for God's sake, get that *mouth* open!'

Dr. Meltzer cursed the photo service people, to whom he meant nothing more than a series of coloured lines in space. Then he added an unkind word or two for the Captain, who had got him into this mess, and started back.

The tadpole creatures seemed to be interested in his progress. They came swarming around him, and now he could see that there were almost a dozen of them. They moved with quick flips of their tails, like the minnows he had once seen back on Earth, where he had attended medical school. Between each pair of flips there was a momentary pause, and when they came close he was able to get a reasonably good look at them. He was surprised to see that they had two rows of eyes each.

Were the eyes functional or vestigial? In the former case, they must spend some part of their life cycle outside the host creature, in places where they had need of the sense of sight. In the latter case, they were at least descended from outside creatures. Maybe I'll try to catch one of them, he thought. Once I get it outside I can give it a real examination.

Once I get it outside, he repeated. Provided I get outside myself.

He waded through the pond again. As he reached the shallow part of the blue liquid, a voice came to him – this time his wife's voice. 'Larry, are you all right?'

'Doing fine. How are the kids?'

'They're with me. They woke up during the excitement, and I brought them along.'

'You didn't tell me that before!'

'I didn't want to upset you.'

'Oh, it doesn't upset me in the least. Nothing like a nice family picnic. But how do you expect them to go to school in the morning?'

'Oh, Larry, what difference does it make if they miss school for once? A chance to be in on something like this happens once in a lifetime.'

'That's a little too often to suit me. Well, now that I know they're here, let me talk to them.'

Evidently they had been waiting for the chance, for Jerry's voice came at once. 'Hiya, Dad.'

'Hiya, Jerry. Having a good time?'

'Swell. You oughtta be out here, Dad. There are a lot of people. They're treatin' us swell.'

Martia cut in. 'Mom, he isn't letting me talk. I want to talk to Daddy too.'

'Let her talk, Jerry. Go ahead, Martia. Say something to Daddy.'

A sudden blast almost knocked out his eardrum. 'Dad, can you hear me?' Martia screamed. 'Can you hear me Dad?'

'I can hear you, and so can these animals. Not so loud, sweetheart.'

'Gee, Dad, you oughtta see all the people. They took pictures of me and Mom. Oh, we're too thrilled!'

'They took pictures of me too,' said Jerry.

'They're sending the pictures all over. To Earth and Venus, and everywhere. We're gonna be on television too, Dad. Isn't it exciting?'

'It's terrific, Martia. You don't know what this does for my morale.'

'Aw, all she thinks about is pictures. Mom, make her get away from the microphone, or I'll push her away.'

'You've had your chance, Martia. Let Jerry talk again.'

'You know what, Dad? Everybody says you're gonna be famous. They say this is the only animal of its kind ever discovered. And you're the only person ever went into it. Can I go down there too, Dad?'

'No!' he yelled.

'Okay, okay. Say, Dad, know what? If you bring it back alive, they're gonna take it to Earth, and put it in a special zoo of its own.'

'Thank them for me. Look, Jerry, did they get the animal's mouth open yet?'

'Not yet, Dad, but they're bringing in a great big machine.'

The Captain's voice again: 'We'll have the mouth open soon. Doctor. Where are you now?'

'Approaching the valve again. Have you heard any-thing that could be useful? Maybe some explorer or

24

hunter might be able to tell you something about space-cows—'

'Sorry, Doctor. Nobody knows anything about space-cows.'

'That's what you said before. All right, Captain, stand by for further news. I've got a shoal of these tadpole beasts in attendance. Let's see what happens now.'

'They're not attacking, are they?'

'Not yet.'

'You feel all right otherwise?'

'Fine. A little short of breath, though. That may be the result of tension. And a little hungry. I wonder how this beast would taste raw – my God!'

The Captain asked anxiously, 'What is it?'

'That valve I paralysed. It's working normally once more!'

'You mean it's opening and closing?'

'The same rhythm as before. And every time it closes, it squeezes those oxygen tubes. That's why I sometimes feel short of breath. I have to get out of here!'

'Do you have enough drug to paralyse the valve again?'

'No, I don't. Keep quiet, Captain, let me figure this out.'

The valve was almost impassable. If he had found a good place to take off from, he might have dived safely through the opening during the near-second when the muscles were far apart. But there was no place for a take-off. He had to approach up a slippery slope, hampered by uniform and lines. And if he misjudged the right moment to go through, he'd be caught when the valve closed again.

He stood there motionless for a moment, sweat pouring down his forehead and into his eyes. Damn it, he thought, I can't even wipe it away. I've got to tackle this thing half blind.

Through one partially fogged eyeplate he noticed the tadpole creature approaching more closely. Were they vicious after all? Were they coming closer because they sensed that he was in danger? Were they closing in for the kill?

One of them plunged straight at him, and involuntarily he ducked. The thing turned barely aside at the last moment, raced past him, slithered out of the blue liquid, and squirmed up the slope towards the valve.

Unexpectedly, the valve opened to twice its previous width, and the creature plunged through without trouble.

'Doctor Meltzer? Are you still all right?'

'I'm alive, if that interests you. Listen, Captain, I'm going to try getting through that valve. One of the tadpole beasts just did it, and the valve opened a lot wider to let it through.'

'Just how do you expect to manage?'

'I'll try grabbing one of the beasts and hitch-hike through. I just hope it isn't vicious, and doesn't turn on me.'

But the tadpole creatures wouldn't let themselves be grabbed. In this, their home territory, they moved a great deal faster than he did, and even though they didn't seem to be using their eyes to see with, they evaded his grasp with great skill.

At last he gave up the attempt and climbed out of the blue pool. The creatures followed him.

One of the biggest of them suddenly dashed forward. Sensing what the thing was going to do, Dr. Meltzer hurried after it. It scurried up the slope, and plunged through the valve. The valve opened wide. Dr. Meltzer, racing desperately forward, threw himself into the opening. The valve paused, then snapped at him. He felt it hit his heel.

The next moment he was gasping for breath. The oxygen lines had become tangled.

He fought frenziedly to untwist them, and failed. Then he realized that he was trying to do too much. All he needed to do was loosen the knot and straighten out the kinks. By the time he finally succeeded, he was seeing black spots in front of his eyes.

'Doctor Meltzer, Doctor Meltzer!'

The sound had been in his ears for some time. 'Still alive,' he gasped.

'Thank God!' We're going to try to open the mouth now, Doctor. If you hurry forward, you'll be in a position to be pulled out.'

'I'm hurrying. By the way, those tadpoles are still with me. They're trailing along as if they'd found a long-lost friend. I feel like a pie-eyed piper.'

'I just hope they don't attack.'

'You're not hoping any harder than I am.'

He could catch his breath now, and with the oxygen lines free, the perspiration that had dimmed his sight slowly evaporated. He caught sight of one of the reddish tumours he had noticed on his forward passage.

'May as well be hung for a sheep as a lamb,' he murmured. 'It would take an axe really to chop that tumour out, but I may as well slice into it and see what I can learn.'

From one of his pockets he took a sharp oversize scalpel, and began to cut around the edges.

The tumour throbbed convulsively.

'Well, well, I may have something here,' he said, with a surgeon's pleasure. He dug deeper.

The tumour erupted. Great blobs of reddish liquid spurted out, and with one of them came another of the tadpole creatures, a small one, half the average size of those he had first encountered.

'Glory be,' he muttered. 'So that's the way they grow.'

The creatures sensed him and darted aside, in the direction of the valve. As it approached, the open valve froze in place, and let the small creature through, further into the host, without enlarging. Then the valve began to close again.

They're adapted to each other, he thought. Probably symbiosis, rather than a one-side parasitism.

He moved upwards, towards the greenish liquid.

An earthquake struck.

The flesh heaved up beneath his feet, tossing him head over heels into the pool. The first shock was followed by a second and a third. A tidal wave hit him, and carried him to the side of the pool. He landed with a thud against the hard side and bounced back.

The sides began to constrict, hemming him in.

'Captain!' he yelled. 'What's going on out there? What are you doing to the beast?'

'Trying to pry open its mouth. It doesn't seem to like the idea. It's threshing around against the walls of the ship.'

'For God's sake, cut it out! It's giving me a beating in here.'

They must have halted their efforts at once, for immediately afterwards the beast's movements became less

27

convulsive. But it was some time before the spasmodic quivering of the side walls came to an end.

Dr. Meltzer climbed out of the pool of liquid, making an automatic and entirely useless gesture to wipe the new perspiration from his forehead.

'Is it better in there, Doctor?'

'It's better. Don't try that again,' he panted.

'We have to get the mouth open some way.'

'Try a bigger electric shock.'

'If you want us to. But it may mean another beating for you, Doctor.'

'Then wait a minute. Wait till I get near the upper part of the gullet.'

'Whenever you say. Just tell us when you're ready.'

Better be ready soon, he thought. My light's beginning to dim. When it goes out altogether, I'll probably be in a real panic. I'll be yelling for him to do anything, just to get me out of there.

And what about the suit and the oxygen lines? I think the digestive fluid's beginning to affect them. It's hard to be sure, now that the light's weakening, but they don't have the clear transparent look they had at first. And when they finally go, I go with them.

He tried to move forward faster, but the surface underfoot was slimy, and when he moved too hastily, he slipped. The lines were getting tangled too. Now that the creature's mouth was closed, it was no use tugging at the cord around his waist. That wouldn't get him up.

'Doctor Meltzer!'

He didn't answer. Instead, he pulled out his lancet and cut the useless cords away. The oxygen lines too were a nuisance, in constant danger of kinking and tangling, now that they were no longer taut. But at least the gas was still flowing through them and would continue to flow – until the digestive fluid ate through.

The tadpole creatures seemed to have developed a positive affection for him. They were all around him, not close enough for him to grab them, but still too close for comfort. At any moment they might decide to take a nip out of his suit or an oxygen line. And with the plastic already weakened, even a slight tear might be fatal.

He reached the sharp slope that signified the gullet. 'Dr. Meltzer?'

'What do you want?'

'Why didn't you answer?'

'I was busy. I cut the cord away from around my waist. Now I'm going to try climbing up inside this thing's throat.'

'Shall we try that sharp electric shock?'

'Go ahead.'

He had a pair of small surgical clamps, and he took one in each hand. The flashlight he put in a holder at his waist. Then, getting down on all fours, he began to crawl up, digging each pair of clamps into the flesh in turn to give him a grip. A slow wave ran away in both directions every time he inserted one of the pairs of clamps into the flesh, but otherwise the beast didn't seem to mind too much.

He was about halfway up, when the earthquakes began again. The first one sent him tumbling head over heels down the slope. The others added some slight injury to the insult, knocking him painfully against the walls. They must have used a powerful electric jolt, for some of it was transmitted through the creature to him, making his skin tingle. He hadn't lost his flashlight, but by now it was exceedingly dim, and shed 'y a feeble circle of light. Far ahead of him, where the mouth was to open, was blackness.

'No luck, Captain?'

'No luck, Doctor. We'll try again.'

'Don't. You just make things worse.'

'Larry, were you hurt? Larry—'

'Don't bother me now, Maida,' he said roughly. 'I have to figure out a way to get out.'

A faint hiss came from the oxygen line. A leak. Time was growing short.

The tadpole creatures were swimming around faster now. They too must have been upset by the shock. One of them darted ahead of him, and wriggled ahead until it was lost in blackness.

That seems to be trying to get out too, he told himself. Maybe we can work this together. There must be some way, something to get this creature to open its mouth. Maybe the Captain can't do it from outside, but I'm in here, where the beast's most sensitive. I can hit it, slash at it, tickle it—

There's a thought. Tickle it. It's a monster, and it'll

29

take some monstrous tickling, but sooner or later, something should affect it.

He stamped hard with his foot. No effect. He took his large lancet from his pocket and slashed viciously with it. A shudder ran through the flesh, but that was all.

And then he had an idea. That green liquid undoubtedly contained hormones. Hormones, enzymes, coenzymes, antibiotics, biological chemicals of all kinds. Stuff to which some tissues would be adapted and some would not. And those that weren't would react violently.

He turned back, filled his hypodermic syringe with the greenish liquid, and ran forward again. The light was almost gone by now, and the hissing from the oxygen line was growing ominously, but he climbed forward as far as he could, before plunging the hypodermic in and injecting its contents.

The creature heaved. He dropped hypodermic, light, and clamps, and let the huge shuddering take him where it would. First it lifted him high. Then it let him fall suddenly – not backwards, but in the same place. Two of the tadpole beasts were thrown against him. Then he was lifted up again, and this time forward. A huge cavern opened before him. Light bathed the grey surface and he was vomited out.

The light began to flicker, and he had time for one last thought. Oxygen lack, he told himself. My suit's ripped, the lines have finally torn.

And then blackness.

When he came to, Maida was at his side. He could see that she had been crying. The Captain stood a little further off, his face drawn, but relieved.

'Larry, dear, are you all right? We thought you'd never get out.'

'I'm fine.' He sat up and saw his two children, standing anxious and awe-stricken on the other side of the bed. Their silence showed how strongly they had been affected. 'I hope you kids didn't worry too much about me.'

'Of course I didn't worry,' said Jerry bravely. 'I knew you were smart, Dad. I knew you'd think of a way to get out.'

'While we're on the subject,' interposed the Captain, 'what *was* the way out?'

'I'll tell you later. How's the patient?'

'Doing fine. Seems to have recovered completely.'

'How many of the tadpoles came out with me?'

'About six. We're keeping them in the same low-oxygen atmosphere as the creature itself. We're going to study them. We figure that if they're parasites—'

'They're not parasites. I finally came to a conclusion about them. They're the young.'

'What?'

'The young. If you take good care of them, they'll eventually grow to be as big as the mother-monster you've got in the ship.'

'Good God, where will we keep them?'

'That's your worry. Maybe you'd better expand that zoo you're preparing. What you'll do for money to feed them, though, I don't know.'

'But what—'

'The trouble with that monster – it's "illness" – was merely that it was gravid.'

'Gravid?'

'That means pregnant,' exclaimed Jerry.

'I know what it means.' The Captain flushed. 'Look, do we have to have these kids in here while we discuss this?'

'Why not? They're a doctor's children. They know what it's all about. They've seen calves and other animals being born.'

'Lots of times,' said Martia.

'Confined as it was on the ship, your beast couldn't get the exercise it needed. And the young couldn't get themselves born.'

'But that was the digestive tract you went down—'

'What of it? Are all animals born the same way? Ask the average kid where a baby grows, and he'll tell you that it's in the stomach.'

'Some kids are dopes,' said Jerry.

'They wouldn't be in this case. What better place to get a chance at the food the mother eats, in all stages from raw to completely digested? All that beast needed to give birth was a little exercise. You gave it some from the outside, but not enough. I finished the job by injecting some of its own digestive fluid into the flesh. That caused a pretty little reaction.'

The Captain scratched his head. 'Doctor, you did a

good job. How would you like to take care of that beast permanently? I could recommend you—'

'To go down inside that monster again? No, thanks. From now on, I treat nothing but small monsters. Sheep, cows – and human beings.'

There was a pounding of feet in the hallway. Then the door swung in, violently. Flashbulbs that gave invisible light began to pop with inaudible bursts of high-frequency sound. Cameras pointed menacingly at him and sent his image winging to Earth and far-off planets. Reporters began to fire their questions.

'My God,' he muttered wearily, 'who let these animals in here? They're worse than the ones I met inside the blue pool.'

'Be nice to them, dear,' chided Maida gently. 'They're turning you into a great man.'

Then Maida and Jerry and Martia grouped themselves around him, and the cameras caught them too. The proud look on their faces was something to see. And he realized that he was glad for their sake.

Opportunity had knocked, and when he had opened the door to it, it had proved to be an exacting guest. Still, he hadn't been a bad host – not a bad host at all, he thought. And slowly his features relaxed into a tired and immediately famous grin.

COUNTRY DOCTOR

The 'space-cow' in this story is by no means as odd a creature as the pyramid-beings in *A Martian Odyssey* or the star-intelligences of *Proof*. The space-cow is at least made up of protein.

The problem set in the story is a very realistic one, given the premise. If we do ever locate advanced forms of life outside the Earth, forms that are not intelligent, how do we handle them? To keep them in zoos, or to exploit them as food, would require us to understand something about their physiology, if only to keep them alive and healthy.

Aside from such purely materialistic considerations, there would be considerable advance in our understanding of life if we could learn details concerning the physiology, if only to keep them alive and healthy.

The most remarkable characteristic of the space-cow is, of course, its sheer size. It nearly fills the spaceship and it is large enough to allow a human being to tramp about its interior. (The realism of that invasion of the animal's gut may be accounted for by the fact that the author, whose real name is Joseph Samachson, has a Ph.D. in chemistry.) The space-cow's mouth is forty feet from the ground and is thirty feet wide and fifty feet deep, so that it ought to be considerably larger than even the largest whale. Yet it would seem to be a land creature.

On Earth, so large a creature would be quite impossible outside the oceans. Without the support of the buoyancy of the ocean, its own weight would crush it. However, it comes from Ganymede, Jupiter's largest satellite, which has a considerably smaller gravitational pull at its surface than Earth has. To be sure, there are many other reasons for supposing Ganymede cannot support a creature such as the space-cow, but here, as in *Surface Tension*, we have an impossible assumption designed merely to start the story.

Questions and Suggestions

1. Investigate the matter of size of living creatures in relation to gravity. What are the most massive land organisms that ever existed? How would their mass compare with that of the largest whale living today?

2. A sperm-whale has a head about a third the length of its body. Assuming the sea-cow is similarly proportioned, estimate its length and its mass. (You might be interested in discovering the size and mass of a large whale's organs; its heart, its tongue; and how its physiology is organized.)

3. What is the gravitational intensity at the surface of Ganymede compared to that on the surface of the Earth? What else is known about Ganymede? What do you think the chances are of finding any kind of life on that world?

4. Do you think there are forms of life on Earth itself as strange as the space-cow, if not as large? When the duck-billed platypus was first discovered in Australia, it was difficult to get biologists back in Europe to believe the descriptions were of real animals and not of hoaxes. What was so strange about the platypus? What other

earthly creatures have to be seen to be believed? What about the Venus's-flytrap? the flying-fox? the mandrill? If you were familiar with all the forms of life on Earth except for *Homo sapiens,* do you think you would be able to predict the existence of man? What in man, if anything, might seem unpredictable?

2. THE HOLES AROUND MARS

Jerome Bixby

Spaceship crews should be selected on the basis of their non-irritating qualities as individuals. No chronic complainers, no hypochondriacs, no bugs on cleanliness – particularly no one-man parties. I speak from bitter experience.

Because on the first expedition to Mars, Hugh Allenby damned near drove us nuts with his puns. We finally got so we just ignored them.

But no one can ignore that classic last one – it's written right into the annals of astronomy, and it's there to stay.

Allenby, in command of the expedition, was first to set foot outside the ship. As he stepped down from the airlock of the *Mars I*, he placed that foot on a convenient rock, caught the toe of his weighted boot in a hole in the rock, wrenched his ankle and smote the ground with his pants.

Sitting there, eyes pained behind the transparent shield of his oxygen-mask, he stared at the rock.

It was about five feet high. Ordinary granite – no special shape. Several inches below its summit, running straight through it in a north-easterly direction, was a neat round four-inch hole.

'I'm *upset* by the *hole* thing,' he grunted.

The rest of us scrambled out of the ship and gathered around his plump form.

'Break anything, Hugh?' asked Burton, our pilot, kneeling beside him.

'Get out of my way, Burton,' said Allenby. 'You're obstructing my view.'

Burton blinked. A man constructed of long bones and

34

caution, he angled out of the way, looking around to see what he was obstructing view *of*.

He saw the rock and the round hole through it. He stood very still, staring. So did the rest of us.

'Well, I'll be damned,' said Janus, our photographer. 'A hole.'

'In a rock,' added Gonzales, our botanist.

'Round,' said Randolph, our biologist.

'An *artifact*,' finished Allenby softly.

Burton helped him to his feet. Silently we gathered around the rock.

Janus bent down and put an eye to one end of the hole. I bent down and looked through the other end. We squinted at each other.

As mineralogist, I was expected to opinionate. 'Not drilled,' I said slowly. 'Not chipped. Not melted. Certainly not eroded.'

I heard a rasping sound by my ear and straightened. Burton was scratching a thumbnail along the rim of the hole. 'Weathered,' he said. 'Plenty old. But I'll bet it's a perfect circle, if we measure.'

Janus was already fiddling with his camera, testing the cooperation of the tiny distant sun with a light-meter.

'Let us see *weather* it is or not,' Allenby said.

Burton brought out a steel tape-measure. The hole was four and three-eighths inches across. It was perfectly circular and about sixteen inches long. And four feet above the ground.

'But why?' said Randolph. 'Why should anyone bore a four-inch tunnel through a rock way out in the middle of the desert?'

'Religious symbol,' said Janus. He looked around, one hand on his gun. 'We'd better keep an eye out – maybe we've landed on sacred ground or something.'

'A totem *hole*, perhaps, Allenby suggested.

'Oh, I don't know,' Randolph said – to Janus, not Allenby. As I've mentioned, we always ignored Allenby's puns. 'Note the lack of ornamentation. Not at all typical of religious articles.'

'On Earth,' Gonzales reminded him. 'Besides, it might be utilitarian, not symbolic.'

'Utilitarian how?' asked Janus.

'An altar for snakes,' Burton said drily.

'Well,' said Allenby, 'you can't deny that it has its *holy* aspects.'

'Get your hands away, will you, Peters?' asked Janus.

I did. When Janus's camera had clicked, I bent again and peered through the hole. 'It sights on that low ridge over there,' I said. 'Maybe it's some kind of surveying setup. I'm going to take a look.'

'Careful,' warned Janus. 'Remember, it may be sacred.'

As I walked away, I heard Allenby say, 'Take some scrapings from the inside of the hole, Gonzales. We might be able to determine if anything is kept in it . . .'

One of the stumpy, purplish, barrel-type cacti on the ridge had a long vertical bite out of it . . . as if someone had carefully carved out a narrow U-shaped section from the top down, finishing the bottom of the U in a neat semicircle. It was as flat and cleancut as the inside surface of a horseshoe magnet.

I hollered. The others came running. I pointed.

'Oh, my God!' said Allenby. 'Another one.'

The pulp of the cactus in and around the U-hole was dried and dead-looking.

Silently Burton used his tape-measure. The hole measured four and three-eighths inches across. It was eleven inches deep. The semicircular bottom was about a foot above the ground.

'This ridge,' I said, 'is about three feet higher than where we landed the ship. I bet the hole in the rock and the hole in this cactus are on the same level.'

Gonzales said slowly, 'This was not done all at once. It is a result of periodic attacks. Look here and here. These overlapping depressions along the outer edges of the hole—' he pointed – 'on this side of the cactus. They are the signs of repeated impact. And the scallop effect on *this* side, where whatever made the hole emerged. There are juices still oozing – not at the point of impact, where the plant is desiccated, but below, where the shock was transmitted—'

A distant shout turned us around. Burton was at the rock, beside the ship. He was bending down, his eye to the far side of the mysterious hole.

He looked for another second, then straightened and came towards us at a lope.

'They line up,' he said when he reached us. 'The

bottom of the hole in the cactus is right in the middle when you sight through the hole in the rock.'

'As if somebody came around and whacked the cactus regularly,' Janus said, looking around warily.

'To keep the line of sight through the holes clear?' I wondered. 'Why not just remove the cactus?'

'Religious,' Janus explained.

We went on past the ridge towards an outcropping of rock about a hundred yards farther on. We walked silently, each of us wondering if what we half-expected would really be there.

It was. In one of the tall, weathered spires in the outcropping, some ten feet below its peak and four feet above the ground, was a round four-inch hole.

Allenby sat down on a rock, nursing his ankle, and remarked that anybody who believed this crazy business was really happening must have holes in the rocks in his head.

Burton put his eye to the hole and whistled. 'Sixty feet long if it's an inch,' he said. 'The other end's just a pinpoint. But you can see it. The damn thing's perfectly straight.'

I looked back the way we had come. The cactus stood on the ridge, with its U-shaped bite, and beyond was the ship, and beside it the perforated rock.

'If we surveyed,' I said, 'I bet the hole would all line up, right to the last millimetre.'

'But,' Randolph complained, 'why would anybody go out and bore holes in things all along a line through the desert?'

'Religious,' Janus muttered. 'It doesn't *have* to make sense.'

We stood there by the outcropping and looked out along the wide, red desert beyond. It stretched flatly for miles from this point, south towards Mars' equator – dead sandy wastes, criss-crossed by the 'canals', which we had observed while landing to be great straggly patches of vegetation, probably strung along underground water-flows.

BLONG-G-G-G- . . . *st-st-st* . . .

We jumped half out of our skins. Ozone bit at our nostrils. Our hair stirred in the electrical uproar.

'L-look,' Janus chattered, lowering his smoking gun.

About forty feet to our left, a small rabbity creature poked its head from behind a rock and stared at us in utter horror.

Janus raised his gun again.

'Don't bother,' said Allenby tiredly. 'I don't think it intends to attack.'

'But—'

'I'm sure it isn't a Martian with religious convictions.'

Janus wet his lips and looked a little shamefaced. 'I guess I'm kind of tense.'

'That's what I *taut*,' said Allenby.

The creature darted from behind its rock and, looking at us over its shoulder, employed six legs to make small but very fast tracks.

We turned our attention again to the desert. Far out, black against Mars' azure horizon, was a line of low hills.

'Shall we go look?' asked Burton, eyes gleaming at the mystery.

Janus lifted his gun nervously. It was still crackling faintly from the discharge. 'I say let's get back to the ship!'

Allenby sighed. 'My leg hurts.' He studied the hills. 'Give me the field-glasses.'

Randolph handed them over. Allenby put them to the shield of his mask and adjusted them.

After a moment he sighed again. 'There's a hole. On a plane surface that catches the Sun. A lousy damned round little impossible hole.'

'Those hills,' Burton observed, 'must be thousands of feet thick.'

The argument lasted all the way back to the ship.

Janus, holding out for his belief that the whole thing was of religious origin, kept looking around for Martians as if he expected them to pour screaming from the hills.

Burton came up with the suggestion that perhaps the holes had been made by a disintegrator-ray.

'It's possible,' Allenby admitted. 'This might have been the scene of some great battle—'

'With only one such weapon?' I objected.

Allenby swore as he stumbled. 'What do you mean?'

'I haven't seen any other lines of holes – only the one. In a battle, the whole joint should be cut up.'

That was good for a few moments' silent thought. Then Allenby said, 'It might have been brought out by one side as a last resort. Sort of an ace in the hole.'

I resisted the temptation to mutiny. 'But would even *one* such weapon, in battle, make only *one* line of holes? Wouldn't it be played in an arc against the enemy? You know it would.'

'Well—'

'Wouldn't it cut slices out of the landscape, instead of boring holes? And wouldn't it sway or vibrate enough to make the holes miles away from it sometimes less than perfect circles?'

'It could have been very firmly mounted.'

'Hugh, does that sound like a practical weapon to you?'

Two second of silence. 'On the other hand,' he said, 'instead of a war, the whole thing might have been designed to frighten some primitive race – or even some kind of beast – the *hole* out of here. A demonstration—'

'Religious,' Janus grumbled, still looking around.

We walked on, passing the cactus on the low ridge.

'Interesting,' said Gonzales. 'The evidence that whatever causes the phenomenon has happened again and again. I'm afraid that the war theory—'

'Oh, my God!' gasped Burton.

We stared at him.

'The ship,' he whispered. 'It's right in line with the holes! If whatever made them is still in operation . . .'

'Run!' yelled Allenby, and we ran like fiends.

We got the ship into the air, out of line with the holes to what we fervently hoped was safety, and then we realized we were admitting our fear that the mysterious hole-maker might still be lurking around.

Well, the evidence was all for it, as Gonzales had reminded us – that cactus had been oozing.

We cruised at twenty thousand feet and thought it over.

Janus, whose only training was in photography, said, 'Some kind of omniverous animal? Or bird? Eats rocks and everything?'

'I will not totally discount the notion of such an animal,' Randolph said. 'But I will resist to the death the suggestion that it forages with geometric precision.'

After a while, Allenby said, 'Land, Burton. By that "canal". Lots of plant life – fauna, too. We'll do a little collecting.'

Burton set us down feather-light at the very edge of the sprawling flat expanse of vegetation, commenting that the scene reminded him of his native Texas pear-flats.

We wandered in the chilly air, each of us except Burton pursuing his speciality. Randolph relentlessly stalked another of the rabbity creatures. Gonzales was carefully digging up plants and stowing them in jars. Janus was busy with his cameras, recording every aspect of Mars transferable to film. Allenby walked around, helping anybody who needed it. An astronomer, he'd done half his work on the way to Mars' would do the other half on the return trip. Burton lounged in the sun, his back against a ship's fin, and played chess with Allenby, calling out his moves in a bull roar. I grubbed for rocks.

My search took me farther and farther away from the others – all I could find around the 'canal' was gravel, and I wanted to chip at some big stuff. I walked towards a long rise a half-mile or so away, beyond which rose an enticing array of house-sized boulders.

As I moved out of earshot, I heard Randolph snarl, 'Burton, *will* you stop yelling, "Kt to B-2 and check?" Every time you open your yap, this critter takes off on me.'

Then I saw the groove.

It started right where the ground began to rise – a thin, shallow, curve-bottomed groove in the dirt at my feet, about half an inch across, running off straight towards higher ground.

With my eyes glued to it, I walked. The ground slowly rose. The groove deepened, widened – now it was about three inches deep.

The ground rose some more. Four and three-eighths inches wide. I didn't have to measure it – I *knew*.

Now, as the ground rose, the edges of the groove began to curve inwards over the groove. They touched. No more groove.

The ground had risen, the groove had stayed level and gone underground.

40

Except that now it wasn't a groove. It was a round tunnel.

A hole.

A few paces farther on, I thumped the ground with my heel where the hole ought to be. The dirt crumbled, and there was the little dark tunnel, running straight in both directions.

I walked on, the ground falling away gradually again. The entire process was repeated in reverse. A hairline appeared in the dirt – widened – became lips that drew slowly apart to reveal the neat straight four-inch groove – which shrank as slowly to a shallow line of the ground – and vanished.

I looked ahead of me. There was one low ridge of ground between me and the enormous boulders. A neat four-inch semi-circle was bitten out of the very top of the ridge. In the house-sized boulder directly beyond was a four-inch hole.

Allenby called the others when I came back and reported.

'The mystery *deepens*,' he told them. He turned to me. 'Lead on, Peters, you're temporary *drill* leader.'

Thank God he didn't say *Fall in*.

The holes went straight through the nest of boulders – there'd be a hole in one and, ten or twenty feet farther on in the next boulder, another hole. And then another, and another – right through the nest in a line. About thirty holes in all.

Burton, standing by the boulder I'd first seen, flashed his flashlight into the hole. Randolph, clear on the other side of the jumbled nest, eye to hole, saw it.

Straight as a string.

The ground sloped away on the far side of the nest – no holes were visible in that direction – just miles of desert. So, after we'd stared at the hole for a while and they didn't go away, we headed back for the canal.

'Is there any possibility,' asked Janus, as we walked, 'that it could be a natural phenomenon?'

'There are no straight lines in nature,' Randolph said, a little shortly. 'That goes for a bunch of circles in a straight line. And for perfect circles, too.'

'A planet is a circle,' objected Janus.

'An oblate spheriod,' Allenby corrected.

'A planet's orbit—'

'An ellipse.'

Janus walked a few steps, frowning. Then he said, 'I remember reading that there *is* something darned near a perfect circle in nature.' He paused a moment. 'Potholes.' And he looked at me, as mineralogist, to corroborate.

'What kind of potholes?' I asked cautiously. 'Do you mean where part of a limestone deposit has dissol—'

'No. I once read that when a glacier passes over a hard rock that's lying on some softer rock, it grinds the hard rock down into the softer, and both of them sort of wear down to fit together, and it all ends up with a round hole in the soft rock.'

'Probably neither stone,' I told Janus, 'would be homogenous. The softer parts would abrade faster in the soft stone. The end result wouldn't be a perfect circle.'

Janus's face fell.

'Now,' I said, 'would anyone care to define this term "perfect circle" we're throwing around so blithely? Because such holes as Janus describes are often pretty damned round.'

Randolph said, 'Well . . .'

'It is settled, then,' Gonzales said, a little sarcastically. 'Your discussion, gentlemen, has established that the long, horizontal holes we have found were caused by glacial action.'

'Oh, no,' Janus argued seriously. 'I once read that Mars never had any glaciers.'

All of us shuddered.

Half on hour later, we spotted more holes, about a mile down the 'canal', still on a line, marching along the desert, through cacti rocks, hills, even through one edge of the low vegetation of the 'canal' for thirty feet or so. It was the damnedest thing to bend down and look straight through all that curling, twisting growth . . . a round tunnel from end to end.

We followed the holes for about a mile, to the rim of an enormous saucer-like valley that sank gradually before us until, miles away, it was thousands of feet deep. We stared out across it, wondering about the other side.

Allenby said determinedly, 'We'll get to the *bottom* of these holes, once and for all. Back to the ship, men!'

We hiked back, climbed in and took off.

At an altitude of fifty feet, Burton lined the nose of the ship on the most recent line of holes and we flew out over the valley.

On the other side was a range of hefty hills. The holes went through them. Straight through. We would approach one hill – Burton would manipulate the front viewscreen until we spotted the hole – we would pass over the hill and spot the other end of the hole in the rear screen.

One hole was two hundred and eighty miles long.

Four hours later, we were halfway around Mars.

Randolph was sitting by a side port, chin on one hand, his eyes unbelieving. 'All around the planet,' he kept repeating. 'All around the planet . . .'

'Halfway at least,' Allenby mused. 'And we can assume that it continues in a straight line, through anything and everything that gets in its way . . .' He gazed out of the front port at the uneven blue-green of a 'canal' off to our left. 'For the love of Heaven, *why*?'

Then Allenby fell down. We all did.

Burton had suddenly slapped at the control board, and the ship braked and sank like a plugged duck. At the last second, Burton propped up the nose with a short burst, the ten-foot wheels hit desert sand, and in five hundred yards we had jounced to a stop.

Allenby got up from the floor. 'Why did you do that?' he asked Burton politely, nursing a bruised elbow.

Burton's nose was almost touching the front port. 'Look!' he said, and pointed.

About two miles away, the Martian village looked like a handful of yellow marbles flung on the desert.

We checked our guns. We put on our oxygen-masks. We checked our guns again. We got out of the ship and made damned sure the airlock was locked.

An hour later, we crawled inch by painstaking inch up a high sand dune and poked our heads over the top.

The Martians were runts — the tallest of them less than five feet tall – and skinny as a pencil. Dried-up and brown, they wore loincloths of woven fibre.

They stood among the dusty-looking inverted-bowl buildings of their village, and every one of them was looking straight up at us with unblinking brown eyes.

43

The six safeties of our six guns clicked off like a rattle of dice. The Martians stood there and gawped.

'Probably a highly developed sense of hearing in this thin atmosphere,' Allenby murmured. 'Heard us coming.'

'They thought that landing of Burton's was an earthquake,' Randolph said sourly.

'Marsquake,' corrected Janus. One look at the village's scrawny occupants seemed to have convinced him that his life was in no danger.

Holding the Martians covered, we examined the village from atop the thirty-foot dune.

The domelike buildings were constructed of something that looked like abobe. No windows – probably built with sandstorms in mind. The doors were about halfway up the sloping sides, and from each door a stone ramp wound down around the house to the ground – again with sandstorms in mind, no doubt, so drifting dunes wouldn't block the entrances.

The centre of the village was a wide street, a long sandy area some thirty feet wide. On either side of it, the houses were scattered at random, as if each Martian had simply hunted for a comfortable place to sit and then built a house around it.

'Look,' whispered Randolph.

One Martian had stepped from a group on the far side of the street from us. He started to cross the street, his round brown eyes on us, his small bare feet plodding sand, and we saw that in addition to a loincloth he wore jewellery – a hammered metal ring, a bracelet on one skinny ankle The Sun caught a copperish gleam on his bald narrow head, and we saw a band of metal there, just above where his eyebrows should have been.

'The super-chief,' Allenby murmured. 'Oh, *shaman* me!'

As the bejewelled Martian approached the centre of the street, he glanced briefly at the ground at his feet. Then he raised his head, stepped with dignity across the exact centre of the street and came on towards us, passing the dusty-looking buildings of his realm and the dusty-looking groups of his subjects.

He reached the slope of the dune we lay on – paused – and raised small hands over his head, palms towards us.

44

'I think,' Allenby said, 'that an anthropologist would give odds on that gesture meaning peace.'

He stood up, holstered his gun – without buttoning the flap – and raised his own hands over his head. We all did.

The Martian language consisted of squeaks.

We made friendly noises, the chief squeaked, and pretty soon we were the centre of a group of wide-eyed Martians, none of whom made a sound. Evidently no one dared peep while the chief spoke – very likely the most articulate Martians simply squeaked themselves into the job. Allenby, of course, said they just *squeaked by*.

He was going through the business of drawing concentric circles in the sand, pointing at the third orbit away from the Sun and thumping his chest. The crowd around us kept growing as more Martians emerged from the dome buildings to see what was going on. Down the winding ramps of the buildings on our side of the wide, sandy street they came – and from the buildings on the other side of the street, plodding through the sand, blinking brown eyes at us, not making a sound.

Allenby pointed at the third orbit and thumped his chest. The chief squeaked and thumped his own chest and pointed at the copperish band around his head. Then he pointed at Allenby.

'I seem to have conveyed to him,' Allenby said drily, 'the fact that I'm chief of our party. Well, let's try again.'

He started over on the orbits. He didn't seem to be getting anyplace, so the rest of us watched the Martians instead. A last handful was struggling across the wide street.

'Curious,' said Gonzales. 'Note what happens when they reach the centre of the street.'

Each Martian, upon reaching the centre of the street, glanced at his feet – just for a moment – without even breaking stride. And then came on.

'What can they be looking at?' Gonzales wondered.

'The chief did it too,' Burton mused. 'Remember when he first came towards us?'

We all stared intently at the middle of the street. We saw absolutely nothing but sand.

The Martians milled around us and watched Allenby

45

and his orbits. A Martian child appeared from between two buildings across the street. On six-inch legs, it started across, got halfway, glanced downward – and came on.

'I don't get it,' Burton said. 'What in hell are they *looking* at?'

The child reached the crowd and squeaked a thin, high note.

A number of things happened at once.

Several members of the group around us glanced down, and along the edge of the crowd nearest the centre of the street there was a mild stir as individuals drifted off to either side. Quite casually – nothing at all urgent about it. They just moved concertedly to get farther away from the centre of the street, not taking their interested gaze off us for one second in the process.

Even the chief glanced up from Allenby's concentric circles at the child's squeak. And Randolph, who had been fidgeting uncomfortably and paying very little attention to our conversation, decided that he must answer nature's call. He moved off into the dunes surrounding the village. Or rather, he started to move.

The moment he set off across the wide street, the little Martian chief was in front of him, brown eyes wide, hands out before him as if to thrust Randolph back.

Again six safeties clicked. The Martians didn't even blink at the sudden appearance of our guns. Probably the only weapon they recognized was a club, or maybe a rock.

'What can the matter be?' Randolph said.

He took another step forward. The chief squeaked and stood his ground. Randolph had to stop or bump into him. Randolph stopped.

The chief squeaked, looking right into the bore of Randolph's gun.

'Hold still,' Allenby told Randolph, 'till we know what's up.'

Allenby made an interrogative sound at the chief. The chief squeaked and pointed at the ground. We looked. He was pointing at his shadow.

Randolph stirred uncomfortably.

'Hold still,' Allenby warned him, and again he made the questioning sound.

The chief pointed up the street. Then he pointed

46

down the street. He bent to touch his shadow, thumping it with thin fingers. Then he pointed at the wall of a house nearby.

We all looked.

Straight lines had been painted on the curved brick-coloured wall, up and down and across, to form small squares about four inches across. In each square was a bit of squiggly writing, in blackish paint, and a small wooden peg jutting from the wall.

Burton said, 'Looks like a damn crossword puzzle.'

'Look,' said Janus. 'In the lower right corner – a metal ring hanging from one of the pegs.'

And that was all we saw on the wall. Hundreds of squares with figures in them – a small peg set in each – and a ring hanging on one of the pegs.

'You know what?' Allenby said slowly. 'I think it's a calendar! Just a second – thirty squares wide by twenty-two high – that's six hundred and sixty. And that bottom line has twenty-six – twenty-*seven* squares. Six hundred and eighty-seven squares in all. That's how many days there are in the Martian year!'

He looked thoughtfully at the metal ring. 'I'll bet that ring is hanging from the peg in the square that represents *today*. They must move it along every day, to keep track . . .'

'What's a calendar got to do with my crossing the street?' Randolph asked in a pained tone.

He started to take another step. The chief squeaked as if it were a matter of desperate concern that he make us understand. Randolph stopped again and swore impatiently.

Allenby made his questioning sound again.

The chief pointed emphatically at his shadow, then at the communal calendar – and we could see now that he was pointing at the metal ring.

Burton said slowly, 'I think he's trying to tell us that this is *today*. And such-and-such a *time* of day. I bet he's using his shadow as a sundial.'

'Perhaps,' Allenby granted.

Randolph said, 'If this monkey doesn't let me go in another minute—'

The chief squeaked, eyes concerned.

47

'Stand still,' Allenby ordered. 'He's trying to warn you of some danger.'

The chief pointed down the street again and, instead of squealing, revealed that there was another sound at his command. He said, 'Whoooooooosh!'

We all stared at the end of the street.

Nothing! Just the wide avenue between the houses, and the high sand dune down at the end of it, from which he had first looked upon the village.

The chief described a large circle with one hand, sweeping the hand above his head, down to his knees, up again, as fast as he could. He pursued his monkey-lips and said, 'Whoooooooosh!' And made the circle again.

A Martian emerged from the door in the side of a house across the avenue and blinked again, this time in interest. He made his way down around the winding ramp and started to cross the street.

About halfway, he paused, eyed the calendar on the house wall, glanced at his shadow. Then he got down on his hands and knees and *crawled* across the middle of the street. Once past the middle, he rose, walked the rest of the way to join one of the groups and calmly stared at us along with the rest of them.

'They're all crazy,' Randolph said disgustedly. 'I'm going to cross that street!'

'Shut up. So it's a certain time of a certain day,' Allenby mused. 'And from the way the chief is acting, he's afraid for you to cross the street. And that other one just *crawled*. By God, do you know what this might tie in with?'

We were silent for a moment. Then Gonzales said, 'Of course!'

And Burton said, 'The *holes*!'

'Exactly,' said Allenby. 'Maybe whatever made – or makes – the holes come right down the centre of the street here. Maybe that's why they built the village this way – to make room for—'

'For what?' Randolph asked unhappily, shifting his feet.

'I don't know,' Allenby said. He looked thoughtfully at the chief. 'That circular motion he made – could he have been describing something that went around and around the planet? Something like – oh, no!' Allenby's eyes glazed. 'I wouldn't believe it in a million years.'

His gaze went to the far end of the street, to the high sand dune that rose there. The chief seemed to be waiting for somthing to happen.

'I'm going to crawl,' Randolph stated. He got to his hands and knees and began to creep across the centre of the avenue.

The chief let him go.

The sand dune at the end of the street suddenly erupted. A forty-foot spout of dust shot straight out from the sloping side, as if a bullet had emerged. Powdered sand hazed the air, yellowed it almost the full length of the avenue. Grains of sand stung the skin and rattled minutely on the houses.

WhoooSSSHHHHH!

Randolph dropped flat on his belly. He didn't have to continue his trip. He had made other arrangements.

That night in the ship, while we all sat around, still shaking our heads every once in a while, Allenby talked with Earth. He sat there, wearing the headphones, trying to make himself understood above the godawful static.

'. . . an exceedingly small body,' he repeated wearily to his unbelieving audience, 'about four inches in diameter. It travels at a mean distance of four feet above the surface of the planet, a velocity yet to be calculated. Its unique nature results in many hitherto unobserved – I might say even unimagined – phenomena.' He stared blankly in front of him for a moment, then delivered the understatement of his life. 'The discovery may necessitate a re-examination of many of our basic postulates in the physical sciences.'

The headphones squawked.

Patiently, Allenby assured Earth that he was entirely serious, and reiterated the results of his observations. I suppose that he, an astronomer, was twice as flabbergasted as the rest of us. On the other hand, perhaps he was better equipped to adjust to the evidence.

'Evidently,' he said, 'when the body was formed, it travelled at such fantastic velocity as to enable it to' – his voice was almost a whisper – 'to punch holes in things.'

The headphones squawked.

'In rocks,' Allenby said, 'in mountains, in anything that got in its way. And now the holes form a large portion of its fixed orbit.'

Squawk.

'Its mass must be in the order of—'

Squawk.

'—process of making the holes slowed it, so that now it travels just fast enough—'

Squawk.

'—maintain its orbit and penetrate occasional objects such as—'

Squawk.

'—and sand dunes—'

Squawk.

'My God, I *know* it's a mathematical monstrosity,' Allenby snarled, '*I* didn't put it there!'

Squawk.

Allenby was silent for a moment. Then he said slowly, 'A name?'

Squawk.

'H'm,' said Allenby. 'Well, well.' He appeared to brighten just a little. 'So it's up to me, as leader of the expedition, to name it?'

Squawk.

'Well, well,' he said.

That chop-licking tone was in his voice. We'd heard it all too often before. We shuddered, waiting.

'Inasmuch as Mar's outermost moon is called Deimos, and the next Phobos,' he said, 'I think I shall name the third moon of Mars — *Bottomos.*'

THE HOLES AROUND MARS

Jerome Bixby, although an excellent piano player, is not an author usually associated with 'scientific' s.f. *The Holes Around Mars* is entertaining and fascinating, but it has many scientific flaws.

Mars has two known moons: Deimos, the outer, which is 12,500 miles above the Martian surface, and Phobos, the inner, which is 3,7000 miles above that surface. Bixby postulates a third satellite, which circles Mars a few feet above its surface.

Bixby supposes this third satellite has the energy to punch holes through any Martian object rising more than those few feet above the surface. But where does the energy to punch holes, sometimes hundreds of miles long, come from?

The kinetic energy of motion depends on the mass and on the square of the velocity of the moving object, and Bixby blames the holes on the vast velocity of the satellite. However, a relatively small object travelling in an orbit about a planet has only one possible velocity, and this depends on the mass of the planet and the distance of the orbiting object from the centre of that planet. If the satellite were to move faster than that, its orbit would curve downward. To maintain a perfectly circular orbit, neither rising further above the surface nor dropping towards it requires an orbital velocity that, in the case of Mars, is not enormously high. It is certainly not high enough to make those holes.

The energy might be due to mass rather than velocity. Suppose that the third satellite were neutronium (see *Proof*). It would then be enormously heavy for its size and it might bore those holes for that reason, but it seems quite certain that a four-inch-across ball of neutronium could not exist by itself. It would explode into ordinary matter as soon as it formed.

Questions and Suggestions

1. What is the orbital velocity of the two known Martian satellites? If you divide the escape velocity from the Martian surface by the square root of two you would obtain the orbital velocity for a satellite revolving in a circular orbit in the neighbourhood of the Martian surface. How much is that in miles per hour? If the satellite were of ordinary granite, what would its kinetic energy be in comparison with that of a .45 bullet shot out of a revolver?

2. If the third satellite were neutronium, how much would it weigh? What would be its kinetic energy at the orbital velocity?

3. Our explorers in *The Holes Around Mars* find that the holes are in a straight line; that is, if you sight through a hole in one place you would see another hole in another place far away. But could you? Is the third satellite travelling in a true straight line or is it follow-

ing the curvature of the Martian surface? How much does the Martian surface curve; that is, in the space of one mile, how far does the Martian surface drop? Calculate how far apart two holes must be so that when sighting through one you can no longer see the other?

4. According to the story, it would seem that the third satellite follows precisely the same path each time it circles the planet. Yet if the orbit were at an angle to the Martian equator, it would follow a different path each time around, for Mars will have rotated part-way during the time of one orbit. What would the orbit look like on a flat map of the Martian surface?

5. If the third satellite were following a path exactly along the Martian equator, the rotation of the planet wouldn't matter and the little satellite would follow its own track each rotation. (Why?) Is it likely, though, that its orbit would be lined up exactly with the Martian equator? What about the orbits of Phobos and Deimos in this respect. Suppose the third satellite's orbit varied from the line of the equator so slightly that it moved four inches south at another. What would that do to the holes?

3. THE DEEP RANGE

Arthur C. Clarke

There was a killer loose on the range. A copter patrol, five hundred miles off Greenland, had seen the great corpse staining the sea crimson as it wallowed in the waves. Within seconds, the intricate warning system had been alerted; men were plotting circles and moving counters on the North Atlantic chart – Don Burley was still rubbing the sleep from his eyes as he dropped silently down to the twenty-fathom line.

The pattern of green lights on the tell-tale was a glowing symbol of security. As long as that pattern was unchanged, as long as none of those emerald stars winked to red, all was well with Don and his tiny craft. Air – fuel – power – this was the triumvirate which ruled his life. If any of them failed, he would be sinking in a steel coffin down towards the pelagic ooze, as Johnnie Tyndall had done the season before last. But there was no reason why they should fail; the accidents one foresaw, Don told himself reassuringly, were never the ones that happened.

He leaned across the tiny control board and spoke into the mike. Sub 5 was still close enough to the mother ship for radio to work, but before long he'd have to switch to the sonics.

'Setting course 255, speed 50 knots, depth 20 fathoms, full sonar coverage. . . . Estimated time to target area, 70 minutes. Will report at 10-minute intervals. That is all. . . . Out.'

The acknowledgement, already weakening with range, came back at once from the *Herman Melville*.

'Message received and understood. Good hunting. What about the hounds?'

Don chewed his lower lip thoughtfully. This might be a job he'd have to handle alone. He had no idea, to within fifty miles either way, where Benj and Susan were at the moment. They'd certainly follow if he signalled for them, but they couldn't maintain his speed and would soon have to drop behind. Besides, he might be heading for a pack of killers, and the last thing he wanted to do was to lead his carefully trained porpoises into trouble. That was common sense and good business. He was also very fond of Susan and Benj.

'It's too far, and I don't know what I'm running into,' he replied. 'If they're in the interception area when I get there, I may whistle them up.'

The acknowledgement from the mother ship was barely audible, and Don switched off the set. It was time to look around.

He dimmed the cabin lights so that he could see the scanner screen more clearly, pulled the polaroid glasses down over his eyes, and peered into the depths. This was the moment when Don felt like a god, able to hold within his hands a circle of the Atlantic twenty miles across, and to see clear down to the still-unexplored deeps, three thousand fathoms below. The slowly rotating beam of inaudible sound was searching the world in which he floated, seeking out friend and foe in the eternal darkness where light could never penetrate. The pattern of soundless shrieks, too shrill even for the hearing of the bats, who had invented sonar a million years before man, pulsed out into the watery night; the faint echoes came tingling back as floating, blue-green flecks on the screen.

Through long practice, Don could read their message with effortless ease. A thousand feet below, stretching out to his submerged horizon, was the scattering layer – the blanket of life that covered half the world. The sunken meadow of the sea, it rose and fell with the passage of the sun, hovering always at the edge of darkness. But the ultimate depths were no concern of his. The flocks he guarded, and the enemies who ravaged them, belonged to the upper levels of the sea.

Don flicked the switch of the depth-selector, and his sonar beam concentrated itself into the horizontal plane. The glimmering echoes from the abyss vanished, but he could see more clearly what lay around him here in the ocean's stratospheric heights. That glowing cloud two miles ahead was a school of fish; he wondered if Base knew about it, and made an entry in his log. There were some larger, isolated *blips* at the edge of the school – the carnivores pursuing the cattle insuring that the endlessly turning wheel of life and death would never lose momentum. But this conflict was no affair of Don's; he was after bigger game.

Sub 5 drove on towards the west, a steel needle swifter and more deadly than any other creature that roamed the seas. The tiny cabin, lit only by the flicker of lights from the instrument board, pulsed with power as the spinning turbines thrust the water aside. Don glanced at the chart and wondered how the enemy had broken through this time. There were still many weak points, for fencing the oceans of the world had been a gigantic task. The tenuous electric fields, fanning out between generators many miles apart, could not always hold at bay the starving monsters of the deep. They were learning, too. When the fences were opened, they would sometimes slip through with the whales and wreak havoc before they were discovered.

The long-range receiver bleeped plaintively, and Don switched over to TRANSCRIBE. It wasn't practical to send speech any distance over an ultrasonic beam, and code had come back into its own. Don had never learned to read it by ear, but the ribbon of paper emerging from the slot saved him the trouble.

COPTER REPORTS SCHOOL 50–100 WHALES HEADING 95

Don started to set the coordinates on the plotting
grid, then saw that it was no longer necessary. At the
extreme edge of his screen, a flotilla of faint stars had
appeared. He altered course slightly, and drove head-on
towards the approaching herd.

The copter was right; they were moving fast. Don felt
a mounting excitement, for this could mean that they
were on the run and luring the killers towards him. At
the rate at which they were travelling he would be
among them in five minutes. He cut the motors and felt
the backward tug of water bringing him swiftly to rest.

Don Burley, a knight in armour, sat in his tiny dim-lit
room fifty feet below the bright Atlantic waves, testing
his weapons for the conflict that lay ahead. In these
moments of poised suspense, before action began, his
racing brain often explored such fantasies. He felt a
kinship with all shepherds who had guarded their flocks
back to the dawn of time. He was David, among ancient
Palestinian hills, alert for the mountain lions that would
prey upon his father's sheep. But far nearer in time, and
far closer in spirit, were the men who had marshalled
the great herds of cattle on the American plains, only a
few lifetimes ago. They would have understood his work,
though his implements would have been magic to them.
The pattern was the same; only the scale had altered. It
made on fundamental difference that the beasts Don
herded weighed almost a hundred tons, and browsed on
the endless savannahs of the sea.

The school was now less than two miles away, and
Don checked his scanner's continuous circling to concentrate on the sector ahead. The picture on the screen
altered to a fan-shaped wedge as the sonar beam started
to flick from side to side; now he could count every
whale in the school, and even make a good estimate of
its size. With a practised eye, he began to look for
stragglers.

Don could never have explained what drew him at
once towards those four echoes at the southern fringe of
the school. It was true that they were a little apart from
the rest, but others had fallen as far behind. There is
some sixth sense that a man acquires when he has stared
long enough into a sonar screen – some hunch which

enables him to extract more from the moving flecks than he has any right to do. Without conscious thought, Don reached for the control which would start the turbines whirling into life. Sub 5 was just getting under way when three leaden thuds reverberated through the hull, as if someone was knocking on the front door and wanted to come in.

'Well, I'm damned,' said Don. 'How did you get here?' He did not bother to switch on the TV; he'd know Benj's signal anywhere. The porpoises must have been in the neighbourhood and had spotted him before he'd even switched on the hunting call. For the thousandth time, he marvelled at their intelligence and loyalty. It was strange that Nature had played the same trick twice – on land with the dog, in the ocean with the porpoise. Why were these graceful sea-beasts so fond of man, to whom they owed so little? It made one feel that the human race was worth something after all, if it could inspire such unselfish devotion.

It had been known for centuries that the porpoise was at least as intelligent as the dog, and could obey quite complex verbal commands. The experiment was still in progress, but if it succeeded, then the ancient partnership between shepherd and sheep dog would have a new lease of life.

Don switched on the speakers recessed into the sub's hull and began to talk to his escorts. Most of the sounds he uttered would have been meaningless to other human ears; they were the product of long research by the animal psychologists of the World Food Administration. He gave his orders twice to make sure that they were understood, then checked with the sonar screen to see that Benj and Susan were following astern as he had told them to.

The four echoes that had attracted his attention were clearer and closer now, and the main body of the whale pack had swept past him to the east. He had no fear of a collision; the great animals, even in their panic, could sense his presence as easily as he could detect theirs, and by similar means. Don wondered if he should switch on his beacon. They might recognize its sound pattern, and it would reassure them. But the still unknown enemy might recognize it, too.

He closed for an interception, and hunched low over

the screen as if to drag from it by sheer will power every scrap of information the scanner could give. There were two large echoes, some distance apart, and one was accompanied by a pair of smaller satellites. Don wondered if he was already too late. In his mind's eye, he could picture the death struggle taking place in the water less than a mile ahead. Those two fainter *blips* would be the enemy – either shark or grampus – worrying a whale while one of its companions stood by in helpless terror, with no weapons of defense except its mighty flukes.

Now he was almost close enough for vision. The TV camera in Sub 5's prow strained through the gloom, but at first could show nothing but the fog of plankton. Then a vast shadowy shape began to form in the centre of the screen, with two smaller companions below it. Don was seeing, with the greater precision but hopelessly limited range of ordinary light, what the sonar scanners had already told him.

Almost at once he saw his mistake. The two satellites were calves, not sharks. It was the first time he had ever met a whale with twins; although multiple births were not unknown, a cow could suckle only two young at once and usually only the stronger would survive. He choked down his disappointment; this error had cost him many minutes and he must begin to search again.

Then came the frantic tattoo on the hull that meant danger. It wasn't easy to scare Benj, and Don shouted his reassurance as he swung Sub 5 round so that the camera could search the turgid waters. Automatically, he had turned towards the fourth *blip* on the sonar screen – the echo he had assumed, from its size, to be another adut whale. And he saw that, after all, he had come to the right place.

'Jesus!' he said softly. 'I didn't know they came that big.' He'd seen larger sharks before, but they had all been harmless vegetarians. This, he could tell at a glance, was a Greenland shark, the killer of the northern seas. It was supposed to grow up to thirty feet long, but this specimen was bigger than Sub 5. It was every inch of forty feet from snout to tail, and when he spotted it, it was already turning in towards the kill. Like the coward it was, it had launched its attack at one of the calves.

Don yelled to Benj and Susan, and saw them racing

ahead into his field of vision. He wondered fleetingly why porpoises had such an overwhelming hatred of sharks; then he loosed his hands from the controls as the autopilot locked on to the target. Twisting and turning as agilely as any other sea-creature of its size, Sub 5 began to close in on the shark, leaving Don free to concentrate on his armament.

The killer had been so intent upon his prey that Benj caught him completely unaware, ramming him just behind the left eye. It must have been a painful blow; an iron-hard snout, backed by a quarter-ton of muscle moving at fifty miles an hour is something not to be laughed at, even by the largest fish. The shark jerked round in an impossibly tight curve, and Don was almost jolted out of his seat as the sub snapped on to a new course. If this kept up, he'd find it hard to use his Sting. But at least the killer was too busy now to bother about his intended victims.

Benj and Susan were worrying the giant like dogs snapping at the heels of an angry bear. They were too agile to be caught in those ferocious jaws, and Don marvelled at the coordination with which they worked. When either had to surface for air, the other would hold off for a minute until the attack could be resumed in strength.

There was no evidence that the shark realized that a far more dangerous adversary was closing in upon it, and that the porpoises were merely a distraction. That suited Don very nicely; the next operation was going to be difficult unless he could hold a steady course for at least fifteen seconds. At a pinch he could use the tiny rocket torps to make a kill. If he'd been alone, and faced with a pack of sharks he would certainly have done so. But it was messy, and there was a better way. He preferred the technique of the rapier to that of the hand-grenade.

Now he was only fifty feet away, and closing in rapidly. There might never be a better chance. He punched the launching stud.

From beneath the belly of the sub, something that looked like a sting-ray hurtled forward. Don had checked the speed of his own craft; there was no need to come any closer now. The tiny, arrow-shaped hydrofoil, only a couple of feet across, could move far faster than his vessel and would close the gap in seconds. As it raced forward, it spun out the thin line of the control wire, like some underwater spider laying its thread. Along that wire passed the energy that powered the Sting, and the signals that steered it to its goal. Don had completely ignored his own larger craft in the effort of guiding this underwater missile. It responded to his touch so swiftly that he felt he was controlling some sensitive high-spirited steed.

The shark saw the danger less than a second before impact. The resemblance of the Sting to an ordinary ray confused it, as the designers had intended. Before the tiny brain could realize that no ray behaved like this, the missile had struck. The steel hypodermic, rammed forward by an exploding cartridge, drove through the shark's horny skin, and the great fish erupted in a frenzy of terror. Don backed rapidly away, for a blow from that tail would rattle him around like a pea in a can and might even cause damage to the sub. There was nothing more for him to do, except to speak into the microphone and call off his hounds.

The doomed killer was trying to arch its body so that it could snap at the poisoned dart. Don had now reeled the Sting back into its hiding place, pleased that he had been able to retrieve the missile undamaged. He watched without pity as the great fish succumbed to its paralysis.

Its struggles were weakening. It was swimming aimlessly back and forth, and once Don had to sidestep smartly to avoid a collision. As it lost control of buoyancy, the dying shark drifted up to the surface. Don did not bother to follow; that could wait until he had attended to more important business.

He found the cow and her two calves less than a mile away, and inspected them carefully. They were uninjured, so there was no need to call the vet in his highly specialized two-man sub which could handle any cetalogical crisis from a stomach-ache to a Caesarean. Don made a note of the mother's number, stencilled just behind the flippers. The calves, as was obvious from their size, were this season's and had not yet been branded.

Don watched for a little while. They were no longer in the least alarmed, and a check on the sonar had shown that the whole school had ceased its panicky flight. He wondered how they knew what had happened; much had been learned about communication among whales, but much was still a mystery.

'I hope you appreciate what I've done for you, old lady,' he muttered. Then, reflecting that fifty tons of mother love was a slightly awe-inspiring sight, he blew his tanks and surfaced.

It was calm, so he cracked the airlock and popped his head out of the tiny conning tower. The water was only inches below his chin, and from time to time a wave made a determined effort to swamp him. There was little danger of this happening, for he fitted the hatch so closely that he was quite an effective plug.

Fifty feet away, a long slate-coloured mound, like an over-turned boat, was rolling on the surface. Don looked at it thoughtfully and did some mental calculations. A brute this size should be valuable; with any luck, there was a chance of a double bonus. In a few minutes he'd radio his report, but for the moment it was pleasant to drink the fresh Atlantic air and to feel the open sky above his head.

A grey thunderbolt shot up out of the depths and smashed back on to the surface of the water, smothering Don with spray. It was Benj's modest way of drawing attention to himself; a moment later the porpoise had swum up to the conning tower, so that Don could reach down and tickle its head. The great, intelligent eyes stared back into his; was it pure imagination, or did an almost human sense of fun also lurk in their depths?

Susan, as usual, circled shyly at a distance until jealousy overpowered her and she butted Benj out of the way. Don distributed caresses impartially, and apologized because he had nothing to give them. He undertook to make up for the omission as soon as he returned to the *Herman Melville*.

'I'll go for another swim with you, too,' he promised, 'as long as you behave yourselves next time.' He rubbed thoughtfully at a large bruise caused by Benj's playfulness, and wondered if he was not getting a little too old for rough games like this.

'Time to go home,' Don said firmly, sliding down into the cabin and slamming the hatch. He suddenly realized that he was very hungry, and had better do something about the breakfast he had missed. There were not many men on earth who had earned a better right to eat their morning meal. He had saved for humanity more tons of meat, oil, and milk than could easily be estimated.

Don Burley was the happy warrior coming home from one battle that man would always have to fight. He was holding at bay the spectre of famine which had confronted all earlier ages, but which would never threaten the world again while the great plankton farms harvested their millions of tons of protein, and the whale herds obeyed their new masters. Man had come back to the sea after aeons of exile; until the oceans froze, he would never be hungry again. . . .

Don glanced at the scanner as he set his course. He smiled as he saw the two echoes keeping pace with the central splash of light that marked his vessel. 'Hang around,' he said. 'We mammals must stick together.' Then, as the auto-pilot took over, he lay back in his chair.

And presently Benj and Susan heard a most peculiar noise, rising and falling against the drone of the turbines. It had filtered faintly through the thick walls of Sub 5, and only the sensitive ears of the porpoises could have detected it. But intelligent beasts though they were, they could hardly be expected to understand why Don Burley was announcing, in a highly unmusical voice, that he was Heading for the Last Round-up. . . .

THE DEEP RANGE

The Deep Range might be considered a science-fiction Western. For cattle, we have whales; for cougars, we have killer sharks; for dogs, we have porpoises; for a cowboy on a horse, we have what we might call a 'whale-boy' in a submarine.

The story ends on a very optimistic note, for it states that once whales are herded for food, man will never starve again. This optimism may not be justified.

There are food chains in which Animal A eats Animal B which eats Animal C which eats Animal D and so on. Usually, we finally reach an animal which lives on plants, and the plants get their energy out of sunlight and their building blocks out of the inanimate environment. Thus, we eat cattle which eats grass or we might eat polar bears, which eat seals which eat fish, which eat minnows, which eat insect larvae, which eat one-celled plants.

At each step of feeding there is considerable waste so that only 10 per cent of the living matter of the creature fed upon is converted into the living matter of the creature who is feeding. The total weight of the polar bears cannot be more than 10 per cent of the total weight of the seals it feeds on which in turn cannot be more than 10 per cent of the fish *it* feeds on, and so on.

Thus, the polar bears weigh only a tenth of a tenth, or one hundredth of the fish the seals feed on. If the polar bears fed on the fish directly, they could weigh, altogether, one tenth the weight of the fish. There would be ten times as many fish-feeding polar bears as seal-feeding polar bears. By cutting out items in the food chain, then, a feeder can do better in terms of its own numbers and mass.

The largest creatures, huge whales and sharks, live on tiny creatures and cut out all the steps in the food chain in between.

Whales can grow larger and more numerous living on tiny shrimp called krill, than they could by living on large fish that lived on smaller fish that lived on krill. If men learned to live on whales, they would have a valuable source of good protein, but suppose they cut out one step of the food chain and learned to harvest and process krill, making it tasty and nourishing. They would then have a food supply ten times as great.

(Clarke, one of the best of the 'scientific' s.f. writers, is best known now for his writing of the screen play of the motion picture *2001*.)

Questions and Suggestions

1. The plant life in the ocean is about four times as great in quantity as the plant life on land. Man's present food supply is based chiefly on land plants and animals. If men could exploit the sea to the same extent as the land, the total food supply would increase fivefold. But man is doubling his numbers every forty-seven years. At the present rate of doubling, how long would it be before the human population increases fivefold? By that time, the amount of food per capita, land and sea, would be no greater than it is now. Is Clarke, in your opinion,

right to be so optimistic over man's food supply? What is needed to make the optimism realistic?

2. The question of the intelligence of porpoises is of great interest to biologists now. Look up some of the work being done with them. If porpoises (and how do they differ from dolphins and from whales, by the way?) are as intelligent as man, as some think, why have they not developed a civilization?

3. If mankind learns to harvest and process krill, what would happen to the great whales?

4. Why has Clarke named the whale-herding ship the *Herman Melville*?

4. THE CAVE OF NIGHT

James E. Gunn

The phrase was first used by a poet disguised in the cynical hide of a newspaper reporter. It appeared on the first day and was widely reprinted. He wrote:

'At eight o'clock, after the Sun has set and the sky is darkening, look up! There's a man up there where no man has ever been.

'He is lost in the cave of night . . .'

The headlines demanded something short, vigorous and descriptive. That was it. It was inaccurate, but it stuck.

If anybody was in a cave, it was the rest of humanity. Painfully, triumphantly, one man had climbed out. Now he couldn't find his way back in to the cave with the rest of us.

What goes up doesn't always come back down.

That was the first day. After it came twenty-nine days of agonized suspense.

The cave of night. I wish the phrase had been mine.

That was it, the tag, the symbol. It was the first thing a man saw when he glanced at the newspaper. It was the way people talked about it: 'What's the latest about the cave?' It summed it all up, the drama, the anxiety, the hope.

Maybe it was the Floyd Collins influence. The papers

63

dug up their files on that old tragedy, reminiscing, comparing; and they remembered the little girl – Kathy Fiscus, wasn't it? – who was trapped in that abandoned California drain pipe; and a number of others.

Periodically, it happens, a sequence of events so accidentally dramatic that men lose their hatreds, their terrors, their shynesses, their inadequacies, and the human race momentarily recognizes its kinship.

The essential ingredients are these: a person must be in unusual and desperate peril. The peril must have duration. There must be proof that the person is still alive. Rescue attempts must be made. Publicity must be widespread.

One could probably be constructed artificially, but if the world ever discovered the fraud, it would never forgive.

Like many others, I have tried to analyse what makes a niggling, squabbling, callous race of beings suddenly share that most human emotion of sympathy, and, like them, I have not succeeded. Suddenly a distant stranger will mean more than their own comfort. Every waking moment, they pray: Live, Floyd! Live, Kathy! Live, Rev!

We pass on the street, we who would not have nodded, and ask, 'Will they get there in time?'

Optimists and pessimists alike, we hope so. We all hope so.

In a sense, this one was different. This was purposeful. Knowing the risk, accepting it because there was no other way to do what had to be done. Rev had gone into the cave of night. The accident was that he could not return.

The news came out of nowhere – literally – to an unsuspecting world. The earliest mention the historians have been able to locate was an item about a ham radio operator in Davenport, Iowa. He picked up a distress signal on a sticky-hot June evening.

The message, he said later, seemed to fade in, reach a peak, and fade out:

. . . and fuel tanks empty –ceiver broke . . . transmitting in clear so someone can pick this up, and . . . no way to get back . . . stuck . . .'

A small enough beginning.

The next message was received by a military base

radio watch near Fairbanks, Alaska. That was early in the morning. Half an hour later, a night-shift worker in Boston heard something on his short-wave set that sent him rushing to the telephone.

That morning, the whole world learned the story. It broke over them, a wave of excitement and concern. Orbiting 1,075 miles above their heads was a man, an officer of the United States Air Force, in a fuelless spaceship.

All by itself, the spaceship part would have captured the world's attention. It was achievement as monumental as anything Man has ever done and far more spectacular. It was liberation from the tyranny of Earth, this jealous mother who had bound her children tight with the apron strings of gravity.

Man was free. It was a symbol that nothing is completely and finally impossible if Man wants it hard enough and long enough.

There are regions that humanity finds peculiarly congenial. Like all Earth's creatures, Man is a product and a victim of environment. His triumph is that the slave became the master. Unlike more specialized animals, he distributed himself across the entire surface of the Earth, from the frozen Antarctic continent to the Arctic icecap.

Man became an equatorial animal, a temperate zone animal, an arctic animal. He became a plain dweller, a valley dweller, a mountain dweller. The swamp and the desert became equally his home.

Man made his own environment.

With his inventive mind and his dexterous hands, he fashioned it, conquered cold and heat, dampness, aridness, land, sea, air. Now, with his science, he had conquered everything. He had become independent of the world that bore him.

It was a birthday cake for all mankind, celebrating its coming of age.

Brutally, the disaster was icing on the cake.

But it was more, too. When everything is considered, perhaps it was the aspect that, for a few, brief days, united humanity and made possible what we did.

It was a sign: Man is never completely independent of Earth; he carries with him his environment; he is always and forever a part of humanity. It was a conquest mellowed by a confession of mortality and error.

It was a statement: Man has within him the qualities of greatness that will never accept the restraints of circumstance, and yet he carries, too, the seeds of fallibility that we all recognize in ourselves.

Rev was one of us. His triumph was our triumph; his peril – more fully and finely – was our peril.

Reverdy L. McMillen, III, first lieutenant, U.S.A.F. Pilot. Rocket jockey. Man. Rev. He was only a thousand miles away, calling for help, but those miles were straight up. We got to know him as well as any member of our own family.

The news came as a great personal shock to me. I knew Rev. We had become good friends in college, and fortune had thrown us together in the Air Force, a writer and a pilot. I had got out as soon as possible, but Rev had stayed in. I knew, vaguely, that he had been testing rocket-powered aeroplanes with Chuck Yeager. But I had no idea that the rocket programme was that close to space.

Nobody did. It was a better-kept secret that the Manhattan Project.

I remember staring at Rev's picture in the evening newspaper – the straight black hair, the thin, rakish moustache, the Clark Gable ears, the reckless, rueful grin – and I felt again, like a physical thing, his great joy in living. It expressed itself in a hundred ways. He loved widely, but with discrimination. He ate well, drank heartily, revelled in expert jazz and artistic inventiveness, and talked incessantly.

Now he was alone and soon all that might be extinguished. I told myself that I would help.

That was a time of wild enthusiasm. Men mobbed the Air Force Proving Grounds at Cocoa, Florida, wildly volunteering their services. But I was no engineer. I wasn't even a welder or a riveter. At best, I was only a poor word mechanic.

But words, at least, I could contribute.

I made a hasty verbal agreement with a local paper and caught the first plane to Washington, D.C. For a long time, I liked to think that what I wrote during the next few days had something to do with subsequent events, for many of my articles were picked up for reprint by other newspapers.

The Washington fiasco was the responsibility of the Senate Investigating Committee. It subpoenaed everybody in sight – which effectively removed them from the vital work they were doing. But within a day, the Committee realized that it had bitten off a bite it could neither swallow nor spit out.

General Beauregard Finch, head of the research and development programme, was the tough morsel the Committee gagged on. Coldly, accurately, he described the development of the project, the scientific and technical research, the tests, the building of the ship, the training of the prospective crewmen, and the winnowing of the volunteers down to one man.

In words more eloquent because of their clipped precision, he described the take-off of the giant three-stage ship, shoved upward on a lengthening arm of combining hydrazine and nitric acid. Within fifty-six minutes, the remaining third stage had reached its orbital height of 1,075 miles.

It had coasted there. In order to maintain that orbit, the motors had to flicker on for fifteen seconds.

At that moment, disaster laughed at Man's careful calculations.

Before Rev could override the automatics, the motors had flamed for almost half a minute. The fuel he had depended upon to slow the ship so that it would drop, re-enter the atmosphere and be reclaimed by Earth was almost gone. His efforts to counteract the excess resulted only in an approximation of the original orbit.

The fact was this: Rev was up there. He would stay there until someone came and got him.

And there was no way to get there.

The Committee took that as an admission of guilt and incompetence; they tried to lever themselves free with it, but General Finch was not to be intimidated. A manned ship had been sent up because no mechanical or electronic computer could contain the vast possibilities for decision and action built into a human being.

The original computer was still the best all-purpose computer.

There had been only one ship built, true. But there

was good reason for that, a completely practical reason – money.

Leaders are, by definition, ahead of the people. But this wasn't a field in which they could show the way and wait for the people to follow. This was no expedition in ancient ships, no light exploring party, no pilot-plant operation. Like a parachute jump, it had to be successful first time.

This was an enterprise into new, expensive fields. It demanded money (billions of dollars), brains (the best available), and the hard, dedicated labour of men (thousands of them).

General Finch became a national hero that afternoon. He said, in bold words, 'With the limited funds you gave us, we have done what we set out to do. We have demonstrated that space flight is possible, that a space platform is feasible.

'If there is an inefficiency, if there is any blame for what has happened, it lies at the door of those who lacked confidence in the courage and ability of their countrymen to fight free of Earth to the greatest glory. Senator, how did you vote on that?'

But I am not writing a history. The shelves are full of them. I will touch on the international repercussions only enough to show that the event was no more a re-specter of national boundaries than was Rev's orbiting ship.

The orbit was almost perpendicular to the equator. The ship travelled as far north as Nome, as far south as Little America on the Antarctic continent. It completed one giant circle every two hours. Meanwhile, the Earth rotated beneath. If the ship had been equipped with adequate optical instruments, Rev could have observed every spot on Earth within twenty-four hours. He could have seen fleets and their dispositions, aircraft carriers and the planes taking off their decks, troop manoeuvres.

In the General Assembly of the United Nations, the Russian ambassador protested this unwarranted and illegal violation of its national boundaries. He hinted darkly that it would not be allowed to continue. The U.S.S.R. had not been caught unprepared, he said. If the violation went on – *'every few hours!'* – drastic steps would be taken.

World opinion reared up in indignation. The U.S.S.R. immediately retreated and pretended, as only it could, that its belligerence had been an unwarranted inference and that it had never said anything of the sort, anyway.

This was not a military observer above our heads. It was a man who would soon be dead unless help reached him.

A world offered what it had. Even the U.S.S.R. announced that it was outfitting a rescue ship, since its space programme was already on the verge of success. And the American public responded with more than a billion dollars within a week. Congress appropriated another billion. Thousands of men and women volunteered.

The race began.

Would the rescue party reach the ship in time? The world prayed.

And it listened daily to the voice of a man it hoped to buy back from death.

The problem shaped up like this:

The trip had been planned to last for only a few days. By careful rationing, the food and water might be stretched out for more than a month, but the oxygen, by cutting down activity to conserve it, couldn't possible last more than thirty days. That was the absolute-outside limit.

I remember reading the carefully detailed calculations in the paper and studying them for some hopeful error. There was none.

Within a few hours, the discarded first stage of the ship had been located floating in the Atlantic Ocean. It was towed back to Cocoa, Florida. Almost a week was needed to find and return to the Proving Grounds the second stage, which had landed 906 miles away.

Both sections were practically undamaged; their fall had been cushioned by ribbon parachute. They could be cleaned, repaired and used again. The trouble was the vital third stage – the nose section. A new one had to be designed and built within a month.

Space-madness became a new form of hysteria. We read statistics, we memorized insignificant details, we studied diagrams, we learned the risks and the dangers and how they would be met and conquered. It all became part of us. We watched the slow progress of the second ship and silently, tautly, urged it upward.

The schedule overhead became part of everyone's daily life. Work stopped while people rushed to windows or outside or to their television sets, hoping for a glimpse, a glint from the high, swift ship, so near, so untouchably far.

And we listened to the voice from the cave of night:

'I've been staring out of the portholes. I never tire of that. Through the one on the right, I see what looks like a black velvet curtain with a strong light behind it. There are pinpoint holes in the curtain and the light shines through, not winking the way stars do, but steady. There's no air up here. That's the reason. The mind can understand and still misinterpret.

'My air is holding out better than I expected. By my figures, it should last twenty-seven days more. I shouldn't use so much of it talking all the time, but it's hard to stop. Talking, I feel as if I'm still in touch with Earth, still one of you, even if I am way up here.

'Through the left-hand window is San Francisco Bay, looking like a dark, wandering arm extended by the ocean octopus. The city itself looks like a heap of diamonds with trails scattered from it. It glitters up cheerfully, an old friend. It misses me, it says. Hurry home, it says. It's gone now, out of sight. Good-bye, Frisco!

'Do you hear me down there? Sometimes I wonder. You can't see me now. I'm in the Earth's shadow. You'll have to wait for the dawn. I'll have mine in a few minutes.

'You're all busy down there. I know that. If I know you, you're all worrying about me, working to get me down, forgetting everything else. You don't know what a feeling that is. I hope to Heaven you never have to, wonderful though it is.

'Too bad the receiver was broken, but if it had to be one or the other, I'm glad it was the transmitter that came through. There's only one of me. There are billions of you to talk to.

'I wish there were some way I could be sure you were hearing me. Just that one thing might keep me from going crazy.'

Rev, you were one in millions. We read all about

70

your selection, your training. You were our representative, picked with our greatest skill.

Out of a thousand who passed the initial **rigid** requirements for education, physical and emotional condition and age, only five could qualify for space. They couldn't be too tall, too stout, too young, too old. Medical and psychiatric tests weeded them out.

One of the training machines – Lord, how we studied this – reproduces the acceleration strains of a blasting rocket. Another trains men for manoeuvring in the weightlessness of space. A third duplicates the cramped, sealed conditions of a spaceship cabin. Out of the final five, you were the only one who qualified.

No, Rev, if any of us could stay sane, it was you.

There were thousands of suggestions, almost all of them useless. Psychologists suggested self-hypnotism; cultists suggested yoga. One man sent a detailed sketch of a giant electromagnet with which Rev's ship could be drawn back to Earth.

General Finch had the only practical idea. He outlined a plan for letting Rev know that we were listening. He picked out Kansas City and set the time. 'Midnight,' he said. 'On the dot. Not a minute earlier or later. At that moment, he'll be right overhead.'

And at midnight, every light in the city went out and came back on and went out and came back on again.

For a few awful moments, we wondered if the man up there in the cave of night had seen. Then came the voice we knew now so well that it seemed it had always been with us, a part of us, our dreams and our waking.

The voice was husky with emotion:

'Thanks . . . Thanks for listening. Thanks, Kansas City. I saw you winking at me. I'm not alone. I know that now. I'll never forget. Thanks.'

And silence then as the ship fell below the horizon. We pictured it to ourselves sometimes, continually circling the Earth, its trajectory exactly matching the curvature of the globe beneath it. We wondered if it would ever stop.

Like the Moon, would it be a satellite of the Earth forever?

We went through our daily chores like automatons while we watched the third stage of the rocket take shape. We raced against a dwindling air supply, and

71

death raced to catch a ship moving at 15,800 miles per hour.

We watched the ship grow. On our television screens, we saw the construction of the cellular fuel tanks, the rocket motors, and the fantastic multitude of pumps, valves, gauges, switches, circuits, transistors, and tubes.

The personnel space was built to carry five men instead of one man. We watched it develop, a Spartan simplicity in the middle of the great complex, and it was as if we ourselves would live there, would watch those dials and instruments, would grip those chair-arm controls for the infinitesimal sign that the automatic pilot had faltered, would feel the soft flesh and the softer internal organs being wrenched away from the unyielding bone, and would hurtle upward into the cave of night.

We watched the plating wrap itself protectively around the vitals of the nose section. The wings were attacked; they would make the ship a huge, metal glider in its unpowered descent to Earth after the job was done.

We met the men who would man the ship. We grew to know them as we watched them train, saw them fighting artificial gravities, testing spacesuits in simulated vacuums, practising manoeuvres in the weightless condition of free fall.

That was what we lived for.

And we listened to the voice that came to us out of the night:

'Twenty-one days. Three weeks. Seems like more. Feel a little sluggish, but there's no room for exercise in a coffin. The concentrated foods I've been eating are fine, but not for a steady diet. Oh, what I'd give for a piece of home-baked apple-pie!

'The weightlessness got me at first. Felt I was sitting on a ball that was spinning in all directions at once. Lost my breakfast a couple of times before I learned to stare at one thing. As long as you don't let your eyes roam, you're okay.

'There's Lake Michigan! My God, but it's blue today! Dazzles the eyes! There's Milwaukee, and how are the Braves doing? It must be a hot day in Chicago. It's a little muggy up here, too. The water absorbers must be overloaded.

'The air smells funny, but I'm not surprised. I must

smell funny, too, after twenty-one days without a bath. Wish I could have one. There are an awful lot of things I used to take for granted and suddenly want more than—

'Forget that, will you? Don't worry about me, I'm fine. I know you're working to get me down. If you don't succeed, that's okay with me. My life wouldn't just be wasted. I've done what I've always wanted to do. I'd do it again.

'Too bad, though, that we only had the money for one ship.'

And again: 'An hour ago, I saw the Sun rise over Russia. It looks like any other land from here, green where it should be green, farther north a sort of mud colour, and then white where the snow is still deep.

'Up here, you wonder why we're so different when the land is the same. You think: we're all children of the same mother planet. Who says we're different?

'Think I'm crazy. Maybe you're right. It doesn't matter much what I say as long as I say something. This is one time I won't be interrupted. Did any man ever have such an audience?'

No, Rev. Never.

The voice from above, historical now, preserved:

'I guess the gadgets are all right. You slide-rule mechanics! You test-tube artists! You finding what you want? Getting the dope on cosmic rays, meteoric dust, those islands you could never map, the cloud formations, wind movements, all the weather data? Hope the tele-metering gauges are working. They're more important than my voice.'

I don't think so, Rev. But we got the data. We built some of it into the new ships. *Ships*, not *ship*, for we didn't stop with one. Before we were finished, we had two complete three-stages and a dozen nose sections.

The voice: 'Air's bad tonight. Can't seem to get a full breath. Sticks in the lungs. Doesn't matter, though. I wish you could all see what I have seen, the vast-spreading universe around Earth, like a bride in a soft veil. You'd know, then, that we belong out here.'

We know, Rev. You led us out. You showed us the way.

We listened and we watched. It seems to me now that we held our breath for thirty days.

At last we watched the fuel pumping into the ship – nitric acid and hydrazine. A month ago, we did not know their names; now we recognize them as the very substance of life itself. It flowed through the long special hoses, dangerous, cautiously grounded, over half a million dollars' worth of rocket fuel.

Statisticians estimate that more than a hundred million Americans were watching their television sets that day. Watching and praying.

Suddenly the view switched to the ship fleeing south above us. The technicians were expert now. The telescopes picked it up instantly, the focus perfect the first time, and tracked it across the sky until it dropped beyond the horizon. It looked no different now than when we had seen it first.

But the voice that came from our speakers was different. It was weak. It coughed frequently and paused for breath.

'Air very bad. Better hurry. Can't last much longer . . . Silly! . . . Of course you'll hurry.

'Don't want anyone feeling sorry for me . . . I've been living fast . . . Thirty days? I've seen 360 sunrises, 360 sunsets . . . I've seen what no man has ever seen before . . . I was the first. That's something . . . worth dying for . . .

'I've seen the stars, clear and undiminished. They look cold, but there's warmth to them and life. They have families of planets like our own Sun, some of them . . . They must. God wouldn't put them there for no purpose . . . They can be homes for our future generations. Or, if they have inhabitants, we can trade with them: goods, ideas, the love of creation . . .

'But – more than this – I have seen the Earth. I have seen it – as no man has ever seen it – turning below me like a fantastic ball, the seas like blue glass in the Sun . . . or lashed into grey storm-peaks . . . and the land green with life . . . the cities of the world in the night, sparkling . . . and the people . . .

'I have seen the Earth – there where I have lived and loved . . . I have known it better than any man and loved it better and known its children better . . . It has been good . . .

'Good-bye . . . I have a better tomb than the greatest conqueror Earth ever bore . . . Do not disturb . . .'

We wept. How could we help it?

Rescue was so close and we could not hurry it. We watched impotently. The crew were hoisted far up into the nose section of the three-stage rocket. It stood as tall as a 24-storey bulding. *Hurry*! we urged. But they could not hurry. The interception of a swiftly moving target is precision business. The takeoff was all calculated and impressed on the metal and glass and free electrons of an electronic computer.

The ship was tightened down methodically. The spectators scurried back from the base of the ship. We waited. The ship waited. Tall and slim as it was, it seemed to crouch. Someone counted off the seconds to a breathless world: ten – nine – eight . . . five, four, three . . . one – *fire*!

There was no flame, and then we saw it spurting into the air from the exhaust tunnel several hundred feet away. The ship balanced, unmoving, on a squat column of incandescence; the column stretched itself, grew tall; the huge ship picked up speed and dwindled into a point of brightness.

The telescopic lenses found it, lost it, found it again. It arched over on its side and thrust itself seaward. At the end of 84 seconds, the rear jets faltered, and our hearts faltered with them. Then we saw that the first stage had been dropped. The rest of the ship moved off on a new fiery trail. A ring-shaped ribbon parachute blossomed out of the third stage and slowed it rapidly.

The second stage dropped away 124 seconds later. The nose section, with its human cargo, its rescue equipment, went on alone. At 63 miles altitude, the flaring exhaust cut out. The third stage would coast up the gravitational hill more than a thousand miles.

Our stomachs were knotted with dread as the rescue ship disappeared beyond the horizon of the farthest television camera. By this time, it was on the other side of the world, speeding towards a carefully planned rendezvous with its sister.

Hang on, Rev! Don't give up!

Fifty-six minutes. That was how long we had to wait. Fifty-six minutes from the take-off until the ship was in

75

its orbit. After that, the party would need time to match speeds, to send a space-suited crewman drifting across the emptiness between, over the vast, eerily turning sphere of the Earth beneath.

In imagination, we followed them.

Minutes would be lost while the rescuer clung to the ship, opened the airlock cautiously so that none of the precious remnants of air would be lost, and passed into the ship where one man had known utter loneliness.

We waited. We hoped.

Fifty-six minutes. They passed. An hour. Thirty minutes more. We reminded ourselves – and were reminded – that the first concern was Rev. It might be hours before we would get any real news.

The tension mounted unbearably. We waited – a nation, a world – for relief.

At eighteen minutes less than two hours – *too soon,* we told ourselves, lest we hope too much – we heard the voice of Captain Frank Pickrell, who was later to become the first commander of the *Doughnut.*

'I have just entered the ship,' he said slowly. 'The airlock was open.' He paused. The implication stunned our emotions; we listened mutely. 'Lieutenant McMillen is dead. He died heroically, waiting until all hope was gone, until every oxygen gauge stood at zero. And then – well, the airlock was open when we arrived.

'In accordance with his own wishes, his body will be left here in its eternal orbit. This ship will be his tomb for all men to see when they look up towards the stars. As long as there are men on Earth, it will circle above them, an everlasting reminder of what men have done and what men can do.

'That was Lieutenant McMillen's hope. This he did not only as an American, but as a man, dying for all humanity, and all humanity can glory for it.

'From this moment, let this be his shrine, sacred to all the generations of spacemen, inviolate. And let it be a symbol that Man's dreams can be realized, but sometimes the price is steep.

'I am going to leave here now. My feet will be the last to touch this deck. The oxygen I released is almost used up. Lieutenant McMillen is in his control chair, staring out towards the stars. I will leave the airlock doors open behind me. Let the airless, frigid arms of

76

space protect and preserve for all eternity the man they would not let go.'

Good-bye, Rev! Farewell! Good night!

Rev was not long alone. He was the first, but not the last to receive a space burial and a hero's farewell.

This, as I said, is no history of the conquest of space. Every child knows the story as well as I and can identify the make of a spaceship more swiftly.

The story of the combined efforts that built the orbital platform irreverently called the *Doughnut* has been told by others. We have learned at length the political triumph that placed it under United Nations control.

Its contribution to our daily lives has received the accolade of the commonplace. It is an observatory, a laboratory, and a guardian. Startling discoveries have come out of that weightless, airless, heartless place. It has learned how weather is made and predicted it with incredible accuracy. It has observed the stars clear of the veil of the atmosphere. And it has insured our peace . . .

It has paid its way. No one can question that. It and its smaller relay stations made possible today's worldwide television and radio network. There is no place on Earth where a free voice cannot be heard or the face of freedom be seen. Sometimes we find ourselves wondering how it could have been any other way.

And we have had adventure. We have travelled to the dead gypsum seas of the Moon with the first exploration party. This year, we will solve the mysteries of Mars. From our armchairs, we will thrill to the discoveries of our pioneers – our stand-ins, so to speak. It has given us a common heritage, a common goal, and for the first time we are united.

This I mention only for background; no one will argue that the conquest of space was not of incalculable benefit to all mankind.

The whole thing came back to me recently, an overpowering flood of memory. I was skirting Times Square, where every face is a stranger's, and suddenly I stopped, incredulous.

'Rev!' I shouted.

The man kept on walking. He passed me without a glance. I turned around and stared after him. I started to run. I grabbed him by the arm. 'Rev!' I said huskily, swinging him around. 'Is it really you?'

The man smiled politely. 'You must have mistaken me for someone else.' He unclamped my fingers easily and moved away. I realized then that there were two men with him, one on each side. I felt their eyes on my face, memorizing it.

Probably it didn't mean anything. We all have our doubles. I could have been mistaken.

But it started me remembering and thinking.

The first thing the rocket experts had to consider was expense. They didn't have the money. The second thing was weight. Even a medium-sized man is heavy when rocket payloads are reckoned, and the stores and equipment essential to his survival are many times heavier.

If Rev had escaped alive, why had they announced that he was dead? But I knew the question was all wrong.

If my speculations were right, Rev had never been up there at all. The essential payload was only a thirty-day recording and a transmitter. Even if the major feat of sending up a manned rocket was beyond their means and their techniques, they could send up that much.

Then they got the money; they got the volunteers and the techniques.

I suppose the telemetered reports from the rocket helped. But what they accomplished in thirty days was an unparalleled miracle.

The timing of the recording must have taken months of work; but the vital part of the scheme was secrecy. General Finch had to know and Captain – now Colonel – Pickrell. A few others – workmen, administrators – and Rev . . .

What could they do with him? Disguise him? Yes. And then hide him in the biggest city in the world. They would have done it that way.

It gave me a funny, sick kind of feeling, thinking about it. Like everybody else, I don't like to be taken in by a phony plea. And this was a fraud perpetrated on all humanity.

Yet it had led us to the planets. Perhaps it would lead us beyond, even to the stars. I asked myself: could they have done it any other way?

I would like to think I was mistaken. This myth has

become part of us. We lived through it ourselves, helped make it. Someday, I tell myself, a spaceman whose reverence is greater than his obedience will make a pilgrimage to that swift shrine and find only an empty shell.

I shudder then.

This pulled us together. In a sense, it keeps us together. Nothing is more important than that.

I try to convince myself that I was mistaken. The straight black hair was grey at the temples now and cut much shorter. The moustache was gone. The Clark Gable ears were flat to the head; that's a simple operation, I understand.

But grins are hard to change. And anyone who lived through those thirty days will never forget that voice.

I think about Rev and the life he must have now, the things he loved and can never enjoy again, and I realize perhaps he made the greater sacrifice.

I think sometimes he must wish he were really in the cave of night, seated in that icy control chair, 1,075 miles above, staring out at the stars.

THE CAVE OF NIGHT

This story was first published in February 1955, two and a half years before the first satellite was orbited, and six and a half years before the first man was put into orbit.

It is interesting to see in what ways James Gunn (who now works in an administrative position at the University of Kansas) foresaw events correctly, and in what ways he did not.

Gunn felt, as science fiction writers had always felt, that it was logical for a man to be inside the first object orbited. Actually, this proved not to be the case. All sorts of objects (including animals) were placed in orbit before the men in charge of the space programmes in either the U.S.A. or the U.S.S.R. would trust men to ride a spaceship safely.

Gunn's final twist has a recording orbited before a man after all (and that is much more nearly correct) and he uses that recording as a device to force mankind of all nations to be willing to invest in a space programme. This was, actually, a remarkable piece of prophecy. The first orbiting vehicle, even though it was very simple, transmitted only a bleep, and did not represent a human life in danger, did arouse enough interest to bring about the spending of billions.

The space effort that resulted, however, was not a united drive aimed at an errand of mercy, but was a nationalistic push on the part of two competing nations, each determined to pull prestige-coups over the other. (This no science fiction writer foresaw.)

Gunn assumed (as all American science fiction writers did) that the American effort would be the first to succeed. He does say the U.S.S.R. announced 'its space programme was already on the verge of success' but Gunn may have intended this ironically as the sort of thing the vainglorious Russians would be bound to say for propaganda reasons. He must have been surprised (as I was) when, in 1957, it was the Russians, after all, who managed to put up a satellite first.

Gunn had the centre of the effort at Cocoa, Florida, which is only fifteen miles west of Cape Canaveral (later Cape Kennedy) where the launchings eventually did take place. On the other hand, his picture of Earth as seen from space seems to envisage a planet with all its land and ocean clearly in view. As it turned out, the most prominent feature visible from space is Earth's cloud cover and very little of its land features can be made out easily at any given moment.

Questions and Suggestions

1. Actually no astronaut or cosmonaut has yet died by being marooned in space. A cosmonaut has died in the process of landing in the U.S.S.R. and three astronauts have died on the ground while testing a capsule in the U.S.A. Do you think that the world would react to a marooned astronaut as described? Or do you think national rivalries would overcome human sympathy? How about world reaction to starvation in Biafra or in India? What about people in crowds who yell 'Jump! Jump!' when someone teeters on a high building ledge? How would *you* feel if it were a Russian who was marooned?

2. Gunn has the rescue vessels designed, built, and launched in the space of thirty days. Do you think this

is practical? Look up data on the space programme and find out how long such things take.

3. Gunn, like all science fiction writers of the time, takes the value of the space effort for granted. He says: 'No one will argue that the conquest of space was not of incalculable benefit to all mankind.' Yet, at the present time, after the Moon has actually been reached, many do argue against the value of the space effort. Look into the matter and assemble points to be made in favour of the space effort and against it.

5. DUST RAG

Hal Clement

'Checking out.'

'Checked, Ridge. See you soon.'

Ridging glanced over his shoulder at Beacon Peak, as the point where the relay station had been mounted was known. The gleaming dome of its leaden meteor shield was visible as a spark; most of the lower peaks of Harpalus were already below the horizon, and with them the last territory with which Ridging or Shandara could claim familiarity. The humming turbine tractor that carried them was the only sign of humanity except each other's faces – the thin crescent of their home world was too close to the sun to be seen easily, and Earth doesn't look very 'human' from outside in any case.

The prospect ahead was not exactly strange, of course, Shandara had remarked several times in the last four weeks that a man who had seen any of the moon had seen all of it. A good many others had agreed with him. Even Ridging, whose temperament kept him normally expecting something new to happen, was beginning to get a trifle bored with the place. It wasn't even dangerous; he knew perfectly well what exposure to vacuum would mean, but checking spacesuit and air-lock valves had become a matter of habit long before.

Cosmic rays went through plastic suits and living bodies like glass, for the most part ineffective because unabsorbed; meteors blew microscopic holes through thin metal, but scarcely marked spacesuits or hulls, as far as current experiences went; the 'dust-hidden crevasses' which they had expected to catch unwary men or vehicles simply didn't exist – the dust was too dry to cover any sort of hole, except by filling it completely. The closest approach to a casualty suffered so far had occurred when a man had missed his footing on the ladder outside the *Albireo*s air lock and narrowly avoided a hundred and fifty foot fall.

Still, Shandara was being cautious. His eyes swept the ground ahead of their tracks, and his gauntleted hands rested lightly on brake and steering controls as the tractor glided ahead.

Harpalus and the relay station were out of sight now. Another glance behind assured Ridging of that. For the first time in weeks he was out of touch with the rest of the group, and for the first time he wondered whether it was such a good idea. Orders had been strict; the radius of exploration settled on long before was not to be exceeded. Ridging had been completely in favour of this; but it was his own instruments which had triggered the change of schedule.

One question about the moon to which no one could more than guess an answer in advance was that of its magnetic field. Once the group was on the surface it had immediately become evident that there was one, and comparative reading had indicated that the south magnetic pole – or *a* south magnetic pole – lay a few hundred miles away. It had been decided to modify the programme to check the region, since the last forlorn chance of finding any trace of a gaseous envelope around the moon seemed to lie in auroral investigation. Ridging found himself, to his intense astonishment, wondering why he had volunteered for the trip and then wondering how such thoughts could cross his mind. He had never considered himself a coward, and certainly had no one but himself to blame for being in the tractor. No one had made him volunteer, and any technician could have set up and operated the equipment.

'Come out of it, Ridge. Anyone would think you were worried.' Shandara's careless tones cut into his thoughts. 'How about running this buggy for a while? I've had her for a hundred kilos.'

'Right.' Ridging slipped into the driver's seat as his companion left it without slowing the tractor. He did not need to find their location on the photographic map clipped beside the panel; he had been keeping a running check almost unconsciously between the features it showed and the landmarks appearing over the horizon. A course had been marked on it, and navigation was not expected to be a problem even without a magnetic compass.

The course was far from straight, though it led over what passed for fairly smooth territory on the moon. Even back on Sinus Roris the tractor had had to weave its way around numerous obstacles; now well on to the Mare Frigoris the situation was no better, and according to the map it was nearly time to turn south through the mountains, which would be infinitely worse. According to the photos taken during the original landing approach the journey would be possible, however, and would lead through the range at its narrowest part out on to Mare Imbrium. From that point to the vicinity of Plato, where the region to be investigated lay, there should be no trouble at all.

Oddly enough, there wasn't. Ridging was moderately surprised; Shandara seemed to take it as a matter of course. The cartographer had eaten, slept, and taken his turn at driving with only an occasional remark. Ridging was beginning to believe by the time they reached their goal that his companion was actually as bored with the moon as he claimed to be. The thought, however, was fleeting; there was work to be done.

About six hundred pounds of assorted instruments were attached to the trailer which had been improvised from discarded fuel tanks. The tractor itself could not carry them; its entire cargo space was occupied by another improvisation – an auxiliary fuel tank which had been needed to make the present journey possible. The instruments had been removed, set up in various spots, and permitted to make their records for the next thirty hours. This would have been a minor task, and possibly even justified a little boredom, had it not been for the fact that some of the 'spots' were supposed to be as high as possible. Both men had climbed Lunar mountains in the last four weeks, and neither was worried about the task; but there was some question as to which mountain would best suit their needs.

They had stopped on fairly level ground south and

somewhat west of Plato — 'sunset' west, that is, not astronomical. There were a number of fairly prominent elevations in sight. None seemed more than a thousand metres or so in height, however, and the men knew that Plato in one direction and the Teneriffe Mountains in the other had peaks fully twice as high. The problem was which to choose.

'We can't take the tractor either way,' pointed out Shandara. 'We're cutting things pretty fine on the fuel question as it is. We are going to have to pack the instruments ourselves, and it's fifty or sixty kilometres to Teneriffe before we even start climbing. Plato's a lot closer.'

'The *near side* of Plato's a lot closer,' admitted Ridging, 'but the measured peaks in its rim must be on the east and west sides, where they can cast shadows across the crater floor. We might have to go as far for a really good peak as we would if we headed south.'

'That's not quite right. Look at the map. The near rim of the crater is fairly straight, and doesn't run straight east and west; it must cast shadows that they could measure from Earth. Why can't it contain some of those two thousand metre humps mentioned in the atlas?'

'No reason why it *can't* but we don't know that it *does*. This map doesn't show.'

'It doesn't show for Teneriffe, either.'

'That's true, but there isn't much choice there, and we know that there's at least one high peak in a fairly small area. Plato is well over three hundred kilometres around.'

'It's still a closer walk, and I don't see why, if there are high peaks at any part of the rim, they shouldn't be fairly common all around the circumference.'

'I don't see *why* either' retorted Ridging, 'but I've seen several craters for which that wasn't true. So have you.' Shandara had no immediate answer to this, but he had no intention of exposing himself to an unnecessarily long walk if he could help it. The instruments to be carried were admittedly light, at least on the moon; but there would be no chance of opening space-suits until the men got back to the tractor, and spacesuits got quite uncomfortable after a while.

* * *

It was the magnetometer that won Shandara's point for him. This pleased him greatly at the time, though he was heard to express a different opinion later. The meter itself did not attract attention until the men were about ready to start, and he had resigned himself to the long walk after a good deal more argument; but a final check of the recorders already operating made Ridging stop and think.

'Say, Shan, have you noticed any sunspots lately?'

'Haven't looked at the sun, and don't plan to.'

'I know. I mean, have any of the astronomers mentioned anything of the sort?'

'I didn't hear them, and we'll never be able to ask until we get back. Why?'

'I'd say there was a magnetic storm of some sort going on. The intensity, dip, and azimuth readings have all changed quite a bit in the last hour.'

'I thought dip was near vertical anyway.'

'It is, but that doesn't keep it from changing. You know, Shan, maybe it would be better if we went to Plato, instead.'

'That's what I've been saying all along. What's changed your mind?'

'This magnetic business. On Earth, such storms are caused by charged particles from the sun, deflected by the planet's magnetic field and forming what amounts to tremendous electric currents which naturally produce fields of their own. If that's what is happening here, it would be nice to get even closer to the local magnetic vertical, if we can; and that seems to be in, or at least near, Plato.'

'That suits me. I've been arguing that way all along. I'm with you.'

'There's one other thing—'

'What?'

'This magnetometer ought to go along with us, as well as the stuff we were taking anyway. Do you mind helping with the extra weight?' Shandara had not considered this aspect of the matter, but since his arguments had been founded on the question of time rather than effort he agreed readily to the additional labour.

'All right. Just a few minutes while I dismount and repack this gadget, and we'll be on our way.' Ridging set to work, and was ready in the specified time, since the apparatus had been designed to be handled by spacesuited men. The carrying racks that took the place of regular packs made the travellers look top-heavy, but they had long since learned to keep their balance under such loads. They turned until the nearly motionless sun was behind them and to their right, and set out for the hills ahead.

These elevations were not the peaks they expected to use; the moon's near horizon made those still invisible. They did, however, represent the outer reaches of the area which had been disturbed by whatever monstrous explosion had blown the ring of Plato in the moon's crust. As far as the men were concerned, these hills simply meant that very little of their journey would be across level ground, which pleased them just as well. Level ground was sometimes an inch or two deep in dust; and whilst dust could not hide deep cracks, it could and sometimes did fill broader hollows and cover irregularities where one could trip. For a top-heavy man, this could be a serious nuisance. Relatively little dust had been encountered by any of the expedition up to this point, since most of their work had involved slopes or peaks; but a few annoying lessons had been learned.

Shandara and Ridging stuck to the relatively dust-free slopes, therefore. The going was easy enough for experienced men, and they travelled at pretty fair speed – some ten or twelve miles per hour, they judged. The tractor soon disappeared, and compasses were useless, but both men had a good eye for country, and were used enough to the Lunar landscape to have no particular difficulty in finding distinctive features. They said little, except to call each other's attention to particularly good landmarks.

The general ground level was going up after the first hour and a half, though there was still plenty of down-hill travel. A relatively near line of peaks ahead was presumably the crater rim; there was little difficulty in deciding on the most suitable one and heading for it. Naturally the footing became worse and the slopes steeper as they approached, but nothing was dangerous even yet. Such crevasses as existed were easy both to see and to jump, and there are few loose rocks on the moon.

*   *   *

It was only about three and a half hours after leaving the tractor, therefore, that the two men reached the peak they had selected, and looked out over the great maulled plain of Plato. They couldn't see all of it, of course; Plato is a hundred kilometres across, and even from a height of two thousand metres the farther side of the floor lies below the horizon. The opposite rim could be seen, of course, but there was no easy way to tell whether any of the peaks visible there were as high as the one from which the men saw them. It didn't really matter; this one was high enough for their purposes.

The instruments were unloaded and set up in half an hour. Ridging did most of the work, with a professional single-mindedness which Shandara made no attempt to emulate. The geophysicist scarcely glanced at the crater floor after his first look around upon their arrival, while Shandara did little else. Ridging was not surprised; he had been reasonably sure that his friend had had ulterior reasons for wanting to come this way.

'All right,' he said, as he straightened up after closing the last switch, 'when do we go down, and how long do we take?'

'Go down where?' asked Shandara innocently.

'Down to the crater floor, I suppose. I'm sure you don't see enough to satisfy you from here. It's just an ordinary crater, of course, but it's three times the diameter of Harpalus even if the walls are less than half as high, and you'll surely want to see every square metre of the floor.'

'I'll want to see *some* of the floor, anyway.' Shandara's tone carried feeling even through the suit radios. 'It's nice of you to realize that we have to go down. I wish you realized why.'

'You mean . . . you mean you really expect to climb down there?' Ridging, in spite of his knowledge of the other's interests, was startled. 'I didn't really mean—'

'I didn't think you did. You haven't looked over the edge once.'

Ridging repaired the omission, letting his gaze sweep carefully over the greyish plain at the foot of the slope. He knew that the floor of Plato was one of the darker areas on the moon, but had never supposed that this fact constituted a major problem.

'I don't get it,' he said at last. 'I don't see anything.

The floor is smoother than that of Harpalus, I'd say, but I'm not really sure even of that, from this distance. It's a couple of kilos down and I don't know how far over.'

'You brought the map.' It was not a question.

'Of course.'

'Look at it. It's a good one.' Ridging obeyed, bewildered. The map was good, as Shandara had said; its scale was sufficient to show Plato some fifteen centimetres across, with plenty of detail. It was basically an enlargement of a map published on Earth, from telescopic observations; but a good deal of detail had been added from photographs taken during the approach and landing of the expedition. Shandara knew that; it was largely his own work.

As a result, Ridging was not long in seeing what his companion meant. The map showed five fairly large craterlets *within* Plato, and nearly a hundred smaller features.

Ridging could see none of them from where he stood.

He looked thoughtfully down the slope, then at the other man.

'I begin to see what you mean. Did you expect something like this? Is that why you wanted to come here? Why didn't you tell me?'

'I didn't expect it, though I had a vague hope. A good many times in the past, observers have reported that the features on the floor of this crater were obscured. Dr. Pickering, at the beginning of the century, thought of it as an active volcanic area; others have blamed the business on clouds – and others, of course, have assumed the observers themselves were at fault, though that is pretty hard to justify. I didn't really expect to get a chance to check up on the phenomenon, but I'm sure you don't expect me to stay up here now.'

'I suppose not.' Ridging spoke in a tone of mock resignation. The problem did not seem to concern his field directly, but he judged rightly that the present situation affected Shandara the way an offer of a genuine fragment of Terrestrial core material would influence Ridging himself. 'What do you plan to take down? I suppose you want to get measures of some sort.'

'Well, there isn't too much here that will apply, I'm afraid. I have my own camera and some filters, which may do some good. I can't see that the magnetic stuff will be any use down there. We don't have any pressure measuring or gas collecting gadgetry; I suppose if we'd brought a spare water container from the tractor we could dump it, but we didn't and I'd bet that nothing would be found in it but water vapour if we did. We'll just have to go down and see what our eyes will tell us, and record anything that seems recordable on film. Are you ready?'

'Ready as I ever will be.' Ridging knew the remark was neither original nor brilliant, but nothing else seemed to fit.

The inner wall of the crater was a good deal steeper than the one they had climbed, but still did not present a serious obstacle. The principal trouble was that much of the way led through clefts where the sun did not shine, and the only light was reflected from distant slopes. There wasn't much of it, and the men had to be careful of their footings – there was an occasional loose fragment here, and a thousand-metre fall is no joke even on the moon. The way did not lead directly towards the crater floor; the serrated rim offered better ways between its peaks, hairpinning back and forth so that sometimes the central plain was not visible at all. No floor details appeared as they descended, but whatever covered them was still below; the stars, whenever the mountains cut off enough sidelight, were clear as ever. Time and again Shandara stopped to look over the great plain, which seemed limitless now that the peaks on the farther side had dropped below the horizon, but nothing in the way of information rewarded the effort.

It was the last few hundred metres of descent that began to furnish something of interest. Shandara was picking his way down an unusually uninviting bit of slope when Ridging, who had already negotiated it, spoke up sharply.

'Shan! Look at the stars over the northern horizon! Isn't there some sort of haze? The sky around them looks a bit lighter.' The other paused and looked.

'You're right. But how could that be? There couldn't suddenly be enough air at this level – gases don't behave that way. Van Maanen's star might have an atmosphere twenty metres deep, but the moon doesn't and never could have.'

'There's *something* between us and the sky.'

'That I admit! but I still say it isn't gas. Maybe dust—'

'What would hold it up? Dust is just as impossible as air.'

'I don't know. The floor's only a few yards down – let's not stand here guessing.' They resumed their descent.

The crater floor was fairly level, and sharply distinguished from the inner slope of the crater wall. Something had certainly filled, partly at least, the vast pit after the original explosion; but neither man was disposed to renew the argument about the origin of Lunar craters just then. They scrambled down the remaining few yards of the journey and stopped where they were, silently.

There *was* something blocking vision; the horizon was no longer visible, nor could the stars be seen for a few degrees above where it should have been. Neither man would have had the slightest doubt about the nature of the obscuring matter had he been on Earth; it bore every resemblance to dust. It *had* to be dust.

But it couldn't be. Granted that dust can be fine enough to remain suspended for weeks or months in Earth's atmosphere when a volcano like Krakatoa hurls a few cubic miles of it aloft, the moon had not enough gas molecules around it to interfere with the trajectory of a healthy virus particle – and no seismometer in the last four weeks had registered crustal activity even approaching the scale of vulcanism. There was nothing on the moon to throw the dust up, and even less to keep it there.

'Meteor splash?' Shandara made the suggestion hesitantly, fully aware that while a meteor might raise dust it could never keep it aloft. Ridging did not bother to answer, and his friend did not repeat the suggestion.

The sky straight overhead seemed clear as ever, whatever the absorbing material was it apparently took more than the few feet above them to show much effect. That could not be right, though, Ridging reflected, if this stuff were responsible for hiding the features which should have been visible from the crater rim. Maybe it was thicker farther in. If so, they'd better go on – there might be some chance of collecting samples after all.

He put this to Shandara, who agreed; and the two started out across the hundred kilometre plain.

The surface *was* fairly smooth, though a pattern of minute cracks suggestive of the joints formed in cooling basalt covered it almost completely. These were not wide enough even to constitute a tripping danger, and the men ignored them for the time being, though Ridging made a mental note to get a sample of the rock if he could detach one.

The obscuration did thicken as they progressed, and by the time they had gone half a dozen kilometres it was difficult to see the crater wall behind them. Looking up, they saw that all but the brighter stars had faded from view even when the men shaded their eyes from the sunlit rock around them.

'Maybe gas is coming from these cracks, carrying dust up with it?' Shandara was no geologist, but had an imagination. He had also read most of the serious articles which had ever been published about the moon.

'We could check. If that were the case, it should be possible to see currents coming from them; the dust would be thicker just above a crack than a few centimetres away. If we had something light, like a piece of paper, it might be picked up.'

'Worth trying. We have the map,' Shandara pointed out. 'That should do for paper; the plastic is thin enough.' Ridging agreed. With some difficulty – spacesuit gloves were not designed for that purpose – he tore a tiny corner off the sheet on which the map was printed, knelt down, and held the fragment over one of the numerous cracks. It showed no tendency to flutter in his grasp, and when he let go it dropped as rapidly as anything ever did on the moon, to lie quietly directly across the crack he had been testing. He tried to pick it up, but could not get a grip on it with his stiff gloves.

'That one didn't seem to pan out,' he remarked, standing up once more.

'Maybe the paper was too heavy – this stuff must be awfully fine – or else it's coming from only a few of the cracks.'

'Possibly; but I don't think it's practical to try them all. It would be smarter to figure some way to get a sample of this stuff, and let people with better lab facilities figure out what it is and what holds it off the surface.'

'Worth trying. If it does, though, we'll have another question – why does it settle there and yet remain suspended long enough to do what is being done? We've been more than an hour coming down the slope, and I'll bet your astronomical friends of the past have reported obscurations longer lasting even than that.'

'They have. Well, even if it does raise more problems it's worth trying. Spread out the map, and we'll wait a few minutes.' Ridging obeyed; then, to keep the score even, came up with an idea of his own.

'Why don't you lay your camera on the ground pointing up and make a couple of time exposures of the stars? You could repeat them after we get back in the clear, and maybe get some data on the obscuring power of this material.'

'Good enough.' Shandara removed the camera from its case, clipped a sun shade over its lens, and looked up to find a section of sky with a good selection of stars. As usual, he had to shield his eyes both from sunlight and from the glare of the nearby hills; but even then he did not seem satisfied.

'This stuff is getting thicker, I think,' he said. 'It's scattering enough light so that it's hard to see any stars at all – harder than it was a few minutes ago, I'd say.' Ridging imitated his manoeuvre, and agreed.

'That's worth recording, too,' he pointed out. 'Better stay here a while and get several shots at different times.' He looked down again. 'It certainly *is* getting thicker. I'm having trouble seeing you, now.'

Human instincts being what they are, the solution to the mystery followed automatically and immediately. A man who fails, for any reason, to see as clearly as he expects usually rubs his eyes – if he can get at them. A man wearing goggles or a space helmet may just possibly control this impulse, but he follows the practically identical one of wiping the panes through which he looks. Ridging did not have a handkerchief within reach, of course, and the gauntlet of a spacesuit is not one of the best windshield wipers imaginable; but without giving a single thought to the action, he wiped his face plate with his gauntlet.

Had there been no results he would not have been surprised; he had no reason to expect any. He would probably have dismissed the matter, perhaps with a faint hope that his companion might not have noticed the futile gesture. However, there were results. Very marked ones.

The points where the plastic of the gauntlet actually touched the face plate were few; but they left trails all the way across – opaque trails. Surprised and still not thinking. Ridging repeated the gesture in an automatic effort to wipe the smears of whatever it was from his helmet; he only made matters worse. He did not quite cover the supposedly transparent area with glove trails – but in the few seconds after he got control of his hand the streaks spread and merged until nothing whatever was possible. He was not quite in darkness; sunlight penetrated the obscuring layer, but he could not see any details.

'Shan!' The cry contained almost a note of panic. 'I can't see at all. Something's covering my helmet!' The cartographer straightened up from his camera and turned towards his friend.

'How come? You look all right from here. I can't see too clearly, though—'

Reflexes are wonderful. It took about five seconds to blind Shandara as thoroughly as Ridging. He couldn't even find his camera to close the shutter.

'You know,' said Ridging thoughtfully after two or three minutes of heavy silence, 'we should have been able to figure all this out without coming down here.'

'Why?'

'Oh, it's plain as anything—'

'Nothing, and I mean *nothing*, is plain right now.'

'I suppose a map maker would joke while he was surveying Gehenna. Look, Shan, we have reason to believe there's a magnetic storm going on, which strongly suggests charged particles from the sun. We are standing, for practical purposes, on the moon's south magnetic pole. Most level parts of the moon are covered with dust – but we walked over bare rock from the foot of the rim to here. Don't those items add up to something?'

'Not to me.'

'Well, then, add the fact that electrical attraction and repulsion are inverse square forces like gravity, but involve a vastly bigger proportionality constant.'

'If you're talking about scale I know all about it, but you still don't paint me a picture.'

'All right. There are, at a guess, protons coming from the sun. They are reaching the moon's surface here – virtually all of them, since the moon has a magnetic field but no atmosphere. The surface material is one of the lousiest imaginable electrical conductors, so the dust normally on the surface picks up *and keeps* a charge. And what, dear student, happens to particles carrying like electrical charges?'

'They are repelled from each other.'

'Head of the class. And if a hundred-kilometre circle with a rim a couple of kilos high is charged all over, what happens to the dust lying on it?'

Shandara did not answer; the question was too obviously rhetorical. He thought for a moment or two, instead, then asked, 'How about our face plates?'

Ridging shrugged – a rather useless gesture, but the time for fighting bad habits had passed some minutes before.

'Bad luck. Whenever two materials rub against each other, electrons come loose. Remember your rubber-and-cat-fur demonstrations in grade school. Unless the materials are of identical electron make-up, which for practical purposes means unless they are the same substance, one of them will hang on to the electrons a little – or a lot – better than the other, so one will have a negative net charge and the other a positive one. It's our misfortune that the difference between the plastic in our face plates and that in the rest of the suits is the wrong way; when we rubbed the two, the face plates picked up a charge opposite to that of the surrounding dust – probably negative, since I suppose the dust is positive and a transparent material should have a good grip on its electrons.'

'Then the rest of our suits, and the gloves we wiped with in particular, ought to be clean.'

'Ought to be. I'd like nothing better than a chance to check the point.'

'Well, the old cat's fur didn't stay charged very long, as I remember. How long will it take this to leak off, do you think?'

'Why should it leak off at all?'

'What? Why, I should think – Hm-m-m.' Shandara was silent for a moment. 'Water *is* pretty wonderful stuff, isn't it?'

'Yep. And air has its uses, too.'

'Then we're . . . Ridge, we've got to *do* something. Our air will last indefinitely, but you still can't stay in a spacesuit too long.'

'I agree that we should do something; I just haven't figured out what. Incidentally, just how sure are you that our air will last? The windows of the regenerators are made, as far as I know, of the same plastic our face plates are. What'll you bet you're not using emergency oxygen right now?'

'I don't know – I haven't checked the gauges.'

'I'll say you haven't. You won't, either; they're outside your helmet.'

'But if we're on emergency now, we could hardly get back to the tractor starting this minute. We've got to get going.'

'Which way?'

'Towards the rim!'

'Be specific, son. Just which way is that? And please don't point; it's rude, and I can't see you anyway.'

'All right, don't rub it in. But Ridge, what *can* we do?'

'While this stuff is on our helmets, and possibly our air windows, nothing. We couldn't climb even if we knew which way the hills were. The only thing which will do us the least good is to get this dust off us; and that will do the trick. As my mathematical friends would say, it is necessary and sufficient.'

'All right, I'll go along with that. We know that the material the suits are made of is worse than useless for wiping, but wiping and electrical discharge seem to be the only method possible. What do we have which by any stretch of the imagination might do either job?'

'What is your camera case made of?' asked Ridging.

'As far as I know, same as the suits. It's a regular clip-on carrier, the sort that came with the suits – remember Tazewell's remarks about the dividends AirTight must have paid when they sold the suits to the Project? It reminded me of the old days when you had to buy a lot of accessories with your automobile whether you wanted them or not—'

'All right, you've made your point. The case is the same plastic. It would be a pretty poor wiper anyway; it's a box rather than a bag, as I remember. What else is there?'

The silence following this question was rather lengthy. The sad fact is that spacesuits don't have outside pockets for handkerchiefs. It did occur to Ridging after a time that he was carrying a set of geological specimen bags; but when he finally did think of these and took one out to use as a wiper, the unfortunate fact developed that it, too, left the wrong charge on the face plate of his helmet. He could see the clear, smooth plastic of the bag as it passed across the plate, but the dust collected so fast behind it that he saw nothing of his surroundings. He reflected ruefully that the charge to be removed was now greater than ever. He also thought of using the map, until he remembered that he had put it on the ground and could never find it by touch.

'I never thought,' Shandara remarked after another lengthy silence, 'that I'd ever miss a damp rag so badly. Blast it, Ridge, there must be *something*.'

'Why? We've both been thinking without any result that I can see. Don't tell me you're one of those fellows who think there's an answer to every problem.'

'I am. It may not be the answer we want, but there is one. Come on, Ridge, you're the physicist; I'm just a high-priced picture-copier. Whatever answer there is, you're going to have to furnish it; all my ideas deal with maps, and we've done about all we can with those at the moment.'

'Hm-m-m. The more I think, the more I remember that there isn't enough fuel on the moon to get a rescue tractor out here, even if anyone knew we were in trouble and could make the trip in time. Still – wait a minute; you said something just then. What was it?'

'I said all my ideas dealt with maps, but—'

'No; before that.'

'I don't recall, unless it was that crack about damp rags, which we don't have.'

'That was it. That's it, Shan; we don't have any rags, but we do have *water*.'

'Yes – inside our spacesuits. Which of us opens up to save the other?'

'Neither one. Be sensible. You know as well as I do that the amount of water in a closed system containing a living person is constantly increasing; we produce it, oxidizing hydrogen in the food we eat. The suits have dryers in the air cycler or we couldn't last two hours in them.'

'That's right; but how do you get the water out? You can't open your air system.'

'You can shut it off, and the check valve will keep air in your suit – remember, there's always the chance someone will have to change emergency tanks. It'll be a job, because we won't be able to see what we're doing, and working by touch through spacesuit gauntlets will be awkward as anything I've ever done. Still, I don't see anything else.'

That means you'll have to work on my suit, then, since I don't know what to do after the line is disconnected. How long can I last before your reconnect? And what do you do, anyway? You don't mean there's a reservoir of liquid water there, do you?'

'No, it's a calcium chloride dryer; and it should be fairly moist by now— You've been in the suit for several hours. It's in several sections, and I can take out one and leave you the others, so you won't suffer from its lack. The air in your suit should do you for four or five minutes, and if I can't make the disconnection and disassembly in that time I can't do it at all. Still, it's your suit, and if I do make a mistake it's your life; do you want to take the chance?'

'What have I to lose? Besides, you always were a pretty good mechanic – or if you weren't, please don't tell me. Get to work.'

'All right.'

As it happened, the job was not started right away, for there was the minor problem of finding Shandara to be solved first. The two men had been perhaps five yards apart when their face plates were first blanked out, but neither could now be sure that he hadn't moved in the meantime, or at least shifted around to face a new direction. After some discussion of the problem, it was agreed that Shandara should stand still, while Ridging walked in what he hoped was the right direction for what he hoped was five yards and then start from wherever he found himself to quarter the area as well as he could by length of stride. He would have to guess at his turns since even the sun no longer could penetrate the layer of dust on the helmets.

It took a full ten minutes to bump into his companion, and even then he felt undeservedly lucky.

Shandara lay down, so as to use a minimum of energy while the work was being done. Ridging felt over the connections several times until he was sure he had them right – they were of course, designed to be handled by spacesuit gauntlets, though not by a blindfold operator. Then he warned the cartographer, closed the main cutoffs at helmet and emergency tanks to isolate the renewer mechanism, and opened the latter. It was a simple device, designed in throwaway units like a piece of electronic gear, with each unit automatically sealing as it was removed – fortunate fact if the alga culture on which Shandara's life for the next few hours depended was to survive the operation.

The calcium chloride cells were easy to locate; Ridging removed two of the half dozen to be on the safe side, replaced and reassembled the renewer, tightened the connections and reopened the valves.

Ridging now had two cans of calcium chloride. He could not tell whether it had yet absorbed enough water actually to go into solution, though he doubted it; but he took no chances. Holding one of the little containers carefully right side up, he opened its perforated top, took a specimen bag and pushed it into the contents. The plastic was not, of course, absorptive – it was not the first time in the past hour he had regretted the change from cloth bags – but the damp crystals should adhere, and the solution if there was any should wet it. He pulled out the material and applied it to his face plate.

It was not until much later that he became sure whether there was any liquid. For the moment it worked, and he found that he could see; he asked no more. Hastily he repeated the process on Shandara's helmet, and the two set out rapidly for the rim. They did not stop to pick up camera or map.

Travel is fast on the moon, but they made less than four hundred metres. Then the face plates were covered again. With a feeling of annoyance they stopped, and Ridging repeated the treatment.

This time it didn't work.

'I suppose you emptied the can while you were jumping,' Shandara remarked in an annoyed tone. 'Try the other one.'

'I didn't empty anything; but I'll try.' The contents of the other container proved equally useless, and the cartographer's morale took another slump.

'What happened?' he asked. 'And please don't tell me it's obvious, because you certainly didn't foresee it.'

'I didn't, but it is. The chloride dried out again.'

'I thought it held on to water.'

'It does, under certain conditions. Unfortunately its equilibrium vapour pressure at this temperature is higher than the local barometer reading. I don't suppose that every last molecule of water has gone, but what's left isn't sufficient to make a conductor. Our face plates are holding charge again – maybe better than before; there must be some calcium chloride dust on them now, though I don't know offhand what effect it would have.'

'There are more chloride cartridges in the cyclers.'

'You have four left, which would get us maybe two kilos at the present rate. We can't use mine, since you can't get them out; and if we use all yours you'd never get up the rim. Drying your air isn't just a matter of comfort, you know; that suit has no temperature controls – it depends on radiation balance and insulation. If your perspiration stops evaporating, your inner insulation is done; and in any case, the cartridges won't get us to the rim.'

'In other words you think we're done – again.'

'I certainly don't have any more ideas.'

'Then I suppose I'll have to do some more pointless chattering. If it gave you the last idea, maybe it will work again.'

'Go ahead. It won't bother me. I'm going to spend my last hours cursing the character who used a different plastic for the face plate than he did for the rest of these suits.'

'All right,' Tazewell snapped as the geophysicist paused. 'I'm supposed to ask you what you did then. You've just told me that that handkerchief of yours is a good windshield wiper; I'll admit I don't see how. I'll even admit I'm curious, if it'll make you happy.'

'It's not a handkerchief, as I said. It's a specimen bag.'

'I thought you tried those and found they didn't work – left a charge on your face plate like the glove.'

'It did. But a remark I made myself about different kinds of plastic in the suits gave me another idea. It occurred to me that if the dust was, say, positively charged—'

'Probably was. Protons from the sun.'

'All right. Then my face plate picked up a negative, and my suit glove a positive, so the dust was attracted to the plate.

'Then when we first tried the specimen bag, it also charged positively and left negative on the face plate.

'Then it occurred to me that the specimen bag *rubbed by the suit* might go negative; and since it was fairly transparent, I could—'

'I get it! You could tie it over your face plate and have a windshield you could see through which would repel the dust.'

'That was the idea. Of course, I had nothing to tie it with; I had to hold it.'

'Good enough. So you got a good idea out of an idle remark.'

'Two of them. The moisture one came from Shan the same way,'

'But yours worked.' Ridging grinned.

'Sorry. It didn't. The specimen bag still came out negative when rubbed on the suit plastic – at least it didn't do the face plate any good.'

Tazewell stared blankly, then looked as though he were about to use violence.

'*All right*! Let's have it, once and for all.'

'Oh, it was simple enough. I worked the specimen bag – I tore it open so it would cover more area across my face plate, pressing tight so there wouldn't be any dust under it.'

'What good would that do? You must have collected more over it right away.'

'Sure. Then I rubbed my face plate, dust rag and all, against Shandara's. We couldn't lose; one of them was bound to go positive. I won, and led him up the rim until the ground charge dropped enough to let the dust stick to the surface instead of us. I'm glad no one was there to take pictures, though; I'd hate to have a photo around which could be interpreted as my kissing Shandara's ugly face – even through a space helmet.'

DUST RAG

During the 1940s and 1950s there was considerable discussion as to whether the Moon was covered by dust and if so, by how much. It seemed that the surface temperature of the Moon dropped very quickly during Lunar eclipses and this meant a large heat loss from the surface. The heat loss wouldn't have been that great if additional heat could only have leaked upwards to the surface from below. Something apparently stopped that leakage, which meant that the material composing the surface of the Earth was a good insulator.

Vacuum is an excellent insulator, so it might be that the Moon's surface consisted of dust particles, touching each other at odd points with vacuum between. There were even speculations that the dust might be very deep and that spaceships trying to land would sink into the dust layer completely.

Even if the dust were not deep, there might be enough to stir up by any disturbance, such as a ship landing, or even the footsteps of a walking man. If that happened, however, the problem would not be a serious one as, in the absence of air, the dust would rise and fall like so many pebbles.

As it happened, close range studies of the Moon's surface, soft-landings of instrument satellites, and finally manned landings on the Moon, showed the dust was not dangerously deep. The footing underneath was crunchy, but firm.

Clement's story written in 1956, over a decade before the close-range studies, predicted that accurately. However, he did want to make the dust dangerous at least under some conditions by having it hover above the Moon's surface even in the absence of air. To do this, he assumed the Moon had a magnetic field and that over the magnetic poles, the dust particles would tend to become charged and to repel each other. In this respect, though, Clement's vision failed. It turned out that the Moon had no magnetic field to speak of.

He did turn out to be correct in supposing that the Moon was bombarded by the Solar wind; that it was continually being struck by charged particles from the Sun. The surface rocks of the Moon contain helium that could have originated only in this fashion.

Questions and Suggestions

1. Most theories of Earth's magnetic field involve the presence of an iron ore at its centre. Do you think the Moon has an iron core? Why or why not? If it lacks an iron core, would that fact be known in 1956? Do you suppose Clement might have suspected the Moon did not have a magnetic field, even while he used one for the purposes of the story?

2. It is likely that Venus has an iron core, yet it has no magnetic field to speak of. How do we know it has none? Why should it not have one despite the iron core? What about other planets: Mars, Jupiter, Saturn? How do we know?

3. Look up the reports on the manned landing on the Moon. What do these have to say about dust?

6. PÂTÉ DE FOIE GRAS

Isaac Asimov

I couldn't tell you my real name if I wanted to and, under the circumstances, I don't want to.

I'm not much of a writer myself, unless you count the kind of stuff that passes muster in a scientific paper, so I'm having Isaac Asimov write this up for me.

I've picked him for several reasons. First, he's a biochemist, so he understands what I tell him; some of it, anyway. Secondly, he can write; or at least he has published considerable fiction, which may not, of course, be the same thing.

But most important of all, he can get what he writes published in science-fiction magazines and he has written two articles on thiotimoline, and that is exactly what I need for reasons that will become clear as we proceed.

I was not the first person to have the honour of meeting The Goose. That belongs to a Texas cotton-farmer named Ian Angus MacGregor, who owned it before it became government property. (The names, places and dates I use are deliberately synthetic. None of you will be able to trace anything through them. Don't bother trying.)

MacGregor apparently kept geese about the place because they ate weeds, but not cotton. In this way, he had automatic weeders that were self-fuelling and, in addition, produced eggs, down, and, at judicious intervals, roast goose.

By summer of 1955, he had sent an even dozen of letters to the Department of Agriculture requesting information on the hatching of goose eggs. The department sent him all the booklets on hand that were anywhere near the subject, but his letters simply got more impassioned and freer in their references to his 'friend', the local congressman.

My connection with this is that I am in the employ of the Department of Agriculture. I have considerable training in agricultural chemistry, plus a smattering of vertebrate physiology. (This won't help you. If you think you can pin my identity out of this, you are mistaken.)

Since I was attending a convention at San Antonio in July of 1955, my boss asked me to stop off at MacGregor's place and see what I could do to help him. We're servants of the public and besides we had finally received a letter from MacGregor's congressman.

On July 17, 1955, I met The Goose.

I met MacGregor first. He was in his fifties, a tall man with a lined face full of suspicion. I went over all the information he had been given, explained about incubators, the values of trace minerals in the diet, plus some late information on Vitamin E, the cobalamins, and the use of antibiotic additives.

He shook his head. He had tried it all and still the eggs wouldn't hatch.

What could I do? I'm a Civil Service employee and not the archangel, Gabriel. I'd told him all I could and if the eggs still wouldn't hatch, they wouldn't and that was that. I asked politely if I might see his geese, just so no one could say afterwards I hadn't done all I possibly could.

He said, 'It's not geese, mister; it's one goose.'

I said, 'May I see the one goose?'

'Rather not.'

'Well, then, I can't help you any further. If it's only one goose, then there's just something wrong with it. Why worry about one goose? Eat it.'

I got up and reached for my hat.

He said, 'Wait!' and I stood there while his lips tightened and his eyes wrinkled and he had a quiet fight with himself.

He said, 'If I show you something, will you swear to keep it secret?'

He didn't seem like the type of man to rely on another's vow of secrecy, but it was as though he had reached such a pit of desperation that he had no other way out.

I said, 'If it isn't anything criminal—'

'Nothing like that,' he snapped.

And then I went out with him to a pen near the house, surrounded by barbed wire, with a locked gate to it, and holding one goose – The Goose.

'That's The Goose,' he said. The way he said it, I could hear the capitals.

I stared at it. It looked like any other goose, Heaven help me, fat, self-satisfied and short-tempered. I said, 'Hm-m-m' in my best professional manner.

MacGregor said, 'And here's one of its eggs. It's been in the incubator. Nothing happens.' He produced it from a capacious overall pocket. There was a queer strain about his manner of holding it.

I frowned. There was something wrong with the egg. It was smaller and more spherical than normal.

MacGregor said, 'Take it.'

I reached out and took it. Or tried to. I gave it the amount of heft an egg like that ought to deserve and it

104

just sat where it was. I had to try harder and then up it came.

Now I knew what was queer about the way MacGregor held it. It weighed nearly two pounds. (To be exact, when we weighed it later, we found its mass to be 852.6 grammes.)

I stared at it as it lay there, pressing down the palm of my hand, and MacGregor grinned sourly. 'Drop it,' he said.

I just looked at him, so he took it out of my hand and dropped it himself.

It hit soggy. It didn't smash. There was no spray of white and yolk. It just lay where it fell with the bottom caved in.

I picked it up again. The white eggshell had shattered where the egg had struck. Pieces of it had flaked away and what shone through was a dull yellow in colour.

My hands trembled. It was all I could do to make my fingers work, but I got some of the rest of the shell flaked away, and stared at the yellow.

I didn't have to run any analyses. My heart told me.

I was face to face with The Goose!

The Goose That Laid The Golden Eggs!

You don't believe me. I'm sure of that. You've got this tabbed as another thiotimoline article.

Good! I'm *counting* on your thinking that. I'll explain later.

Meanwhile, my first problem was to get MacGregor to give up that golden egg. I was almost hysterical about it. I was almost ready to clobber him and make off with the egg by force if I had to.

I said, 'I'll give you a receipt. I'll guarantee you payment. I'll do anything in reason. You can't cash the gold unless you can explain how it came into your possession. Holding gold is illegal. And how do you expect to explain? If the government—'

'I don't want the government butting in,' he said, stubbornly.

But I was twice as stubborn. I followed him about. I pleaded. I yelled. I threatened. It took me hours. Literally. In the end, I signed a receipt and he dogged me out to my car and stood in the road as I drove away, following me with his eyes.

He never saw that egg again. Of course, he was compensated for the value of the gold – $656.47 after taxes had been subtracted – but that was a bargain for the government.

When one considers the potential value of that egg—

The *potential* value! That's the irony of it. That's the reason for this article.

The head of my section at the Department of Agriculture is Louis P. Bronstein. (Don't bother looking him up. The 'P.' stands for Pittfield if you want more misdirection.)

He and I are on good terms and I felt I could explain things without being placed under immediate observation. Even so, I took no chances. I had the egg with me and when I got to the tricky part, I just laid it on the desk between us.

Finally, he touched it with his fingers as though it were hot.

I said, 'Pick it up.'

It took him a long time, but he did, and I watched him take two tries at it as I had.

I said, 'It's a yellow metal and it could be brass only it isn't because it's inert to concentrated nitric acid. I've tried that already. There's only a shell of gold because it can be bent with moderate pressure. Besides, if it were solid gold, the egg would weigh over ten pounds.'

Bronstein said, 'It's some sort of hoax. It *must* be.'

'A hoax that uses real gold? Remember, when I first saw this thing, it was covered completely with authentic unbroken eggshell. It's been easy to check a piece of the eggshell. Calcium carbonate. That's a hard thing to gimmick. And if we look inside the egg – I didn't want to do that on my own, chief – and find real egg, then we've got it, because that would be impossible to gimmick. Surely, this is worth an official project.'

'How can I approach the Secretary with—' He stared at the egg.

But he did in the end. He made phone calls and sweated out most of a day. One or two of the department brass came to look at the egg.

Project Goose was started. That was July 20, 1955.

I was the responsible investigator to begin with and

remained in titular charge throughout, though matters quickly got beyond me.

We began with one egg. Its average radius was 35 millimetres (major axis, 72 millimetres; minor axis, 68 millimetres). The gold shell was 2.45 millimetres in thickness. Studying other eggs later on, we found this value to be rather high. The average thickness turned out to be 2.1 millimetres.

Inside *was* egg. It looked like egg and it smelled like egg.

Aliquots were analysed and the organic constituents were reasonably normal. The white was 9.7 per cent albumin. The yolk had the normal complement of vitellin, cholesterol, phospholipid and carotenoid. We lacked enough material to test for trace constituents but later on with more eggs at our disposal we did and nothing unusual showed up as far as the contents of vitamins, coenzymes, nucleotides, sulfhydryl groups, et cetera, et cetera were concerned.

One important gross abnormality that showed was the egg's behaviour on heating. A small portion of the yolk, heated, 'hard-boiled' almost at once. We fed a portion of the hard-boiled egg to a mouse. It survived.

I nibbled at another bit of it. Too small a quantity to taste, really, but it made me sick. Purely psychosomatic, I'm sure.

Boris W. Finley, of the Department of Biochemistry of Temple University – a department consultant – supervised these tests.

He said, referring to the hard-boiling, 'The ease with which the egg-proteins are heat-denatured indicates a partial denaturation to begin with and, considering the nature of the shell, the obvious guilt would lie at the door of heavy-metal contamination.'

So a portion of the yolk was analysed for inorganic constituents, and it was found to be high in chloraurate ion, which is a singly-charged ion containing an atom of gold and four of chlorine, the symbol for which is $AuCl_4$. (The 'Au' symbol for gold comes from the fact that the Latin word for gold is 'aurum'.) When I say the chloraurate ion content was high, I mean it was 3.2 parts per thousand, or 0.32 per cent. That's high enough to form insoluble complexes of 'gold-protein' which would coagulate easily.

Finley said, 'It's obvious this egg cannot hatch. Nor can any other such egg. It is heavy-metal poisoned. Gold may be more glamorous than lead but it is just as poisonous to proteins.'

I agreed gloomily, 'At least it's safe from decay, too.'

'Quite right. No self-respecting bug would live in this chlorauriferous soup.'

The final spectrographic analysis of the gold of the shell came in. Virtually pure. The only detectable impurity was iron which amounted to 0.23 per cent of the whole. The iron content of the egg yolk had been twice normal, also. At the moment, however, the matter of the iron was neglected.

One week after Project Goose was begun, an expedition was sent into Texas. Five biochemists went – the accent was still on biochemistry, you see – along with three truckloads of equipment, and a squadron of army personnel. I went along, too, of course.

As soon as we arrived, we cut MacGregor's farm off from the world.

That was a lucky thing, you know – the security measures we took right from the start. The reasoning was wrong at first, but the results were good.

The Department wanted Project Goose kept quiet at the start simply because there was always the thought that this might still be an elaborate hoax and we couldn't risk the bad publicity, if it were. And if it weren't a hoax, we couldn't risk the newspaper hounding that would definitely result over any goose-and-golden-egg story.

It was only well after the start of Project Goose, well after our arrival at MacGregor's farm, that the real implications of the matter became clear.

Naturally, MacGregor didn't like the men and equipment settling down all about him. He didn't like being told The Goose was government property. He didn't like having his eggs impounded.

He didn't like it but he agreed to it – if you can call it agreeing when negotiations are being carried on while a machine gun is being assembled in a man's barnyard and ten men, with bayonets fixed, are marching past while the arguing is going on.

He was compensated, of course. What's money to the government?

The Goose didn't like a few things, either – like having blood samples taken. We didn't dare anaesthetize it for fear of doing anything to alter is metabolism, and it took two men to hold it each time. Ever try to hold an angry goose?

The Goose was put under a twenty-four hour guard with the threat of summary court-martial to any man who let anything happen to it. If any of those soldiers read this article, they may get a sudden glimmering of what was going on. If so, they will probably have the sense to keep shut about it. At least, if they know what's good for them, they will.

The blood of The Goose was put through every test conceivable.

It carried 2 parts per hundred thousand (0.002 per cent) of chloraurate ion. Blood taken from the hepatic vein was richer than the rest, almost 4 parts per hundred thousand.

Finley grunted. 'The liver,' he said.

We took X-rays. On the X-ray negative, the liver was cloudy mass of light grey, lighter than the viscera in its neighbourhood, because it stopped more of the X-rays, because it contained more gold. The blood vessels showed up lighter than the liver proper and the ovaries were pure white. No X-rays got through the ovaries at all.

It made sense and in an early report, Finley stated it as bluntly as possible. Paraphrasing the report, it went, in part:

'The chloraurate ion is secreted by the liver into the blood stream. The ovaries act as a trap for the ion, which is there reduced to metallic gold and deposited as a shell about the developing egg. Relatively high concentrations of unreduced chloraurate ion penetrate the contents of the developing egg.

'There is little doubt that The Goose finds this process useful as a means of getting rid of the gold atoms which, if allowed to accumulate, would undoubtedly poison it. Excretion by egg-shell may be novel in the animal kingdom, even unique, but there is no denying that it is keeping The Goose alive.

'Unfortunately, however, the ovary is being locally

poisoned to such an extent that few eggs are laid, probably not more than will suffice to get rid of the accumulating gold, and those few eggs are definitely unhatchable.'

That was all he said in writing, but to the rest of us, he said, 'That leaves one peculiarly embarrasing question.'

I knew what it was. We all did.

Where was the gold coming from?

No answer to that for a while, except for some negative evidence. There was no perceptible gold in The Goose's feed, nor were there any gold-bearing pebbles about that it might have swallowed. There was no trace of gold anywhere in the soil of the area and a search of the house and grounds revealed nothing. There were no gold coins, gold jewellery, gold plate, gold watches or gold anything. No one on the farm even had as much as gold fillings in his teeth.

There was Mrs. MacGregor's wedding ring, of course, but she had only had one in her life and she was wearing that one.

So where was the gold coming from?

The beginnings of the answer came on August 16, 1955.

Albert Nevis, of Purdue, was forcing gastric tubes into The Goose – another procedure to which the bird objected strenuously – with the idea of testing the contents of its alimentary canal. It was one of our routine searches for exogenous gold.

Gold *was* found, but only in traces and there was every reason to suppose those traces had accompanied the digestive secretions and were, therefore, endogenous – from within, that is – in origin.

However, something else showed up, or the lack of it, anyway.

I was there when Nevis came into Finley's office in the temporary building we had put up overnight – almost – near the goosepen.

Nevis said, 'The Goose is low in bile pigment. Duodenal contents show about none.'

Finley frowned and said, 'Liver function is probably

knocked loop-the-loop because of its gold concentration. It probably isn't secreting bile at all.'

'It *is* secreting bile,' said Nevis. 'Bile acids are present in normal quantity. Near normal, anyway. 'It's just the bile pigments that are missing. I did a faecal analysis and that was confirmed. No bile pigments.'

Let me explain something at this point. Bile acids are steroids secreted by the liver into the bile and *via* that are poured into the upper end of the small intestine. These bile acids are detergentlike molecules which help to emulsify the fat in our diet– or The Goose's – and distribute them in the form of tiny bubbles through the watery intestinal contents. This distribution, or homogenization, if you'd rather, makes it easier for the fat to be digested.

Bile pigments, the substances that were missing in The Goose, are something entirely different. The liver makes them out of haemoglobin, the red oxygen-carrying protein of the blood. Worn out haemoglobin is broken up in the liver, the haeme part being split away. The haeme is made up of a squarish molecule – called a 'porphyrin' – with an iron atom in the centre. The liver takes the iron out and stores it for future use, then breaks the squarish molecule that is left. This broken porphyrin is bile pigment. It is coloured brownish or greenish – depending on further chemical changes – and is secreted into the bile.

The bile pigments are of no use to the body. They are poured into the bile as waste products. They pass through the intestines and come out with the faeces. In fact, the bile pigments are responsible for the colour of the faeces.

Finley's eyes began to glitter.

Nevis said, 'It looks as though porphyrin catabolism isn't following the proper course in the liver. Doesn't it to you?'

It surely did. To me, too.

There was tremendous excitement after that. This was the first metabolic abnormality, not directly involving gold, that had been found in The Goose!

We took a liver biopsy (which means we punched a cylindrical sliver out of The Goose reaching down into the liver). It hurt The Goose but didn't harm it. We took more blood samples, too.

This time, we isolated haemoglobin from the blood and small quantities of the cytochromes from our liver samples. (The cytochromes are oxidizing enzymes that also contain haeme.) We separated out the haeme and in acid solution some of it precipitated in the form of a brilliant orange substance. By August 22, 1955, we had 5 microgrammes of the compound.

The orange compound was similar to haeme, but it was not haeme. The iron in haeme can be in the form of a doubly charged ferrous ion ($Fe + +$) or a triply charged ferric ion ($Fe + + +$), in which latter case, the compound is called haematin. (Ferrous and ferric, by the way, come from the Latin word for iron, which is 'ferrum'.)

The orange compound we had separated from haeme had the porphyrin portion of the molecule all right, but the metal in the centre was gold, to be specific, a triply charged auric ion ($Au + + +$). We called this compound 'auraeme', which is simply short for 'auric haeme.'

Auraeme was the fist naturally-occurring gold-containing organic compound ever discovered. Ordinarily, it would rate headline news in the world of biochemistry. But now it was nothing; nothing at all in comparison to the further horizons its mere existence opened up.

The liver, it seemed, was not breaking up the haeme to bile pigment. Instead it was converting it to auraeme; it was replacing iron with gold. The auraeme, in equilibrium with chloraurate ion, entered the blood stream and was carried to the ovaries where the gold was separated out and the porphyrin portion of the molecule disposed of by some as yet unidentified mechanism.

Further analyses showed that 29 per cent of the gold in the blood of The Goose was carried in the plasma in the form of chloraurate ion. The remaining 71 per cent was carried in the red blood corpuscles in the form of 'auraemoglobin'. An attempt was made to feed The Goose traces of radioactive gold so that we could pick up radioactivity in plasma and corpuscles and see how readily the auraemoglobin molecules were handled in the ovaries. It seemed to us the auraemoglobin should be much more slowly disposed of than the dissolved chloraurate ion in the plasma.

The experiment failed, however, since we detected no radioactivity. We put it down to inexperience since none of us were isotopes men which was too bad since the failure was highly significant, really, and by not realizing it, we lost several weeks.

The auraemoglobin was, of course, useless as far as carrying oxygen was concerned, but it only made up about 0.1 per cent of the total haemoglobin of the red blood cells so there was no interference with the respiration of The Goose.

This still left us with the question of where the gold came from and it was Nevis who first made the crucial suggestion.

'Maybe,' he said, at a meeting of the group held on the evening of August 25, 1955, 'The Goose doesn't replace the iron with gold. Maybe it *changes* the iron to gold.'

Before I met Nevis personally that summer, I had known him through his publications – his field is bile chemistry and liver function – and had always considered him a cautious, clear-thinking person. Almost overcautious. One wouldn't consider him capable for a minute of making any such completely ridiculous statement.

It just shows the desperation and demoralization involved in Project Goose.

The desperation was the fact that there was nowhere, literally nowhere, that the gold could come from. The Goose was excreting gold at the rate of 38.9 grammes of gold a day and had been doing it over a period of months. That gold had to come from somewhere and, failing that – absolutely failing that – it had to be made from something.

The demoralization that led us to consider the second alternative was due to the mere fact that we were face to face with The Goose That Laid The Golden Eggs; the undeniable GOOSE. With that, everything became possible. All of us were living in a fairy-tale world and all of us reacted to it by losing all sense of reality.

Finley considered the possibility seriously. 'Haemoglobin', he said, 'enters the liver and a bit of auraemoglobin comes out. The gold shell of the eggs has iron as its only impurity. The egg yolk is high in only two things; in gold, of course, and also, somewhat, in iron. It all makes a horrible kind of distorted sense. We're going to need help, men.'

We did and it meant a third stage of the investigation. The first stage had consisted of myself alone. The second was the biochemical task-force. The third, the greatest, the most important of all, involved the invasion of the nuclear physicists.

On September 5, 1955, John L. Billings of the University of California arrived. He had some equipment with him and more arrived in the following weeks. More temporary structures were going up. I could see that within a year we would have a whole research institution built about The Goose.

Billings joined our conference the evening of the 5th.

Finley brought him up to date and said, 'There are a great many serious problems involved in this iron-to-gold idea. For one thing, the total quantity of iron in The Goose can only be of the order of half a gramme, yet nearly 40 grammes of gold a day are being manufactured.'

Billings had a clear, high-pitched voice. He said, 'There's a worse problem than that. Iron is about at the bottom of the packing fraction curve. Gold is much higher up. To convert a gramme of iron to a gramme of gold takes just about as much energy as is produced by the fissioning of one gramme of U-235.

Finley shrugged. 'I'll leave the problem to you.'

Billings said, 'Let me think about it.'

He did more than think. One of the things done was to isolate fresh samples of haeme from The Goose, ash it and send the iron oxide to Brookhaven for isotopic analysis. There was no particular reason to do that particular thing. It was just one of a number of individual investigations, but it was the one that brought results.

When the figures came back, Billings choked on them. He said, 'There's no Fe^{56}.'

'What about the other isotopes?' asked Finley at once.

'All present,' said Billings, 'in the appropriate relative ratios, but no detectable Fe^{56}.'

I'll have to explain again: iron, as it occurs naturally, is made up of four different isotopes. These isotopes are varieties of atoms that differ from one another in atomic weight. Iron atoms with an atomic weight of 56, or Fe^{56}, makes up 91.6 per cent of all the atoms in iron. The other atoms have atomic weights of 54, 57 and 58.

The iron from the haeme of The Goose was made up only of Fe^{54}, Fe^{57}, Fe^{58}. The implication was obvious Fe^{56} was disappearing while the other isotopes weren't and this meant a nuclear reaction was taking place. A nuclear reaction could take one isotope and leave others be. An ordinary chemical reaction, any chemical reaction at all, would have to dispose of all isotopes equally.

'But it's energically impossible,' said Finley.

He was only saying that in mild sarcasm with Billings's initial remark in mind. As biochemists, we knew well enough that many reactions went on in the body which required an input of energy and that this was taken care of by coupling the energy-demanding reaction with an energy-producing reaction.

However, chemical reactions gave off or took up a few kilocalories per mole. Nuclear reactions gave off or took up millions. To supply energy for an energy-demanding nuclear reaction required, therefore, a second, and energy-producing, nuclear reaction.

We didn't see Billings for two days.

When he did come back, it was to say, 'See here. The energy-producing reaction must produce just as much energy per nucleon involved as the energy-demanding reaction uses up. If it produces even slightly less, then the overall reaction won't go. If it produces even slightly more, then considering the astronomical number of nucleons involved, the excess energy produced would vapourize The Goose in a fraction of a second.'

'So? said Finley.

'So the number of reactions possible is very limited. I have been able to find only one plausible system. Oxygen-18, if converted to iron-56 will produce enough energy to drive the iron-56 on to gold-197. It's like going down one side of a roller-coaster and then up the other. We'll have to test this.'

'How?'

'First suppose we check the isotopic composition of the oxygen in 'The Goose.'

Oxygen is made up of three stable isotopes, almost all of it O^{16}. O^{18} makes up only one oxygen atom out of 250.

Another blood sample. The water content was distilled off in vacuum and some of it put through a mass spectograph. There was O^{18} there but only one oxygen atom out of 1300. Fully 80 per cent of the O^{18} we expected wasn't there.

Billings said, 'That's corroborative evidence. Oxygen-18 is being used up. It is being supplied constantly in the food and water fed to The Goose, but it is still being used up. Gold-197 is being produced. Iron-56 is one intermediate and since the reaction that uses up iron-56 is faster than the one that produces it, it has no chance to reach significant concentration and isotopic analysis shows its absence.'

We weren't satisfied, so we tried again. We kept The Goose on water that had been enriched with O^{18} for a week. Gold production went up almost at once. At the end of a week, it was producing 45.8 grammes while the O^{18} content of its body water was no higher than before.

'There's no doubt about it,' said Billings.

He snapped his pencil and stood up. 'That Goose is a living nuclear reactor.'

The Goose was obviously a mutation.

A mutation suggested radiation among other things and radiation brought up the thought of nuclear tests conducted in 1952 and 1953 several hundred miles away from the site of MacGregor's farm. (If it occurs to you that no nuclear tests have been conducted in Texas, it just shows two things; I'm not telling you everything and you don't know everything.)

I doubt that at any time in the history of the atomic era was background radiation so thoroughly analysed and the radioactive content of the soil so rigidly sifted.

Back records were studied. It didn't matter how top-secret they were. By this time, Project Goose had the highest priority that had ever existed.

Even weather records were checked in order to follow the behaviour of the winds at the time of the nuclear tests.

Two things turned up.

One: The background radiation at the farm was a bit higher than normal. Nothing that could possibly do harm, I hasten to add. There were indications, however, that at the time of the birth of The Goose, the farm had been subjected to the drifting edge of at least

116

two fallouts. Nothing really harmful, I again hasten to add.

Second: The Goose, alone of all geese on the farm, in fact, alone of all living creatures on the farm that could be tested, including the humans, showed no radioactivity at all. Look at it this way: *everything* shows traces of radioactivity; that's what is meant by background radiation. But The Goose showed none.

Finley sent one report on December 6, 1955, which I can paraphrase as follows:

'The Goose is a most extraordinary mutation, born of a high-level radioactivity environment which at once encouraged mutations in general and which made this particular mutation a beneficial one.

'The Goose has enzyme systems capable of catalysing various nuclear reactions. Whether the enzyme system consists of one enzyme or more than one is not known. Nor is anything known of the nature of the enzymes in question. Nor can any theory be yet advanced as to how an enzyme can catalyse a nuclear reaction, since these involve particular interactions with forces five orders of magnitude higher than those involved in the ordinary chemical reactions commonly catalysed by enzymes.

'The overall nuclear change is from oxygen-18 to gold-197. The oxygen-18 is plentiful in its environment, being present in significant amount in water and all organic foodstuffs. The gold-197 is excreted via the ovaries. One known intermediate is iron-56 and the fact that auraemoglobin is formed in the process leads us to suspect that enzyme or enzymes involved may have haeme as a prosthetic group.

'There has been considerable thought devoted to the value this overall nuclear change might have to the goose. The oxygen-18 does it no harm and the gold-197 is troublesome to be rid of, potentially poisonous, and a cause of its sterility. Its formation might possibly be a means of avoiding greater danger. This danger—'

But just reading it in the report, friend, makes it all seem so quiet, almost pensive. Actually, I never saw a man come closer to apoplexy and survive than Billings did when he found out about our own radioactive gold experiments which I told you about earlier – the ones

117

in which we detected no radioactivity in the goose, so that we discarded the results as meaningless.

Many times over he asked how we could possibly consider it unimportant that we had lost radioactivity.

'You're like the cub reporter,' he said. 'who was sent to cover a society wedding and on returning said there was no story because the groom hadn't shown up.

'You fed The Goose radioactive gold and lost it. Not only that, you failed to detect any natural radioactivity about The Goose. Any carbon-14. Any potassium-40. And you called it failure.'

We started feeding The Goose radioactive isotopes. Cautiously, at first, but before the end of January of 1956 we were shovelling it in.

The Goose remained nonradioactive.

'What it amounts to,' said Billings, 'is that this enzyme-catalysed nuclear process of The Goose manages to convert any unstable isotope into a stable isotope.'

'Useful,' I said.

'Useful? It's a thing of beauty. It's the perfect defence against the atomic age. Listen, the conversion of oxygen-18 to gold-197 should liberate eight and a fraction positrons per oxygen atom. That means eight and a fraction gamma rays as soon as each position combines with an electron. No gamma rays either. The Goose must be able to absorb gamma rays harmlessly.'

We irradiated The Goose with gamma rays. As the level rose, The Goose developed a slight fever and we quit in panic. It was just fever, though, not radiation sickness. A day passed, the fever subsided, and The Goose was as good as new.

'Do you see what we've got?' demanded Billings.

'A scientific marvel,' said Finley.

'Man, don't you see the practical applications? If we could find out the mechanism and duplicate it in the test tube, we've got a perfect method of radioactive ash disposal. The most important drawback preventing us from going ahead with a full-scale atomic economy is the headache of what to do with the radioactive isotopes manufactured in the process. Sift them through an enzyme preparation in large vats and that would be it.

'Find out the mechanism, gentlemen, and you can stop worrying about fallouts. We would find a protection against radiation sickness.

'Alter the mechanism somehow and we can have Geese excreting any element needed. How about uranium-235 eggshells?

'The mechanism! The mechanism!'

We sat there, all of us, staring at The Goose.

If only the eggs would hatch. If only we could get a tribe of nuclear-reactor Geese.

'It must have happened before,' said Finley. 'The legends of nuclear-reactor Geese.

'It must have happened before,' said Finley. 'The legends of such Geese must have started somehow.'

'Do you want to wait?' asked Billings.

If we had a gaggle of such Geese, we could begin taking a few apart. We could study its ovaries. We could prepare tissue slices and tissue homogenates.

That might not do any good. The tissue of a liver biopsy did not react with oxygen-18 under any conditions we tried.

But then we might perfuse an intact liver. We might study intact embryos, watch for one to develop the mechanism.

But with only one Goose, we could do none of that.

We don't dare kill The Goose That Lays The Golden Eggs.

The secret was in the liver of that fat Goose.

Liver of fat goose! *Pâté de foie gras!* No delicacy to us!

Nevis said, thoughtfully, 'We need an idea. Some radical departure. Some crucial thought.'

'Saying it won't bring it,' said Billings despondently.

And in a miserable attempt at a joke, I said, 'We could advertise in the newspapers,' and that gave *me* an idea.

'Science fiction!' I said.

'What?' said Finley.

'Look, science-fiction magazines print gag articles. The readers consider it fun. They're interested.' I told them about the thiotimoline articles Asimov wrote and which I had once read.

The atmosphere was cold with disapproval.

'We won't even be breaking security regulations,' I said, 'because no one will believe it.' I told them about the time in 1944 when Cleve Cartmill wrote a story describing the atom bomb one year early and the F.B.I. kept its temper.

'And science-fiction readers have ideas. Don't underrate them. Even if they think it's a gag article, they'll send their notions in to the editor. And since we have no ideas of our own; since we're up a dead-end street, what can we lose?'

They still didn't buy it.

So I said, 'And you know – The Goose won't live forever.'

That did it, somehow.

We had to convince Washington; then I got in touch with John Campbell and he got in touch with Asimov.

Now the article is done. I've read it, I approve, and I urge you all not to believe it. Please don't.

Only—

Any ideas?

PÂTÉ DE FOIE GRAS

Since this story is my own, I can tell you how it originated. It began with a deliberate attempt to pick something utterly unscientific and surround it with the trappings of science in so plausible a manner as to make it legitimate science fiction.

The fantasy I chose was that of the goose that lays the golden eggs. The question was how such a goose, which has no gold in its diet, can produce golden eggs. Gold must be produced out of other elements and that requires nuclear reactions in quantity. But nuclear reactions do not take place in living tissue in quantity, the assumption that it does is the impossible point that starts the story.

This impossible assumption must be surrounded with a wealth of quite authentic chemical and biochemical reasoning, and with an accurate picture of what scientific research is like. And since I have a Ph.D. in chemistry and spent years teaching biochemistry at a medical school, I could manage it – and have little to add here to what I said in the story.

1. How are nuclear reactions different from ordinary chemical reactions? What arguments can you bring forward against (or for) the possibility of nuclear reactions in living tissue? Cosmic rays and other hard radiation can indeed bring about nuclear reactions in living tissue (with what effects?') but how does this differ from the sort of thing dealt with in *Pâté de Foie Gras*?

2. Have you any suggestions that may help answer the problem posed at the end of the story?

7. OMNILINGUAL

H. Beam Piper

Martha Dane paused, looking up at the purple-tinged copper sky. The wind had shifted since noon, while she had been inside, and the dust storm that was sweeping the high deserts to the east was now blowing out over Syrtis. The sun, magnified by the haze, was a gorgeous magenta ball, as large as the sun of Terra, at which she could look directly. Tonight, some of that dust would come sifting down from the upper atmosphere to add another film to what had been burying the city for the last fifty thousand years.

The red loess lay over everything, covering the streets and the open spaces of park and plaza, hiding the small houses that had been crushed and pressed flat under it and the rubble that had come down from the tall buildings when roofs had caved in and walls had toppled outward. Here where she stood, the ancient streets were a hundred to a hundred and fifty feet below the surface; the breach they had made in the wall of the building behind her had opened into the sixth storey. She could look down on the cluster of prefabricated huts and sheds, on the brush-grown flat that had been the waterfront when this place had been a seaport on the ocean that was now Syrtis Depression; already, the bright metal was thinly coated with red dust. She thought, again, of what clearing this city would mean, in terms of time and labour, of people and supplies and equipment brought across fifty million miles of space. They'd have to use machinery; there was no other way it could be done. Bulldozers and power shovels and draglines; they were fast, but they were rough and indiscriminate. She remembered the digs around Harappa and Mohenjo-Daro, in the Indus Valley, and the careful, patient native labourers – the painstaking foremen, the pick-men and spademen, the long files of basketmen carrying away the earth. Slow and primitive as the civilization whose ruins they were uncovering, yes, but she could count on the fingers of one hand the times one of her pickmen had damaged a valuable object in the ground. If it hadn't been for the underpaid and uncomplaining native labourer, archaeology would still be back where Wincklemann had found it. But on Mars there was no native labour; the last Martian had died five hundred centuries ago.

Something started banging like a machine gun, four or five hundred yards to her left. A solenoid jack-hammer; Tony Lattimer must have decided which building he wanted to break into next. She became conscious, then, of the awkward weight of her equip-ment, and began redistributing it, shifting the straps of her oxy-tank pack, slinging the camera from one shoulder and the board and drafting tools from the other, gathering the notebooks and sketchbooks under her left arm. She started walking down the road, over hillocks of buried rubble, around snags of wall jutting up out of the loess, past buildings still standing, some of them already breached and explored, and across the brush-grown flat to the huts.

There were ten people in the main office room of Hut One when she entered. As soon as she had disposed of her oxygen equipment, she lit a cigarette, her first since noon, then looked from one to another of them. Old Selim von Ohlmhorst, the Turco-German, one of her two fellow archaeologists, sitting at the end of the long table against the farther wall, smoking his big curved pipe and going through a looseleaf notebook. The girl ordnance officer, Sachiko Koremitsu, between two drop-lights at the other end of the table, her head bent over her work. Colonel Hubert Penrose, the Space Force CO, and Captain Field, the intelligence officer, listening to the report of one of the airdyne pilots, returned from his afternoon survey flight. A couple of girl lieutenants from Signals, going over the script of the evening tele-cast, to be transmitted to the *Cyrano*, on orbit five thousand miles off planet and relayed from thence to Terra via Lunar. Sid Chamberlain, the Trans-Space News Service man, was with them. Like Selim and her-self, he was a civilian; he was advertising the fact with a white shirt and a sleeveless blue sweater. And Major Lindemann, the engineer officer, and one of his assis-tants, arguing over some plans on a drafting board. She hoped, drawing a pint of hot water to wash her hands and sponge her face, that they were doing something about the pipeline.

She started to carry the notebooks and sketchbooks over to where Selim von Ohlmhorst was sitting, and then, as she always did, she turned aside and stopped to watch Sachiko. The Japanese girl was restoring what had been a book, fifty thousand years ago; her eyes were masked by a binocular loup, the black headband invisible against her glossy black hair, and she was pick-delicately at the crumpled page with a hair-fine wire set in a handle of copper tubing. Finally, loosening a particle as tiny as a snowflake, she grasped it with tweezers, placed it on the sheet of transparent plastic on which she was reconstructing the page, and set it with a mist of fixative from a little spraygun. It was a sheer joy to watch her; every movement was as graceful and precise as though done to music after being re-hearsed a hundred times.

'Hello, Martha. It isn't cocktail-time yet, is it?' The girl at the table spoke without raising her head, almost without moving her lips, as though she were afraid that the slightest breath would disturb the flaky stuff in front of her.

'No, it's only fifteen-thirty. I finished my work, over there. I didn't find any more books, if that's good news for you.'

Sachiko took off the loup and leaned back in her chair, her palms cupped over her eyes.

'No, I like doing this. I call it micro-jigsaw puzzles. This book, here, really is a mess. Selim found it lying open, with some heavy stuff on top of it; the pages were simply crushed.' She hesitated briefly. 'If only it would mean something, after I did it.'

There could be a faintly critical overtone to that. As she replied, Martha realized that she was being defensive.

'It will, some day. Look how long it took to read Egyptian hieroglyphics, even after they had the Rosetta Stone.'

Sachiko smiled. 'Yes, I know. But they did have the Rosetta Stone.'

'And we don't. There is no Rosetta Stone, not anywhere on Mars. A whole race, a whole species, died while the first Cro-Magnon cave-artist was daubing pictures of reindeer and bison, and across fifty thousand years and fifty million miles there was no bridge of understanding.'

'We'll find one. There must be something, somewhere, that will give us the meaning of a few words, and we'll use them to pry meaning out of more words, and so on. We may not live to learn this language, but we'll make a start, and some day somebody will.'

Sachiko took her hands from her eyes, being careful not to look towards the unshaded lights, and smiled again. This time Martha was sure that it was not the Japanese smile of politeness, but the universally human smile of friendship.

'I hope so, Martha; really I do. It would be wonderful for you to be the first to do it, and it would be wonderful for all of us to be able to read what these people wrote. It would really bring this dead city to life again.' The smile faded slowly. 'But it seems so hopeless.'

'You haven't found any more pictures?'

Sachiko shook her head. Not that it would have meant much if she had. They had found hundreds of pictures with captions; they had never been able to establish a positive relationship between any picture object and any printed word. Neither of them said anything more, and after a moment Sachiko replaced the loup and bent her head forward over the book.

Selim von Ohlmhorst looked up from his notebook, taking his pipe out of his mouth.

'Everything finished over there?' he asked, releasing a puff of smoke.

'Such as it was.' She laid the notebooks and sketches

on the table. 'Captain Gicquel's started airsealing the building from the fifth floor down, with an entrance on the sixth; he'll start putting in oxygen generators as soon as that's done. I have everything cleared up where he'll be working.'

Colonel Penrose looked up quickly, as though making a mental note to attend to something later. Then he returned his attention to the pilot, who was pointing something out on a map.

Von Ohlmhorst nodded. 'There wasn't much to it, at that,' he agreed. 'Do you know which building Tony has decided to enter next?'

'The tall one with the conical thing like a candle extinguisher on top, I think. I heard him drilling for the blasting shots over that way.'

'Well, I hope it turns out to be one that was occupied up to the end.'

The last one hadn't. It had been stripped of its contents and fittings, a piece of this and a bit of that, haphazardly, apparently over a long period of time, until it had been almost gutted. For centuries, as it had died, this city had been consuming itself by a process of autocannibalism. She said something to that effect.

'Yes. We always find that – except, of course, at places like Pompeii. Have you seen any of the other Roman cities in Italy?' he asked. 'Minturnae, for instance? First the inhabitants tore down this to repair that, and then, after they had vacated the city, other people came along and tore down what was left, and burned the stones for lime, or crushed them to mend roads, till there was nothing left but the foundation traces. That's where we are fortunate; this is one of the places where the Martian race perished, and there were no barbarians to come later and destroy what they had left.' He puffed slowly at his pipe. 'Some of these days, Martha, we are going to break into one of these buildings and find that it was one in which the last of these people died. Then we will learn the story of the end of their civilization.'

And if we learn to read their language, we'll learn the whole story, not just the obituary. She hesitated, not putting the thought into words. 'We'll find that, some time, Selim,' she said, then looked at her watch.

'I'm going to get some more work done on my lists, before dinner.'

For an instant, the old man's face stiffened in disapproval; he started to say something, thought better of it, and put his pipe back into his mouth. The brief wrinkling around his mouth and the twitch of his white moustache had been enough, however; she knew what he was thinking. She was wasting time and effort, he believed; time and effort belonging not to herself but to the expedition. He could be right, too, she realized. But he had to be wrong; there had to be a way to do it. She turned from him silently and went to her own packing case seat, at the middle of the table.

Photographs, and photostats of restored pages of books, and transcripts of inscriptions, were piled in front of her, and the notebooks in which she was compiling her lists. She sat down, lighting a fresh cigarette, and reached over to a stack of unexamined material, taking off the top sheet. It was a photostat of what looked like the title page and contents of some sort of a periodical. She remembered it; she had found it herself, two days before, in a closet in the basement of the building she had just finished examining.

She sat for a moment, looking at it. It was readable, in the sense that she had set up a purely arbitrary but consistently pronounceable system of phonetic values for the letters. The long vertical symbols were vowels. There were only ten of them; not too many, allowing separate characters for long and short sounds. There were twenty of the short horizontal letters, which meant that sounds like -ng or -ch or -sh were single letters. The odds were millions to one against her system being anything like the original sound of the language, but she had listed several thousand Martian words, and she could pronounce all of them.

And that as far as it went. She could pronounce between three and four thousand Martian words, and she couldn't assign a meaning to one of them. Selim von Ohlmhorst believed that she never would. So did Tony Lattimer, and he was a great deal less reticent about saying so. So, she was sure, did Sachiko Koremitsu. There were times, now and then, when she began to be afraid that they were right.

126

The letters on the page in front of her began squirming and dancing, slender vowels with fat little consonants. They did that, now, every night in her dreams. And there were other dreams, in which she read them as easily as English; waking, she would try desperately and vainly to remember. She blinked, and looked away from the photostated page; when she looked back, the letters were behaving themselves again. There were three words at the top of the page, over-and-under-lined, which seemed to be the Martian method of capitalization. *Mastharnorvod Tadavas Sornhulva.* She pronounced them mentally, leafing through her notebooks to see if she had encountered them before, and in what contexts. All three were listed. In addition, *masthar* was a fairly common word, and so was *norvod,* and so was *nor,* but *-vod* was a suffix and nothing but a suffix. *Davas,* was a word, too, and *ta-* was a common prefix; *sorn* and *hulva* were both common words. This language, she had long ago decided, must be something like German; when the Martians had needed a new word, they had just pasted a couple of existing words together. It would probably turn out to be a grammatical horror. Well, they had published magazines, and one of them had been called *Mastharnorvod Tadavas Sornhulva.* She wondered if it had been something like the *Quarterly Archaeological Review*, or something more on the order of *Sexy Stories.*

A smaller line, under the title, was plainly the issue number and date; enough things had been found numbered in series to enable her to identify the numerals and determine that a decimal system of numeration had been used. This was the one thousand and seven hundred and fifty-fourth issue, for Doma, 14837; then Doma must be the name of one of the Martian months. The word had turned up several times before. She found herself puffing furiously on her cigarette as she leafed through notebooks and piles of already examined material.

Sachiko was speaking to somebody, and a chair scraped at the end of the table. She raised her head, to see a big man with red hair and a red face, in Space Force green, with the single star of a major on his shoulder, sitting down. Ivan Fitzgerald, the medic. He was lifting weights from a book similar to the one the girl ordnance officer was restoring.

'Haven't had time, lately,' he was saying, in reply to Sachiko's question. 'The Finchley girl's still down with whatever it is she has, and it's something I haven't been able to diagnose yet. And I've been checking on bacteria cultures, and in what spare time I have, I've been dissecting specimens for Bill Chandler. Bill's finally found a mammal. Looks like a lizard, and it's only four inches long, but it's a real warm-blooded, gamogenetic, placental, viviparous mammal. Burrows, and seems to live on what pass for insects here.'

'Is there enough oxygen for anything like that?' Sachiko was asking.

'Seems to be, close to the ground.' Fitzgerald got the headband of his loup adjusted, and pulled it down over his eyes. 'He found this thing in a ravine down on the sea bottom— Ha, this page seems to be intact; now, if I can get it out all in one piece—'

He went on talking inaudibly to himself, lifting the page a little at a time and sliding one of the transparent plastic sheets under it, working with minute delicacy. Not the delicacy of the Japanese girl's small hands, moving like the paws of a cat washing her face, but like a steam-hammer cracking a peanut. Field archaeology requires a certain delicacy of touch, too, but Martha watched the pair of them with envious admiration. Then she turned back to her own work, finishing the table of contents.

The next page was the beginning of the first article listed; many of the words were unfamiliar. She had the impression that this must be some kind of scientific or technical journal; that could be because such publications made up the bulk of her own periodical readings. She doubted if it were fiction; the paragraphs had a solid, factual look.

At length, Ivan Fitzgerald gave a short, explosive grunt.

'Ha! Got it!'

She looked up. He had detached the page and was cementing another plastic sheet on to it.

'Any pictures?' she asked.

'None on this side. Wait a moment.' He turned the sheet. 'None on this side, either.' He sprayed another sheet of plastic to sandwich the page, then picked up his pipe and relighted it.

'I get fun out of his, and it's good practice for my hands, so don't think I'm complaining,' he said, 'but, Martha, do you honestly think anybody's ever going to get anything out of this?'

Sachiko held up a scrap of the silicone plastic the Martians had used for paper with her tweezers. It was almost an inch square.

'Look; three whole words on this piece,' she crowed. 'Ivan, you took the easy book.'

Fitzgerald wasn't being sidetracked. 'This stuff's absolutely meaningless,' he continued. 'It had a meaning fifty thousand years ago, when it was written, but it has none at all now.'

She shook her head. 'Meaning isn't something that evaporates with time,' she argued. 'It has just as much meaning now as it ever had. We just haven't learned how to decipher it.'

'That seems like a pretty pointless distinction,' Selim von Ohlmhorst joined the conversation. 'There no longer exists a means of deciphering it.'

'We'll find one.' She was speaking, she realized, more in self-encouragement than in controversy.

'How? From pictures and captions? We've found captioned pictures, and what have they given us? A caption is intended to explain the picture, not the picture to explain the caption. Suppose some alien to our culture found a picture of a man with a white beard and moustache sawing a billet from a log. He would think the caption meant, "Man Sawing Wood." How would he know that it was really, "Wilhelm II in Exile at Doorn"?'

'Well, of course, if we found something like that,' von Ohlmhorst began.

'Michael Ventris found something like that, back in the Fifties,' Hubert Penrose's voice broke in from directly behind her.

She turned her head. The colonel was standing by the archaeologists' table; Captain Field and the airdyne pilot had gone out.

'He found a lot of Greek inventories of military stores,' Penrose continued. 'They were in Cretan Linear B script, and at the head of each list was a little picture,

129

a sword or a helmet or a cooking tripod or a chariot wheel. That's what gave him the key to the script.'

'Colonel's getting to be quite an archaeologist,' Fitzgerald commented. 'We're all learning each other's specialities, on this expedition.'

'I heard about that long before this expedition was even contemplated.' Penrose was tapping a cigarette on his gold case. 'I heard about that back before the Thirty Days' War, at Intelligence School, when I was a lieutenant. As a feat of cryptanalysis, not an archaeological discovery.'

'Yes, cryptanalysis,' von Ohlmhorst pounced. 'The reading of a known language in an unknown form of writing. Ventris's lists were in the known language, Greek. Neither he nor anybody else ever read a word of the Cretan language until the finding of the Greek-Cretan bilingual in 1963, because only with a bilingual text, one language already known, can be unknown ancient language be learned. And what hope, I ask you, have we of finding anything like that here? Martha, you've been working on these Martian texts ever since we landed here – for the last six months. Tell me, have you found a single word to which you can positively assign a meaning?'

'Yes, I think I have one.' She was trying hard not to sound too exultant. '*Doma*. It's the name of one of the months of the Martian calendar.'

'Where did you find that?' von Ohlmhorst asked. 'And how did you establish—'

'Here.' She picked up the photostat and handed it along the table to him. 'I'd call this the title page of a magazine.'

He was silent for a moment, looking at it. 'Yes, I would say so, too. Have you any of the rest of it?'

'I'm working on the first page of the first article, listed there. Wait till I see; yes, here's all I found, together, here.' She told him where she had got it. 'I just gathered it up, at the time, and gave it to Geoffrey and Rosita to photostat; this is the first time I've really examined it.'

The old man got to his feet, brushing tobacco ashes from the front of his jacket, and came to where she was sitting, laying the title page on the table and leafing quickly through the stack of photostats.

'Yes, and here is the second article, on page eight, and here's the next one.' He finished the pile of photostats. 'A couple of pages missing at the end of the last article. This is remarkable; surprising that a thing like a magazine would have survived so long.'

'Well, this silicone stuff the Martians used for paper is pretty durable,' Hubert Penrose said. 'There doesn't seem to have been any water or any other fluid in it originally, so it wouldn't dry out with time.'

'Oh, it's not remarkable that the material would have survived. We've found a good many books and papers in excellent condition. But only a really vital culture, an organized culture, will publish magazines, and this civilization had been dying for hundreds of years before the end. It might have been a thousand years before the time they died out completely that such activities as publishing ended.'

'Well, look where I found it; in a closet in a cellar. Tossed in there and forgotten, and then ignored when they were stripping the building. Things like that happen.'

Penrose had picked up the title page and was looking at it.

'I don't think there's any doubt about this being a magazine, at all.' He looked again at the title, his lips moving silently. *Mastharnorvod Tadavas Sornhulva.* Wonder what it means. But you're right about the date — *Doma* seems to be the name of a month. Yes, you have a word, Dr. Dane.'

Sid Chamberlain, seeing that something unusual was going on, had come over from the table at which he was working. After examining the title page and some of the inside pages, he began whispering into the stenophone he had taken from his belt.

'Don't try to blow this up to anything big, Sid,' she cautioned. 'All we have is the name of a month, and Lord only knows how long it'll be till we even find out which month it was.'

'Well, it's a start, isn't it?' Penrose argued. 'Grotefend only had the word for "king" when he started reading Persian cuneiform.'

'But I don't have the word for month; just the name of a month. Everybody knew the names of the Persian kings, long before Grotefend.'

'That's not the story,' Chamberlain said. 'What the public back on Terra will be interested in is finding out that the Martians published magazines, just like we do. Something familiar; make the Martians seem more real. More human.'

Three men had come in, and were removing their masks and helmets and oxy-tanks, and peeling out of their quilted coveralls. Two were Space Force lieutenants; the third was a youngish civilian with close-cropped blond hair in a checked woollen shirt. Tony Lattimer and his helpers.

'Don't tell me Martha finally got something out of that stuff?' he asked, approaching the table. He might have been commenting on the antics of the village half-wit, from his tone.

'Yes; the name of one of the Martian months,' Hubert Penrose went on to explain, showing the photostat.

Tony Lattimer took it, glanced at it, and dropped it on the table.

'Sounds plausible, of course, but just an assumption. That word may not be the name of a month, at all – could mean "published" or "authorized" or "copyrighted" or anything like that. Fact is, I don't think it's more than a wild guess that that thing's anything like a periodical.' He dismissed the subject and turned to Penrose. 'I picked out the next building to enter; that tall one with the conical thing on top. It ought to be in pretty good shape inside; the conical top wouldn't allow dust to accumulate, and from the outside nothing seems to be in caved in or crushed. Ground level's higher than the other one, about the seventh floor. I found a good place and drilled for the shots; tomorrow I'll blast a hole in it, and if you can spare some people to help, we can start exploring it right away.'

'Yes, of course, Dr. Lattimer. I can spare about a dozen, and I suppose you can find a few civilian volunteers,' Penrose told him. 'What will you need in the way of equipment?'

'Oh, about six demolition-packets; they can all be shot together. And the usual thing in the way of lights, and breaking and digging tools, and climbing equipment in case we run into broken or doubtful stairways. We'll divide into two parties. Nothing ought to be entered

132

for the first time without a qualified archaeologist along. Three parties, if Martha can tear herself away from this catalogue of systematized incomprehensibilities she's making long enough to do some real work.'

She felt her chest tighten and her face become stiff. She was pressing her lips together to lock in a furious retort when Hubert Penrose answered for her.

'Dr. Dane's been doing as much work, and as important work, as you have,' he said brusquely. 'More important work, I'd be inclined to say.'

Von Ohlmhorst was visibly distressed; he glanced once towards Sid Chamberlain, then looked hastily away from him. Afraid of a story of dissension among archaeologists getting out.

'Working out a system of pronunciation by which the Martian language could be translated was a most important contribution,' he said. 'And Martha did that almost unassisted.'

'Unassisted by Dr. Lattimer, anyway,' Penrose added. 'Captain Field and Lieutenant Koremitsu did some work, and I helped out a little, but nine-tenths of it she did herself.'

'Purely arbitrary,' Lattimer disdained. 'Why, we don't even know that the Martians could make the same kind of vocal sounds we do.'

'Oh, yes, we do,' Ivan Fitzgerald contradicted, safe on his own ground. 'I haven't seen any actual Martian skulls – these people seem to have been very tidy about disposing of their dead – but from statues and busts and pictures I've seen, I'd say that their vocal organs were identical with our own.'

'Well, grant that. And grant that it's going to be impressive to rattle off the names of Martian notables whose statues we find, and that if we're ever to attribute any place-names, they'll sound a lot better than this horse-doctor's Latin the old astronomers splashed all over the map of Mars,' Lattimer said. 'What I object to is her wasting time on this stuff, of which nobody will ever be able to read a word if she fiddles around with those lists till there's another hundred feet of loess on this city, when there's so much real work to be done and we're as shorthanded as we are.'

That was the first time that had come out in just so

many words. She was glad Lattimer had said it and not Selim von Ohlmhorst.

'What you mean,' she retorted, 'is that it doesn't have the publicity value that digging up statues has.'

For an instant, she could see that the shot had scored. Then Lattimer, with a side glance at Chamberlain, answered:

'What I mean is that you're trying to find something that any archaeologist, yourself included, should know doesn't exist. I don't object to your gambling your professional reputation and making a laughing-stock of yourself; what I object to is that the blunders of one archaeologist discredit the whole subject in the eyes of the public.'

That seemed to be what worried Lattimer most. She was framing a reply when the communication-outlet whistled shrilly, and then squawked: 'Cocktail time! One hour to dinner; cocktails in the library, Hut Four!'

The library, which was also lounge, recreation room, and general gathering-place, was already crowded; most of the crowd was at the long table topped with sheets of glasslike plastic that had been wall panels out of one of the ruined buildings. She poured herself what passed, here, for a martini, and carried it over to where Selim von Ohlmhorst was sitting alone.

For a while, they talked about the building they had just finished exploring, then drifted into reminiscences of their work on Terra – von Ohlmhorst's in Asia Minor, with the Hittite Empire, and hers in Pakistan, excavating the cities of the Harappa civilization. They finished their drinks – the ingredients were plentiful; alcohol and flavouring extracts synthesized from Martian vegetation – and von Ohlmhorst took the two glasses to the table for refills.

'You know, Martha,' he said, when he returned. 'Tony was right about one thing. You are gambling your professional standing and reputation. It's against all archaeological experience that a language so completely dead as this one could be deciphered. There was a continuity between all the other ancient languages – by knowing Greek, Champollion learned to read Egyptian; by knowing Egyptian, Hittite was learned. That's why you and your colleagues have never been able to translate the

Harappa hieroglyphics; no such continuity exists there. If you insist that this utterly dead language can be read, your reputation will suffer for it.'

'I heard Colonel Penrose say, once, that an officer who's afraid to risk his military reputation seldom makes much of a reputation. It's the same with us. If we really want to find things out, we have to risk making mistakes. And I'm a lot more interested in finding things out that I am in my reputation.'

She glanced across the room, to where Tony Lattimer was sitting with Gloria Standish, talking earnestly, while Gloria sipped one of the counterfeit Martinis and listened. Gloria was the leading contender for the title of Miss Mars, 1996, if you liked big bosomy blondes, but Tony would have been just as attentive to her if she'd looked like the Wicked Witch in the *Wizard of Oz*, because Gloria was the Pan-Federation Telecast System commentator with the expedition.

'I know you are,' the old Turco-German was saying. 'That's why, when they asked me to name another archaeologist for this expedition, I named you.'

He hadn't named Tony Lattimer; Lattimer had been pushed on to the expedition by his university. There'd been a lot of high-level string-pulling to that; she wished she knew the whole story. She'd managed to keep clear of universities and university politics; all her digs had been sponsored by non-academic foundations or art museums.

'You have an excellent standing; much better than my own, at your age. That's why it disturbs me to see you jeopardizing it by this insistence that the Martian language can be translated. I can't, really, see how you can hope to succeed.'

She shrugged and drank some more of her cocktail, then lit another cigarette. It was getting tiresome to try to verbalize something she only felt.

'Neither do I, now, but I will. Maybe I'll find something like the picture-books Sachiko was talking about. A child's primer, maybe; surely they had things like that. And if I don't, I'll find something else. We've only been here six months. I can wait the rest of my life, if I have to, but I'll do it some time.'

'I can't wait so long,' von Ohlmhorst said. 'The rest of my life will only be a few years, and when the

Schiaparelli orbits in, I'll be going back to Terra on the *Cyrano*.'

'I wish you wouldn't. This is a whole new world of archaeology. Literally.'

'Yes.' He finished the cocktail and looked at his pipe as though wondering whether to re-light it so soon before dinner, then put it in his pocket. 'A whole new world – but I've grown old, and it isn't for me. I've spent my life studying the Hittites. I can speak the Hittite language, though maybe King Muwatallis wouldn't be able to understand my modern Turkish accent. But the things I'd have to learn, here – chemistry, physics, engineering, how to run analytic tests on steel girders and beryllo-silver alloys and plastics and silicones. I'm more at home with a civilization that rode in chariots and fought with swords and was just learning how to work iron. Mars is for young people. This expedition is a cadre of leadership – not only the Space Force people, who'll be the commanders of the main expedition, but us scientists, too. And I'm just an old cavalry general who can't learn to command tanks and aircraft. You'll have time to learn about Mars. I won't.'

His reputation as the dean of Hittitologists was solid and secure, too, she added mentally. Then she felt ashamed of the thought. He wasn't to be classed with Tony Lattimer.

'All I came for was to get the work started,' he was continuing. 'The Federation Government felt that an old hand should do that. Well, it's started, now; you and Tony and whoever comes out on the *Schiaparelli* must carry it on. You said it, yourself; you have a whole new world. This is only one city of the last Martian civilization. Behind this, you have the Late Upland Culture, and the Canal Builders, and all the civilizations and races and empires before them, clear back to the Martian Stone Age.' He hesitated for a moment. 'You have no idea what you have to learn, Martha. This isn't the time to start specializing too narrowly.'

They all got out of the truck and stretched their legs and looked up the road to the tall building with the queer conical cap askew on its top. The four little figures that had been busy against its wall climbed into the jeep and started back slowly, the smallest of them,

136

Sachiko Koremitsu, paying out an electric cable behind. When it pulled up beside the truck, they climbed out; Sachiko attached the free end of the cable to a nuclear-electric battery. At once, dirty grey smoke and orange dust puffed out from the wall of the building, and, a second later, the multiple explosion banged.

She and Tony Lattimer and Major Lindemann climbed on to the truck, leaving the jeep standing by the road. When they reached the building, a satisfying wide breach had been blown in the wall. Lattimer had placed his shots between two of the windows; they were both blown out along with the wall between, and lay unbroken on the ground. Martha remembered the first building they had entered. A Space Force officer had picked up a stone and thrown it at one of the windows, thinking that would be all they'd need to do. It had bounced back. He had drawn his pistol – they'd all carried guns, then, on the principle that what they didn't know about Mars might easily hurt them – and fired four shots. The bullets had ricochetted, screaming thinly; there were four coppery smears of jacket-metal on the window, and a little surface spalling. Somebody tried a rifle; the 4000-f.s. bullet had cracked the glasslike pane without penetrating. An oxy-acetylene torch had taken an hour to cut the window out; the lab crew, abroad the ship, were still trying to find out just what the stuff was.

Tony Lattimer had gone forward and was sweeping his flashlight back and forth, swearing petulantly, his voice harshened and amplified by his helmet-speaker.

'I thought I was blasting into a hallway; this lets us into a room. Careful; there's about a two-foot drop to the floor, and a lot of rubble from the blast just inside.'

He stepped down through the breach; the others began dragging equipment out of the trucks – shovels and picks and crowbars and sledges, portable floodlights, cameras, sketching materials, an extension ladder, even Alpinists' ropes and crampons and pickaxes. Hubert Penrose was shouldering something that looked like a surrealist machine gun but which was really a nuclear-electric jack-hammer. Martha selected one of the spike-shod mountaineer's ice axes, with which she could dig or chop or poke or pry or help herself over rough footing.

The windows, grimed and crusted with fifty millennia of dust, filtered in a dim twilight; even the breach in the wall, in the morning shade, lighted only a small patch of floor. Somebody snapped on a floodlight, aiming it at the ceiling. The big room was empty and bare; dust lay thick on the floor and reddened the once-white walls. It could have been a large office, but there was nothing left in it to indicate its use.

'This one's been stripped up to the seventh floor!' Lattimer exclaimed. 'Street level'll be cleaned out, completely.'

'Do for living quarters and shops, then,' Lindemann said. 'Added to the others, this'll take care of everybody on the *Schiaparelli*.'

'Seem to have been a lot of electric or electronic apparatus over along this wall,' one of the Space Force officers commented. 'Ten or twelve electric outlets.' He brushed the dusty wall with his glove, then scraped on the floor with his foot. 'I can see where things were pried loose.'

The door, one of the double sliding things the Martians had used, was closed. Selim von Ohlmhorst tried it, but it was stuck fast. The metal latch-parts had frozen together, molecule bonding itself to molecule, since the door had last been closed. Hubert Penrose came over with the jack-hammer, fitting a spear-point chisel into place. He set the chisel in the joint between the doors, braced the hammer against his hip, and squeezed the trigger-switch. The hammer banged briefly like the weapon it resembled, and the doors popped a few inches apart, then stuck. Enough dust had worked into the recesses into which it was supposed to slide to block it on both sides.

That was old stuff; they ran into that every time they had to force a door, and they were prepared for it. Somebody went outside and brought in a power-jack and finally one of the doors inched back to the doorjamb. That was enough to get the lights and equipment through; they all passed from the room to the hallway beyond. About half the other doors were open; each had a number and a single word, *Darfhulva*, over it.

One of the civilian volunteers, a woman professor of

natural ecology from Penn State University, was looking up and down the hall.

'You know,' she said, 'I feel at home here. I think this was a college of some sort, and these were classrooms. That word, up there; that was the subject taught, or the department. And those electronic devices, all where the class would face them; audio-visual teaching aids.'

'A twenty-five-storey university?' Lattimer scoffed. 'Why, a building like this would handle thirty thousand students.'

'Maybe there were that many. This was a big city, in its prime,' Martha said, moved chiefly by a desire to oppose Lattimer.

'Yes, but think of the snafu in the halls, every time they changed classes. It'd take half an hour to get everybody back and forth from one floor to another.' He turned to von Ohlmhorst. 'I'm going up above this floor. This place has been looted clean up to here, but there's a chance there may be something above,' he said.

'I'll stay on this floor, at present,' the Turco-German replied. 'There will be much coming and going, and dragging things in and out. We should get this completely examined and recorded first. Then Major Lindemann's people can do their worst, here.'

'Well, if nobody else wants it, I'll take the downstairs,' Martha said.

'I'll go along with you,' Hubert Penrose told her. 'If the lower floors have no archaeological value, we'll turn them into living quarters. I like this building; it'll give everybody room to keep out from under everybody else's feet.' He looked down the hall. We ought to find escalators at the middle.'

The hallway, too, was thick underfoot with dust. Most of the open rooms were empty, but a few contained furniture, including small seat-desks. The original proponent of the university theory pointed these out as just what might be found in classroms. There were escalators, up and down, on either side of the hall, and more on the intersecting passage to the right.

'That's how they handled the students, between classes,' Martha commented. 'And I'll bet there are more ahead, there.'

They came to a stop where the hallway ended at a great square central hall. There were elevators, there, on two of the sides, and four escalators, still usable as stairways. But it was the walls, and the paintings on them, that brought them up short and staring.

They were clouded with dirt — she was trying to imagine what they must have looked like originally, and at the same time estimating the labour that would be involved in cleaning them — but they were still distinguishable, as was the word, *Darfhulva*, in golden letters above each of the four sides. It was a moment before she realized, from the murals, that she had at last found a meaningful Martian word. They were a vast historical panorama, clockwise around the room. A group of skin-clad savages squatting around a fire. Hunters with bows and spears, carrying the carcass of an animal slightly like a pig. Nomads riding long-legged, graceful mounts like hornless deer. Peasants sowing and reaping; mud-walled hut villages, and cities; processions of priests and warriors; battles with swords and bows, and with cannon and muskets; galleys, and ships with sails, and ships without visible means of propulsion, and aircraft. Changing costumes and weapons and machines and styles of architecture. A richly fertile landscape, gradually merging into barren deserts and bushlands — the time of the great planet-wide drought. The Canal Builders — men with machines recognizable as steam-shovels and derricks, digging and quarrying driving across the empty plains with aqueducts. Many cities — seaports on the shrinking oceans; dwindling, half-deserted cities; an abandoned city, with four tiny humanoid figures and a thing like a combat-car in the middle of a brush-grown plaza, they and their vehicle dwarfed by the huge lifeless buildings around them. She had not the least doubt; *Darfhulva* was History.

'Wonderful!' von Ohlmhorst was saying. 'The entire history of this race. Why, if the painter depicted appropriate costumes and weapons and machines for each period, and got the architecture right, we can break the history of this planet into eras and periods and civilizations.'

'You can assume they're authentic. The faculty of this university would insist on authenticity in the *Darfhulva* — History - Department,' she said.

'Yes! *Darfhulva* – History! And your magazine was a journal of *Sornhulva*!' Penrose exclaimed. 'You have a word, Martha!' It took her an instant to realize that he had called her by her first name, and not Dr. Dane. She wasn't sure if that weren't a bigger triumph than learning a word of the Martian language. Or a more auspicious start. 'Alone, I suppose that *hulva* means something like science or knowledge, or study; combined, it would be equivalent to our 'ology. And *darf* would mean something like past, or old times, or human events, or chronicles.'

'That gives you three words, Martha!' Sachiko jubilated. 'You did it.'

'Let's don't go too fast,' Lattimer said, for once not derisively. 'I'll admit that *darfhulva* is the Martian word for history as a subject of study; I'll admit that *hulva* is the general word and *darf* modifies it and tells us which subject is meant. But as for assigning specific meanings, we can't do that because we don't know just how the Martians thought, scientifically or otherwise.'

He stopped short, startled by the blue-white light that blazed as Sid Chamberlain's Kliegettes went on. When the whirring of the camera stopped, it was Chamberlain who was speaking:

'This is the biggest thing yet; the whole history of Mars, Stone Age to the end, all on four walls. I'm taking this with the fast shutter, but we'll telecast it in slow motion, from the beginning to the end. Tony, I want you to do the voice for it – running commentary, interpretation of each scene as it's shown. Would you do that?'

Would he do that! Martha thought. If he had a tail, he'd be wagging it at the very thought.

'Well, there ought to be more murals on the other floors,' she said. 'Who wants to come downstairs with us?'

Sachiko did; immediately, Ivan Fitzgerald volunteered. Sid decided to go upstairs with Tony Lattimer and Gloria Standish decided to go upstairs, too. Most of the party would remain on the seventh floor, to help Selim von Ohlmhorst get it finished. After poking tentatively at the escalator with the spike of her axe, Martha led the way downward.

* * *

The sixth floor was *Darfhulva*, too; military and technological history, from the character of the murals. They looked around the central hall, and went down to the fifth; it was like the floors above except that the big quadrangle was stacked with dusty furniture and boxes. Ivan Fitzgerald, who was carrying the floodlight, swung it slowly around. Here the murals were of heroic-sized Martians, so human in appearance as to seem members of her own race, each holding some object – a book, or a test tube, or some bit of scientific apparatus, and behind them were scenes of laboratories and factories, flame and smoke, lightning-flashes. The word at the top of each of the four walls was one with which she was already familiar – *Sornhulva*.

'Hey, Martha; there's that word,' Ivan Fitzgerald exclaimed. 'The one in the title of your magazine.' He looked at the paintings. 'Chemistry, or physics.'

'Both,' Hubert Penrose considered. 'I don't think the Martians made any sharp distinction between them. See, the old fellow with the scraggly whiskers must be the inventor of the spectroscope; he has one in his hands, and he has a rainbow behind him. And the woman in the blue smock, beside him, worked in organic chemistry; see the diagrams of long-chain molecules behind her. What word would convey the idea of chemistry and physics taken as one subject?'

'*Sornhulva*,' Sachiko suggested. 'If *hulva's* something like science, *sorn* must mean matter, or substance, or physical object. You were right, all along, Martha. A civilization like this would certainly leave something like this, that would be self-explanatory.'

'This'll wipe a little more of that superior grin off Tony Lattimer's face,' Fitzgerald was saying, as they went down the motionless escalator to the floor below. 'Tony wants to be a big shot. When you want to be a big shot, you can't bear the possibility of anybody else being a bigger big shot, and whoever makes a start on reading this language will be the biggest big shot archaeology ever saw.'

That was true. She hadn't thought of it, in that way, before, and now she tried not to think about it. She didn't want to be a big shot. She wanted to be able to read the Martian language, and find things out about the Martians.

142

Two escalators down, they came out on a mezzanine around a wide central hall on the street level, the floor forty feet below them and the ceiling forty feet above. Their lights picked out object after object below – a huge group of sculptured figures in the middle; some kind of a motor vehicle jacked up on trestles for repairs; things that looked like machine guns and auto-cannon; long tables, tops litered with a dust-covered miscellany; machinery; boxes and crates and containers.

They made their way down and walked among the clutter, missing a hundred things for every one they saw, until they found a escalator to the basement. There were three basements, one under another, until at last they stood at the bottom of the last escalator, on a bare concrete floor, swinging the portable floodlight over stacks of boxes and barrels and drums, and heaps of powdery dust. The boxes were plastic – nobody had ever found anything made of wood in the city – and the barrels and drums were of metal or glass or some glass-like substance. They were outwardly intact. The powdery heaps might have been anything organic, or anything containing fluid. Down here, where wind and dust could not reach, evaporation had been the only force of destruction after the minute life that caused putrefaction had vanished.

They found refrigeration rooms, too, and using Martha's ice axe and the pistol-like vibratool Sachiko carried on her belt, they pounded and pried one open, to find desiccated piles of what had been vegetables, and leathery chunks of meat. Samples of that stuff, rocketed up to the ship, would give a reliable estimate, by radio-carbon dating, of how long ago this building had been occupied. The refrigeration unit, radically different from anything their own culture had produced, had been electrically powered. Sachiko and Penrose, poking into it, found the switches still on; the machine had only ceased to function when the power-source, whatever that had been, had failed.

The middle basement had also been used, at least towards the end, for storage; it was cut in half by a partition pierced by but one door. They took half an hour to force this, and were on the point of sending above for heavy equipment when it yielded enough for them to squeeze through. Fitzgerald, in the lead with the light, stopped short, looked around, and then gave a groan that came through his helmet-speaker like a foghorn.

'Oh, no! *No*!'

'What's the matter, Ivan?' Sachiko, entering behind him, asked anxiously.

He stepped aside. 'Look at it, Sachi! Are we going to have to do all that?'

Martha crowded through behind her friend and looked around, then stood motionless, dizzy with excitement. Books. Case on case of books, half an acre of cases, fifteen feet to the ceiling. Fitzgerald, and Penrose, who had pushed in behind her, were talking in rapid excitement; she only heard the sound of their voices, not their words. This must be the main stacks of the university library – the entire literature of the vanished race of Mars. In the centre, down an aisle between the cases, she could see the hollow square of the librarian's desk, and stairs and a dumb-waiter to the floor above.

She realized that she was walking forward, with the others, towards this. Sachiko was saying: 'I'm the lightest; let me go first.' She must be talking about the spidery metal stairs.

'I'd say they were safe,' Penrose answered. 'The trouble we've had with doors around here shows that the metal hasn't deteriorated.'

In the end, the Japanese girl led the way, more catlike than ever in her caution. The stairs were quite sound, in spite of their fragile appearance, and they all followed her. The floor above was a duplicate of the room they had entered, and seemed to contain about as many books. Rather than waste time forcing the door here, they returned to the middle basement and came up by the escalator down which they had originally descended.

The upper basement contained kitchens – electric stoves, some with pots and pans still on them – and a big room that must have been, originally, the students' dining room, though when last used it had been a workshop. As they expected, the library reading room was on the street-level floor, directly above the stacks. It seemed to have been converted into a sort of common living room for the building's last occupants. An adjoining auditorium had been made into a chemical works; there were vats and distillation apparatus, and a metal frac-

144

tionating tower that extended through a hole knocked in the ceiling seventy feet above. A good deal of plastic furniture of the sort they had been finding everywhere in the city was stacked about, some of it broken up, apparently for reprocessing. The other rooms on the street floor seemed also to have been devoted to manufacturing and repair work; a considerable industry, along a number of lines, must have been carried on here for a long time after the university had ceased to function as such.

On the second floor, they found a museum; many of the exhibits remained, tantalizingly half-visible in grimed glass cases. There had been administrative offices there, too. The doors of most of them were closed, and they did not waste time trying to force them, but those that were open had been turned into living quarters. They made notes, and rough floorplans, to guide them in future more thorough examination; it was almost noon before they had worked their way back to the seventh floor.

Selim von Ohlmhorst was in a room on the north side of the building, sketching the position of things before examining them and collecting them for removal. He had the floor checker-boarded with a grid of chalked lines, each numbered.

'We have everything on this floor photographed,' he said. 'I have three gangs – all the floodlights I have – sketching and making measurements. At the rate we're going, with time out for lunch, we'll be finished by the middle of the afternoon.'

'You've been working fast. Evidently you aren't being high-church about a "qualified archaeologist" entering rooms first,' Penrose commented.

'Ach, childishness!' the old man exclaimed impatiently. 'These officers of yours aren't fools. All of them have been to Intelligence School and Criminal Investigation School. Some of the most careful amateur archaeologists I ever knew were retired soldiers or policemen. But there isn't much work to be done. Most of the rooms are either empty or like this one – a few bits of furniture and broken trash and scraps of paper. Did you find anything down on the lower floors?'

'Well, yes,' Penrose said, a hint of mirth in his voice. 'What would you say, Martha?'

She started to tell Selim. The others, unable to restrain their excitement, broke in with interruptions. Von Ohlmhorst was staring in incredulous amazement.

'But this floor was looted almost clean, and the buildings we've entered before were all looted from the street level up,' he said, at length.

'The people who looted this one lived here,' Penrose replied. 'They had electric power to the last; we found refrigerators full of food, and stoves with the dinner still on them. They must have used the elevators to haul things down from the upper floor. The whole first floor was converted into workshops and laboratories. I think that this place must have been something like a monastery in the Dark Ages in Europe, or what such a monastery would have been like if the Dark Ages had followed the fall of a highly developed scientific civilization. For one thing, we found a lot of machine guns and light auto-cannon on the street level, and all the doors were barricaded. The people here were trying to keep a civilization running after the rest of the planet had gone back to barbarism; I suppose they'd have to fight off raids by the barbarians now and then.'

'You're not going to insist on making this building into expedition quarters, I hope colonel?' von Ohlmhorst asked anxiously.

'Oh, no! This place is an archaeological treasure-house. More than that; from what I saw, our technicians can learn a lot, here. But you'd better get this floor cleaned up as soon as you can, though. I'll have the subsurface part, from the sixth floor down, airsealed. Then we'll put in oxygen generators and power units, and get a couple of elevators into service. For the floors above, we can use temporary airsealing floor by floor, and portable equipment; when we have things atmosphered and lighted and heated, you and Martha and Tony Lattimer can go to work systematically and in comfort, and I'll give you all the help I can spare from the other work. This is one of the biggest things we've found yet.'

Tony Lattimer and his companions came down to the seventh floor a little later.

'I don't get this, at all,' he began, as soon as he joined them. 'This building wasn't stripped the way the others were. Always, the procedure seems to have been to strip from the bottom up, but they seem to have stripped the top floors first, here. All but the very top. I found out what that conical thing is, by the way. It's a wind-rotor, and under it there's an electric generator. This building generated its own power.'

'What sort of condition are the generators in?' Penrose aksed.

'Well, everything's full of dust that blew in under the rotor, of course, but it looks to be in pretty good shape. Hey, I'll bet that's it! They had power, so they used the elevators to haul stuff down. That's just what they did. Some of the floors above here don't seem to have been touched, though.' He paused momentarily; back of his oxy-mask, he seemed to be grinning. 'I don't know that I ought to mention this in front of Martha, but two floors above we hit a room – it must have been the reference library for one of the departments – that had close to five hundred books in it.'

The noise that interrupted him, like the squawking of a Brobdingnagian parrot, was only Ivan Fitzgerald laughing through his helmet-speaker.

Lunch at the huts was a hasty meal, with a gabble of full-mouthed and excited talking. Hubert Penrose and his chief subordinates snatched their food in a huddled consultation at one end of the table; in the afternoon, work was suspended on everything else and the fifty-odd men and women of the expedition concentrated their efforts on the university. By the middle of the afternoon, the seventh floor had been completely examined, photographed and sketched, and the murals in the square central hall covered with protective tarpaulins, and Laurent Gicquel and his airsealing crew had moved in and were at work. It had been decided to seal the central hall at the entrances. It took the French-Canadian engineer most of the afternoon to find all the ventilation-ducts and plug them. An elevator-shaft on the north side was found reaching clear to the twenty-fifth floor; this would give access to the top of the building; another shaft, from the centre, would take care of the floors below. Nobody seemed willing to trust the ancient elevators, themselves; it was the next evening before a couple of cars and the necessary machinery could be fabricated in the machine shop aboard the ship and sent down by landing-rocket. By that time, the airsealing was finished, the nuclear-electric energy-converters were in place, and the oxygen generators set up.

Martha was in the lower basement, an hour or so before lunch the day after, when a couple of Space Force officers came out of the elevator, bringing extra lights with them. She was still using oxygen-equipment; it was a moment before she realized that the newcomers had no masks, and that one of them was smoking. She took off her own helmet-speaker, throat-mike and mask and unslung her tank-pack, breathing cautiously. The air was chilly, and musty-acrid with the odour of antiquity – the first Martian odour she had smelled – but when she lit a cigarette, the lighter flamed clear and steady and the tobacco caught and burned evenly.

The archaeologists, many of the other civilian scientists, a few of the Space Force officers and the two newscorrespondents, Sid Chamberlain and Gloria Standish, moved in that evening, setting up cots in vacant rooms. They installed electric stoves and a refrigerator in the old library reading room, and put in a bar and lunch counter. For a few days, the place was full of noise and activity, then, gradually, the Space Force people and all but a few of the civilians returned to their own work. There was still the business of airsealing the more habitable of the buildings already explored, and fitting them up in readiness for the arrival, in a year and a half, of the five hundred members of the main expedition. There was work to be done enlarging the landing field for the ship's rocket craft, and building new chemical-fuel tanks.

There was the work of getting the city's ancient reservoirs cleared of silt before the next spring thaw brought more water down the underground aqueducts everybody called canals in mistranslation of Schiaparelli's Italian word, though this was proving considerably easier than anticipated. The ancient Canal Builders must have anticipated a time when their descendants would no longer be capable of maintenance work, and had prepared against it. By the day after the university had been made completely habitable, the actual work there was being done by Selim, Tony Lattimer and herself, with half a dozen Space Force officers, mostly girls, and four or five civilians, helping.

* * *

148

They worked up from the bottom, dividing the floor-surfaces into numbered squares, measuring and listing and sketching and photographing. They packaged samples of organic matter and sent them up to the ship for carbon-14 dating and analysis; they opened cans and jars and bottles, and found that everything fluid in them had evaporated, through the porosity of glass and metal and plastic if there were no other way. Wherever they looked, they found evidence of activity suddenly suspended and never resumed. A vice with a bar of metal in it, half cut through and the hacksaw beside it. Pots and pans with hardened remains of food in them; a leathery cut of meat on a table, with the knife ready at hand. Toilet articles on washstands; unmade beds, the bedding ready to crumble at a touch but still retaining the impress of the sleeper's body; papers and writing materials on desks, as though the writer had got up, meaning to return and finish in a fifty-thousand-year-ago moment.

It worried her. Irrationally, she began to feel that the Martians had never left this place; that they were still around her, watching disapprovingly every time she picked up something they had laid down. They haunted her dreams, now, instead of their enigmatic writing. At first, everybody who had moved into the university had taken a separate room, happy to escape the crowding and lack of privacy of the huts. After a few nights, she was glad when Gloria Standish moved in with her, and accepted the newswoman's excuse that she felt lonely without somebody to talk to before falling asleep. Sachiko Koremitsu joined them the next evening, and before going to bed, the girl officer cleaned and oiled her pistol, remarking that she was afraid some rust may have got into it.

The others felt it, too. Selim von Ohlmhorst developed the habit of turning quickly and looking behind him, as though trying to surprise somebody or something that was stalking him. Tony Lattimer, having a drink at the bar that had been improvised from the librarian's desk in the reading room, set down his glass and swore.

'You know what this place is? It's an archaeological *Marie Celeste*!' he declared. 'It was occupied right up to the end – we've all seen the shifts these people used

149

to keep a civilization going here – but what was the end? What happened to them? Where did they go?

'You didn't expect them to be waiting out front, with a red carpet and a big banner, *Welcome Terrans,* did you, Tony?' Gloria Standish asked.

'No, of course not; they've all been dead for fifty thousand years. But if they were the last of the Martians, why haven't we found their bones, at least? Who buried them, after they were dead?' He looked at the glass, a bubble-thin goblet, found, with hundreds of others like it, in a closet above, as though debating with himself whether to have another drink. Then he voted in the affirmative and reached for the cocktail pitcher. 'And every door on the old ground level is either barred or barricaded from the inside. How did they get out? And why did they leave?'

The next day, at lunch, Sachiko Koremitsu had the answer to the second question. Four or five electrical engineers had come down by rocket from the ship, and she had been spending the morning with them, in oxy-masks, at the top of the building.

'Tony, I thought you said those generators were in good shape,' she began, catching sight of Lattimer. 'They aren't. They're in the most unholy mess I ever saw. What happened, up there, was that the supports of the wind-rotor gave way, and weight snapped the main shaft, and smashed everything under it.'

'Well, after fifty thousand years, you can expect something like that,' Lattimer retorted. 'When an archaeologist says something's in good shape, he doesn't necessarily mean it'll start as soon as you shove a switch in.'

'You didn't notice that it happened when the power was on, did you,' one of the engineers asked, nettled at Lattimer's tone. 'Well, it was. Everything's burned out or shorted or fused together; I saw one busbar eight inches across melted clean in two. It's a pity we didn't find things in good shape, even archaeologically speaking. I saw a lot of interesting things, things in advance of what we're using now. But it'll take a couple of years to get everything sorted out and figure what it looked like originally.'

'Did it look as though anybody'd made any attempt to fix it?' Martha asked.

Sachiko shook her head. 'They must have taken one

look at it and given up. I don't believe there would have been any possible way to repair anything.'

'Well, that explains why they left. They needed electricity for lighting, and heating, and all their industrial equipment was electrical. They had a good life, here, with power; without it, this place wouldn't have been habitable.'

'Then why did they barricade everything from the inside, and how did they get out?' Lattimer wanted to know.

'To keep other people from breaking in and looting. Last man out probably barred the last door and slid down a rope from upstairs,' von Ohlmhorst suggested. 'This Houdini-trick doesn't worry me too much. We'll find out about it eventually.'

'Yes, about the time Martha starts reading Martian,' Lattimer scoffed.

'That may be just when we'll find out,' von Ohlmhorst replied seriously. 'It wouldn't surprise me if they left something in writing when they evacuated this place.'

'Are you really beginning to treat this pipe dream of hers as a serious possibility, Selim?' Lattimer demanded. 'I know, it would be a wonderful thing, but wonderful things don't happen just because they're wonderful. Only because they're possible, and this isn't. Let me quote that distinguished Hittitologist, Johannes Friedrich: "Nothing can be translated out of nothing." Or that later but no less distinguished Hittitologist, Selim von Ohlmhorst: "Where are you going to get your bilingual?"'

'Friedrich lived to see the Hittite language deciphered and read,' von Ohlmhorst reminded him.

'Yes, when they found Hittite-Assyrian bilinguals.' Lattimer measured a spoonful of coffee-powder into his cup and added hot water. 'Martha, you ought to know, better than anybody, how little chance you have. You've been working for years in the Indus Valley; how many words of Harappa have you or anybody else ever been able to read?'

'We never found a university, with a half-million-volume library, at Harappa or Mohenjo-Daro.'

'And, the first day we entered this building, we established meaning for several words,' Selim von Ohlm-

151

horst added.

'And you've never found another meaningful word since,' Lattimer added. 'And you're only sure of general meaning, not specific meaning of word-elements, and you have a dozen different interpretations for each word.'

'We made a start,' von Ohlmhorst maintained. 'We have Grotefend's word for "king". But I'm going to be able to read some of those books, over there, if it takes me the rest of my life here. It probably will, anyhow.'

'You mean you've changed your mind about going home on the *Cyrano*?' Martha asked. 'You'll stay on here?'

The old man nodded. 'I can't leave this. There's too much to discover. The old dog will have to learn a lot of new tricks, but this is where my work will be, from now on.'

Lattimer was shocked. 'You're nuts!' he cried. 'You mean you're going to throw away everything you've accomplished in Hittitology and start all over again here on Mars? Martha, if you've talked him into his crazy decision, you're a criminal!'

'Nobody talked me into anything,' von Ohlmhorst said roughly. 'And as for throwing away what I've accomplished in Hittitology, I don't know what the devil you're talking about. Everything I know about the Hittite Empire is published and available to anybody. Hittitology's like Egyptology; it's stopped being research and archaeology and become scholarship and history. And I'm not a scholar or a historian; I'm a pick-and-shovel field archaeologist – a highly skilled and specialized grave-robber and junk-picker – and there's more pick-and-shovel work on this planet than I could do in a hundred lifetimes. This is something new; I was a fool to think I could turn my back on it and go back to scribbling footnotes about Hittite kings.'

'You could have anything you wanted, in Hittitology. There are a dozen universities that'd sooner have you than a winning football team. But no! You have to be the top man in Martiology, too. You can't leave that for anybody else—' Lattimer shoved his chair back and got to his feet, leaving the table with an oath that was almost a sob of exasperation.

Maybe his feelings were too much for him. Maybe he realized, as Martha did, what he had betrayed. She sat, avoiding the eyes of the others, looking at the ceiling, as embarrassed as though Lattimer had flung something dirty on the table in front of them. Tony Lattimer had, desperately, wanted Selim to go home on the *Cyrano*. Martiology was a new field; if Selim entered it, he would bring with him the reputation he had already built in Hittitology, automatically stepping into the leading role that Lattimer had coveted for himself. Ivan Fitzgerald's words echoed back to her – when you want to be a big shot, you can't bear the possibility of anybody else being a bigger big shot. His derision of her own efforts became comprehensible, too. It wasn't that he was convinced that she would never learn to read the Martian language. He had been afraid that she would.

Ivan Fitzgerald finally isolated the germ that had caused the Finchley girl's undiagnosed illness. Shortly afterwards, the malady turned into a mild fever, from which she recovered. Nobody else seemed to have caught it. Fitzgerald was still trying to find out how the germ had been transmitted.

They found a globe of Mars, made when the city had been a seaport. They located the city, and learned that its name had been Kukan – or something with a similar vowel-consonant ratio. Immediately, Sid Chamberlain and Gloria Standish began giving their telecasts a Kukan dateline, and Hubert Penrose used the name in his official reports. They also found a Martian calendar; the year had been divided into ten more or less equal months, and one of them had been Doma. Another month was Nor, and that was a part of the name of the scientific journal Martha had found.

Bill Chandler, the zoologist, had been going deeper and deeper into the old sea bottom of Syrtis. Four hundred miles from Kukan, and at fifteen thousand feet lower altitude, he shot a bird. At least, it was a something with wings and what were almost but not quite feathers, though it was more reptilian than avian in general characteristics. He and Ivan Fitzgerald skinned and mounted it, and then dissected the carcass almost tissue by tissue. About seven-eighths of its body capacity was lungs; it certainly breathed air containing at least half enough oxygen to support human life, or five times as much as the air around Kukan.

That took the centre of interest away from archaeology, and started a new burst of activity. All the expedition's aircraft – four jetticopters and three wingless
airdyne reconnaisance fighters – were thrown into in-
tensified exploration of the lower sea bottoms, and the
bio-science boys and girls were wild with excitement and
making new discoveries on each flight.

The university was left to Selim and Martha and
Tony Lattimer, the latter keeping to himself while she
and the old Turco-German worked together. The
civilian specialists in other fields, and the Space Force
people who had been holding tape lines and making
sketches and snapping cameras, were all flying to lower
Syrtis to find out how much oxygen there was and what
kind of life it supported.

Sometimes Sachiko dropped in; most of the time she
was busy helping Ivan Fitzgerald dissect specimens. They
had four or five species of what might loosely be called
birds, and a carnivorous mammal the size of a cat with
birdlike claws, and a herbivore almost identical with
the piglike thing in the big *Darfhulva* mural, and
another like a gazelle with a single horn in the middle
of its forehead.

The high point came when one party, at thirty thousand feet below the level of Kukan, found breathable
air. One of them had a mild attack of *sorroche* and had
to be flown back for treatment in a hurry, but the others
showed no ill effects.

The daily newscasts from Terra showed a correspond-
ing shift in interest at home. The discovery of the university had focused attention on the dead past of Mars;
now the public was interested in Mars as a possible
home for humanity. It was Tony Lattimer who brought
archaeology back into the activities of the expedition
and the news at home.

Martha and Selim were working in the museum on
the second floor, scrubbing the grime from the glass
cases, noting contents, and grease-pencilling numbers;
Lattimer and a couple of Space Force officers were going
through what had been the administrative offices on the
other side. It was one of these, a young second lieutenant,
who came hurrying in from the mezzanine, almost burst-
ing with excitement.

'Hey, Martha! Dr. von Ohlmhorst!' he was shouting. 'Where are you? Tony's found the Martians!'

Selim dropped his rag back in the bucket; she laid her clipboard on top of the case beside her.

'Where?' they asked together.

'Over on the north side.' The lieutenant took hold of himself and spoke more deliberately. 'Little room, back of one of the old faculty offices – conference room. It was locked from the inside, and we had to burn it down with a torch. That's where they are. Eighteen of them, around a long table—'

Gloria Standish, who had dropped in for lunch, was on the mezzanine, fairly screaming into a radio-phone extension:

'. . . Dozen and a half of them! Well, of course, they're dead. What a question! They look like skeletons covered with leather. No, I do not know what they died of. Well, forget it; I don't care if Bill Chandler's found a three-headed hippopotamus. Sid, don't you get it? We've found the *Martians*!'

She slammed the phone back on its hook, rushing away ahead of them.

Martha remembered the closed door; on the first survey, they hadn't attempted opening it. Now it was burned away at both sides and lay, still hot along the edges, on the floor of the big office room in front. A floodlight was on in the room inside, and Lattimer was going around looking at things while a Space Force officer stood by the door. The centre of the room was filled by a long table; in armchairs around it sat the eighteen men and women who had occupied the room for the last fifty millennia. There were bottles and glasses on the table in front of them, and, had she seen them in a dimmer light, she would have thought that they were merely dozing over their drinks. One had a knee hooked over his chair-arm and was curled in foetus-like sleep. Another had fallen forward on to the table, arms extended, the emerald set of a ring twinkling dully on one finger. Skeletons covered with leather, Gloria Standish had called them, and so they were – faces like skulls, arms and legs like sticks, the flesh shrunken on to the bones under it.

'Isn't this something!' Lattimer was exulting. 'Mass suicide, that's what it was. Notice what's in the corners?'

Braziers, made of perforated two-gallon-odd metal cans the white walls smudged with smoke above them. Von Ohlmhorst had noticed them at once, and was poking into one of them with his flashlight.

'Yes; charcoal. I noticed a quantity of it around a couple of hand-forges in the shop on the first floor. That's why you had so much trouble breaking in; they'd sealed the room on the inside.' He straightened and went around the room, until he found a ventilator, and peered into it. 'Stuffed with rags. They must have been all that were left, here. Their power was gone, and they were old and tired, and all around them their world was dying. So they just came in here and lit the charcoal, and sat drinking together till they all fell asleep. Well, we know what became of them, now, anyhow.'

Sid and Gloria made the most of it. The Terran public wanted to hear about Martians, and if live Martians couldn't be found, a room full of dead ones was the next best thing. Maybe an even better thing; it had been only sixty-odd years since the Orson Welles invasion-scare. Tony Lattimer, the discoverer, was beginning to cash in on his attentions to Gloria and his ingratiation with Sid; he was always either making voice-and-image talks for telecast or listening to the news from the home planet. Without question, he had become, overnight, the most widely known archaeologist in history.

'Not that I'm interested in all this, for myself,' he disclaimed, after listening to the telecast from Terra two days after his discovery. 'But this is going to be a big thing for Martian archaeology. Bring it to the public attention; dramatize it. Selim, can you remember when Lord Carnarvon and Howard Carter found the tomb of Tutankhamen?'

'In 1923? I was two years old, then,' von Ohlmhorst chuckled. 'I really don't know how much that publicity ever did for Egyptology. Oh, the museums did devote more space to Egyptian exhibits, and after a museum department head gets a few extra showcases, you know how hard it is to make him give them up. And, for a while, it was easier to get financial support for new

156

excavations. But I don't know how much good all this public excitement really does, in the long run.'

'Well, I think one of us should go back on the *Cyrano*, when the *Schiaparelli* orbits in,' Lattimer said. 'I'd hoped it would be you; your voice would carry the most weight. But I think it's important that one of us go back, to present the story of our work, and what we have accomplished and what we hope to accomplish, to the public and to the universities and the learned societies, and to the Federation Government. There will be a great deal of work that will have to be done. We must not allow the other scientific fields and the so-called practical interests to monopolize public and academic support. So, I believe I shall go back at least for a while, and see what I can do—'

Lectures. The organization of a Society of Martian Archaeology, with Anthony Lattimer, Ph.D., the logical candidate for the chair. Degrees, honours; the deference of the learned, and the adulation of the lay public. Positions, with impressive titles and salaries. Sweet are the uses of publicity.

She crushed out her cigarette and got to her feet. 'Well, I still have the final lists of what we found in *Halvhulva* – Biology – Department to check over. I'm starting on Sornhulva tomorrow, and I want that stuff in shape for expert evaluation.'

That was the sort of thing Tony Lattimer wanted to get away from, the detail-work and the drudgery. Let the infantry do the slogging through the mud; the brass-hats got the medals.

She was halfway through the fifth floor, a week later, and was having midday lunch in the reading room on the first floor when Hubert Penrose came over and sat down beside her, asking her what she was doing. She told him.

'I wonder if you could find me a couple of men, for an hour or so,' she added. 'I'm stopped by a couple of jammed doors at the central hall. Lecture room and library, if the layout of that floor's anything like the ones below it.'

'Yes. I'm a pretty fair door-buster, myself.' He looked around the room. 'There's Jeff Miles; he isn't doing much of anything. And we'll put Sid Chamberlain to work, for a change, too. The four of us ought to get your doors open.' He called to Chamberlain, who was carrying his tray over to the dishwasher. 'Oh, Sid; you doing anything for the next hour or so?'

'I was going up to the fourth floor, to see what Tony's doing.'

'Forget it. Tony's bagged his season limit of Martians. I'm going to help Martha bust in a couple of doors; we'll probably find a whole cemetery full of Martians.'

Chamberlain shrugged. 'Why not. A jammed door can have anything back of it, and I know what Tony's doing – just routine stuff.'

Jeff Miles, the Space Force captain, came over, accompanied by one of the lab-crew from the ship who had come down on the rocket the day before.

'This ought to be up your alley, Mort,' he was saying to his companion. 'Chemistry and Physics Department. Want to come along?'

The lab man, Mort Tranter, was willing. Seeing the sights was what he'd come down from the ship for. She finished her coffee and cigarette, and they went out into the hall together, gathered equipment and rode the elevator to the fifth floor.

The lecture hall door was the nearest; they attacked it first. With proper equipment and help, it was no problem and in ten minutes they had it open wide enough to squeeze through with the floodlights. The room inside was quite empty, and, like most of the rooms behind closed doors, comparatively free from dust. The students, it appeared, had sat with their backs to the door, facing a low platform, but their seats and the lecturer's table and equipment had been removed. The two side walls bore inscriptions: on the right, a pattern of concentric circles which she recognized as a diagram of atomic structure, and on the left a complicated table of numbers and words, in two columns. Tranter was pointing at the diagram on the right.

'They got as far as the Bohr atom, anyhow,' he said. 'Well, not quite. They knew about electron shells, but they have the nucleus pictured as a solid mass. No indication of proton-and-neutron structure. I'll bet, when you come to translate their scientific books, you'll find that they taught that the atom was the ultimate and indivisible particle. That explains why you people

158

never found any evidence that the Martians used nuclear energy.'

'That's a uranium atom,' Captain Miles mentioned.

'It is?' Sid Chamberlain asked, excitedly. 'Then they did know about atomic energy. Just because we haven't found any pictures of A-bomb mushrooms doesn't mean—'

She turned to look at the other wall. Sid's signal reactions were getting away from him again; uranium meant nuclear power to him, and the two words were interchangeable. As she studied the arrangement of the numbers and words, she could hear Tranter saying:

'Nuts, Sid. We knew about uranium a long time before anybody found out what could be done with it. Uranium was discovered on Terra in 1789, by Klaproth.'

There was something familiar about the table on the left wall. She tried to remember what she had been taught in school about physics, and what she had picked up by accident afterwards. The second column was a continuation of the first: there were forty-six items in each, each item numbered consecutively—

'Probably used uranium because it's the largest of the natural atoms,' Penrose was saying. 'The fact that there's nothing beyond it there shows that they hadn't created any of the transuranics. A student could go to that thing and point out the outer electron of any of the ninety-two elements.'

Ninety-two! That was it: there were ninety-two items in the table on the left wall! Hydrogen was Two; that was *Tirfaldsorn*. She couldn't remember which element came next, but in Martian it was *Sarfalddavas. Sorn* must mean matter, or substance, then. And *davas;* she was trying to think of what it could be. She turned quickly to the others, catching hold of Hubert Penrose's arm with one hand and waving her clipboard with the other.

'Look at this thing, over here,' she was clamouring excitedly. 'Tell me what you think it is. Could it be a table of the elements?'

They all turned to look Mort Tranter stared at it for a moment.

'Could be. If I only knew what those squiggles meant—'

That was right; he'd spent his time aboard the ship.

'If you could read the numbers, would that help?' she asked, beginning to set down the Arabic digits and their Martian equivalents. 'It's decimal system, the same as we use.'

'Sure. If that's a table of elements, all I'd need would be the numbers. Thanks,' he added as she tore off the sheet and gave it to him.

Penrose knew the numbers, and was ahead of him. 'Ninety-two items, numbered consecutively. The first number would be the atomic number. Then a single word, the name of the element. Then the atomic weight—'

She began reading off the names of the elements. 'I know hydrogen and helium; what's *tirfalddavas*, the third one?'

'Lithium,' Tranter said. 'The atomic weights aren't run out past the decimal point. Hydrogen's one plus, if that double-hook dingus is a plus sign; Helium's four-plus, that's right. And lithium's given as seven, that isn't right. It's six-point-nine-four-oh. Or is that thing a Martian minus sign?'

'Of course! Look! A plus sign is a hook, to hang things together; a minus sign is a knife, to cut something off from something – see, the little loop is the handle and the long pointed loop is the blade. Stylized, of course, but that's what it is. And the fourth element, *Kiradavas*; what's that?'

'Beryllium. Atomic weight given as nine-and-a-hook; actually it's nine-point-oh-two.'

Sid Chamberlain had been disgruntled because he couldn't get a story about the Martians having developed atomic energy. It took him a few minutes to understand the newest development, but finally it dawned on him.

'Hey! You're reading that!' he cried. 'You're reading Martian!'

'That's right,' Penrose told him. 'Just reading it right off. I don't get the two items after the atomic weight, though. They look like months of the Martian calendar. What ought they to be, Mort?'

Tranter hesitated. 'Well, the next information after

160

the atomic weight ought to be the period and group numbers. But those are words.'

'What would the numbers be for the first one, hydrogen?'

'Period One, Group One. One electron shell, one electron in the outer shell,' Tranter told her. 'Helium's period one, too, but it has the outer – only – electron shell full, so it's in the group of inert elements.'

'*Trav, Trav. Trav's* the first month of the year. And helium's *Trav, Yenth; Yenth* is the eight month.'

'The inert elements could be called Group Eight, yes. And the third element, lithium, is Period Two, Group One. That check?'

'It certainly does. *Sanv, Trav; Sanv's* the second month. What's the first element in Period Three?'

'Sodium, Number Eleven.'

'That's right; it's *Krav, Trav.* Why, the names of the months are simply numbers, one to ten, spelled out.'

'*Doma's* the fifth month. That was your first Martian word, Martha,' Penrose told her. 'The word for five. And if *davas* is the word for metal, and *sornhulva* is chemistry and/or physics, I'll bet *Tadavas Sornhulva* is literally translated as: 'Of-Metal Matter-Knowledge.' Metallurgy, in other words. I wonder what *Mastharnorvod* means.' It surprised her that, after so long and with so much happening in the meantime, he could remember that. 'Something like "Journal", or "Review", or maybe "Quarterly".'

'We'll work that out, too,' she said confidently. After this, nothing seemed impossible. 'Maybe we can find—' Then she stopped short. 'You said "Quarterly", I think it was "Monthly", instead. It was dated for a specific month, the fifth one. And if *nor* is ten, *Mastharnorvod* could be "Year-Tenth". And I'll bet we'll find that *masthar* is the word for year.' She looked at the table on the wall again. 'Well, let's get all these words down, with translations for as many as we can.'

'Let's take a break for a minute,' Penrose suggested, getting out his cigarettes. 'And then, let's do this in comfort. Jeff, suppose you and Sid go across the hall and see what you find in the other room in the way of a desk or something like that, and a few chairs. There'll be a lot of work to do on this.'

Sid Chamberlain had been squirming as though he

were afflicted with ants, trying to contain himself. Now he let go with an excited jabber.

'This is really it! *The* it, not just it-of-the-week, like finding the reservoirs or those statues or this building, or even the animals and the dead Martians! Wait till Selim and Tony see this! Wait till Tony sees it; I want to see his face! And when I get this on telecast, all Terra's going to go nuts about it!' He turned to Captain Miles. 'Jeff, suppose you take a look at that other door, while I find somebody to send to tell Selim and Tony. And Gloria; wait till she sees this—'

'Take it easy, Sid,' Martha cautioned. 'You'd better let me have a look at your script, before you go too far overboard on the telecast. This is just a beginning; it'll take years and years before we're able to read any of those books downstairs.'

'It'll go faster than you think, Martha,' Hubert Penrose told her. 'We'll all work on it, and we'll teleprint material to Terra, and people there will work on it. We'll send them everything we can . . . everything we work out, and copies of books, and copies of your word-lists—'

And there would be other tables – astronomical tables, tables in physics and mechanics, for instance – in which words and numbers were equivalent. The library stacks, below, would be full of them. Transliterate them into Roman alphabet spellings and Arabic numerals, and somewhere, somebody would spot each numerical significance, as Hubert Penrose and Mort Tranter and she had done with the table of elements. And pick out all the chemistry textbooks in the library; new words would take on meaning from contexts in which the names of elements appeared. She'd have to start studying chemistry and physics, herself—

Sachiko Koremitsu peeped in through the door, then stepped inside.

'Is there anything I can do—?' she began. 'What's happened? Something important?'

'Important?' Sid Chamberlain exploded. 'Look at that, Sachi! We're reading it! Martha's found out how to read Martian!' He grabbed Captain Miles by the arm. 'Come on, Jeff; let's go. I want to call on the

162

others—' He was still babbling as he hurried from the room.

Sachi looked at the inscription. 'It it true?' she asked, and then, before Martha could more than begin to explain, flung her arms around her. 'Oh, it really is! You are reading it! I'm so happy!'

She had to start explaining again when Selim von Ohlmhorst entered. This time, she was able to finish.

'But, Martha, can you be really sure? You know, by now, that learning to read this language is as important to me as it is to you, but how can you be so sure that those words really mean things like hydrogen and helium and boron and oxygen? How do you know that their table of elements was anything like ours?'

Tranter and Penrose and Sachiko all looked at him in amazement.

'That isn't just the Martian table of elements; that's *the* table of elements. It's the only one there is,' Mort Tranter almost exploded. 'Look, hydrogen has one proton and one electron. If it had more or either, it wouldn't be hydrogen, it'd be something else. And the same with all the rest of the elements. And hydrogen on Mars is the same as hydrogen on Terra, or on Alpha Centauri, or in the next galaxy—'

'You just set up those numbers, in that order, and any first-year chemistry student could tell you what elements they represented,' Penrose said. 'Could if he expected to make a passing grade, that is.'

The old man shook his head, slowly, smiling. 'I'm afraid I wouldn't make a passing grade. I didn't know, or at least didn't realize, that. One of the things I'm going to place an order for, to be brought on the *Schiaparelli*, will be a set of primers in chemistry and physics, of the sort intended for a bright child of ten or twelve. It seems that a Martiologist has to learn a lot of things the Hittites and the Assyrians never heard about.'

Tony Lattimer, coming in, caught the last part of the explanation. He looked quickly at the walls and, having found out just what had happened, advanced and caught Martha by the hand.

'You really did it, Martha! You found your bilingual! I never believed that it would be possible; let me congratulate you!'

163

He probably expected that to erase all the jibes and sneers of the past. If he did, he could have it that way. His friendship would mean as little to her as his derision – except that his friends had to watch their backs and his knife. But he was going home on the *Cyrano*, to be a big shot. Or had this changed his mind for him again?

'This is something we can show the world, to justify any expenditure of time and money on Martian archaeological work. When I get back to Terra, I'll see that you're given full credit for this achievement—'

On Terra, her back and his knife would be out of her watchfulness.

'We won't need to wait that long,' Hubert Penrose told him dryly. 'I'm sending off an official report, tomorrow; you can be sure Dr. Dane will be given full credit, not only for this but for her previous work, which made it possible to exploit this discovery.'

'And you might add, work done in spite of the doubts and discouragements of her colleagues,' Selim von Ohlmhorst said. 'To which I am ashamed to have to confess my own share.'

'You said we had to find a bilingual,' she said. 'You were right, too.'

'This is better than a bilingual, Martha,' Hubert Penrose said. 'Physical science expresses universal facts; necessarily it is a universal language. Heretofore archaeologists have dealt only with pre-scientific cultures.'

OMNILINGUAL

In the 1870s, thin, long markings were observed on Mars which, from their straightness, seemed sure to be artificial. They were called 'canals' and many people (including professional astronomers) felt they were the artifacts of a high civilization trying to survive the gradual desiccation of the small planet.

Science fiction writers seized upon this and for half a century there were innumerable stories of civilizations on Mars, usually slowly dying, sometimes malevolent.

Twentieth-century studies of Mars made this all seem increasingly unlikely. Few astronomers could actually make out the canals and the opinion grew more common that they were optical illusions; that the eye made straight lines out of barely visable irregular markings. The atmosphere seemed very thin indeed and it was difficult to detect water or free oxygen.

Even so, as late as 1957, when *Omnilingual* was published there was still some faint reason to hope for life on Mars.

Since then, however, unmanned probes have skimmed past Mars and taken photographs and made measurements. The atmosphere is thinner than the most pessimistic earlier estimates had made it appear and there are no canals. There are numerous craters and the state of weathering would seem to indicate that the atmosphere has been this thin for many millions of years. What's more, there is no free oxygen and the atmosphere, what there is of it, seems to be entirely or almost entirely carbon dioxide.

Then, too, the temperature seems lower than had been thought and the polar ice caps on Mars, which had been thought to be frozen water, now seem more likely to be frozen carbon dioxide.

It seems quite unlikely, therefore, that there is, or ever was, intelligent life on Mars; and it is even increasingly doubtful that there is life of any sort.

Piper's speculations would seem to be quite wrong, therefore. He not only assumed intelligent life almost at the level of our own but had it existing as late as 50,000 years ago. What's more, he had the Martian atmosphere dense enough to support a flying creature, and had it contain enough oxygen to support it chemically as well as mechanically. (He did, however, make its internal organs mostly lung.)

But then, one unlikely, or even impossible assumption, is allowed to start a science fiction story, and Piper's purpose was to tackle the problem of an unknown language – as unknown as possible – and its decipherment. That intention he fulfilled admirably.

Questions and Suggestions

1. The decipherment of numerous unknown languages are mentioned in the story. Look up the story of the decipherment of Egyptian hieroglyphics and Babylonian

cuneiform and decide what made the decipherment possible.

2. Why are the two ships in the story named *Schiaparelli* and *Cyrano*?

3. What is the meaning of *Omnilingual*? Is it reasonable to use that adjective to describe the periodic table of the elements? If so, why? Could any ancient languages have been deciphered through omnilingual inscriptions? Can omnilingual situations arise in a non-technological civilization?

4. Do you think a civilization can develop and reach a high state of technology, yet do so without duplicating any of our theories, and without ever working out the periodic table of the elements, for instance? Or, having worked it out, might an alien civilization represent the table in such a way as to have it unrecognizable? In other words, is intelligence intelligence, or are there different kinds that can be mutually incomprehensible?

5. What is the periodic table of the elements, by the way?

8. THE BIG BOUNCE

Walter S. Tevis

'Let me show you something,' Fansworth said. He set his near-empty drink – a Bacardi Martini – on the mantel and waddled out of the room towards the basement.

I sat in my big leather chair, feeling very peaceful with the world, watching the fire. Whatever Farnsworth would have to show tonight would be far more entertaining than watching TV – my custom on other evenings. Farnsworth, with his four labs in the house and his very tricky mind, never failed to provide my best night of the week.

When he returned, after a moment, he had with him a small box, about three inches square. He held this carefully in one hand and stood by the fireplace dramatically – or as dramatically as a very small, very fat man with pink cheeks can stand by a fireplace of the sort that seems to demand a big man with tweeds, pipe and, perhaps, a sabre wound.

Anyway, he held the box dramatically and he said, 'Last week, I was playing around in the chem lab, trying to make a new kind of rubber eraser. Did quite well with the other drafting equipment, you know, especially the dimensional curve and the photosensitive ink. Well, I approached the job trying for a material that would absorb graphite without abrading paper.'

I was a little disappointed with this; it sounded pretty tame. But I said, 'How did it come out?'

He screwed his pudgy face up thoughtfully. 'Synthesized the material, all right, and it seems to work, but the interesting thing is that it has a certain – ah – secondary property that would make it quite awkward to use. Interesting property, though. Unique, I am inclined to believe.'

This began to sound more like it. 'And what property is that?' I poured myself a shot of straight rum from the bottle sitting on the table beside me. I did not like straight rum, but I preferred it to Farnsworth's rather imaginative cocktails.

'I'll show you, John,' he said. He opened the box and I could see that it was packed with some kind of batting. He fished in this and withdrew a grey ball about the size of a golfball and set the box on the mantel.

'And that's the – eraser?' I asked.

'Yes, he said. Then he squatted down, held the ball about a half inch from the floor, dropped it.

It bounced, naturally enough. Then it bounced again. And again. Only this was not natural, for on the second bounce the ball went higher in the air than on the first, and on the third bounce higher still. After a half minute, my eyes were bugging out and the little ball was bouncing four feet in the air and going higher each time.

I grabbed my glass. 'What the hell!' I said.

Farnsworth caught the ball in a pudgy hand and held it. He was smiling a little sheepishly. 'Interesting effect, isn't it?'

'Now wait a minute,' I said, beginning to think about it. 'What's the gimmick? What kind of motor do you have in that thing?'

His eyes were wide and a little hurt. 'No gimmick, John. None at all. Just a very peculiar molecular structure.'

'Structure!' I said. 'Bouncing balls just don't pick up energy out of nowhere, I don't care how their molecules are put together. And you don't get energy out without putting energy in.'

'Oh,' he said, 'that's the really interesting thing. Of course you're right; energy *does* go into the ball. Here, I'll show you.'

He let the ball drop again and it began bouncing, higher and higher, until it was hitting the ceiling. Farnsworth reached out to catch it, but he fumbled and the thing glanced off his hand, hit the mantelpiece and zipped across the room. It banged into the far wall, ricocheted, banked off three other walls, picking up speed all the time.

When it whizzed by me like a rifle bullet. I began to get worried, but it hit against one of the heavy draperies by the window and this damped its motion enough so that it fell to the floor.

It started bouncing again immediately, but Farnsworth scrambled across the room and grabbed it. He was perspiring a little and he began instantly to transfer the ball from one hand to another and back again as if it were hot.

'Here,' he said, and handed it to me.

I almost dropped it.

'It's like a ball of ice!' I said. 'Have you been keeping it in the refrigerator?'

'No. As a matter of fact, it was at room temperature a few minutes ago.'

'Now wait a minute,' I said. 'I only teach physics in high school, but I know better than that. Moving around in warm air doesn't make anything cold except by evaporation.'

'Well, there's your input and output, John,' he said. 'The ball lost heat and took on motion. Simple conversion.'

My jaw must have dropped to my waist. 'Do you mean that that little thing is converting heat to kinetic energy?'

'Apparently.'

'But that's impossible!'

He was beginning to smile thoughtfully. The ball

was not as cold now as it had been and I was holding it in my lap.

'A steam engine does it,' he said, 'and a steam turbine. Of course, they're not very efficient.'

'They work mechanically, too, and only because water expands when it turns to steam.'

'This seems to do it differently,' he said, sipping thoughtfully at his dark-brown Martini. 'I don't know exactly how – maybe something piezo-electric about the way its molecules slide about. I ran some tests – measured its impact energy in foot pounds and compared that with the heat loss in BTUs. Seemed to be about 98 per cent efficient, as close as I could tell. Apparently it converts heat into bounce very well. Interesting, isn't it?'

'*Interesting*?' I almost came flying out of my chair. My mind was beginning to spin like crazy. 'If you're not pulling my leg with this thing. Farnsworth, you've got something by the tail there that's just a little bigger than the discovery of fire.'

He blushed modestly. 'I'd rather thought that myself,' he admitted.

'Good Lord, look at the heat that's available!' I said, getting really excited now.

Farnsworth was still smiling, very pleased with himself. 'I suppose you could put this thing in a box, with convection fins, and let it bounce around inside—'

'I'm away ahead of you,' I said. 'But that wouldn't work. All your kinetic energy would go right back to heat, on impact – and eventually that little ball would build up enough speed to blast its way through any box you could build.'

'Then how would you work it?'

'Well,' I said, choking down the rest of my rum, 'you'd seal the ball in a big steel cylinder, attach the cylinder to a crankshaft and flywheel, give the thing a shake to start the ball bouncing back and forth, and let it run like a gasoline engine or something. It would get all the heat it needed from the air in a normal room. Mount the apparatus in your house and it would pump your water, operate a generator and keep you cool at the same time!'

I sat down again, shakily, and began pouring myself another drink.

Farnsworth had taken the ball from me and was carefully putting it back in its padded box. He was visibly showing excitement, too; I could see that his cheeks were ruddier and his eyes even brighter than normal. 'But what if you want the cooling and don't have any work to be done?'

'Simple,' I said. 'You just let the machine turn a flywheel or lift weights and drop them, or something like that, outside your house. You have an air intake inside. And if in the winter, you don't want to lose heat, you just mount the thing in an outside building, attach it to your generator and use the power to do whatever you want – heat your house, say. There's plenty of heat in the outside air even in December.'

'John,' said Farnsworth, 'you are very ingenious. It might work.'

'Of course it'll work.' Pictures were beginning to light up in my head. 'And don't you realize that this is the answer to the solar power problem? Why, mirrors and selenium are, at best, ten per cent efficient! Think of big pumping stations on the Sahara! All that heat, all that need for power, for irrigation!' I paused a moment for effect. 'Farnsworth, this can change the very shape of the Earth!'

Farnsworth seemed to be lost in thought. Finally he looked at me strangely and said, 'Perhaps we had better try to build a model.'

I was so excited by the thing that I couldn't sleep that night. I kept dreaming of power stations, ocean liners, even automobiles, being operated by balls bouncing back and forth in cylinders.

I even worked out a spaceship in my mind, a bullet-shaped affair with a huge rubber ball on its end, gyrocopes to keep it oriented properly, the ball serving as solution to that biggest of missile-engineering problems, excess heat. You'd built a huge concrete launching field, supported all the way down to bedrock, hop in the ship and start bouncing. Of course it would be kind of a rough ride . . .

In the morning, I called my superintendent and told him to get a substitute for the rest of the week; I was going to be busy.

Then I started working in the machine shop in Farnsworth's basement, trying to turn out a working model of a device that, by means of a crankshaft, oleo dampers and a reciprocating cylinder, would pick up some of that random kinetic energy from the bouncing ball and do something useful with it, like turning a drive shaft. I was just working out a convection-and-air-pump system for circulating hot air around the ball when Farnsworth came in.

He had tucked carefully under his arm a sphere of about the size of a basketball and, if he had made it to my specifications, weighing thirty-five pounds. He had a worried frown on his forehead.

'It looks good,' I said. 'What's the trouble?'

'There seems to be a slight hitch,' he said. 'I've been testing for conductivity. It seems to be quite low.'

'That's what I'm working on now. It's just a mechanical problem of pumping enough warm air back into the ball. We can do it with no more than a twenty per cent efficiency loss. In an engine, that's nothing.'

'Maybe you're right. But this material conducts heat even less than rubber does.'

'The little ball yesterday didn't seem to have any trouble,' I said.

'Naturally not. It had had plenty of time to warm up before I started it. And its mass-surface area relationship was pretty low – the larger you make a sphere, of course, the more mass inside in proportion to the outside area.'

'You're right, but I think we can whip it. We may have to honeycomb the ball and have part of the work the machine does operate a big hot air pump; but we can work it out.'

All that day, I worked with lathe, milling machine and hacksaw. After clamping the new big ball securely to a workbench, Farnsworth pitched in to help me. But we weren't able to finish by nightfall and Farnsworth turned his spare bedroom over to me for the night. I was too tired to go home.

And too tired to sleep soundly, too. Farnsworth lived on the edge of San Francisco, by a big truck by-pass, and almost all night I wrestled with the pillow and sheets, listening half-consciously to those heavy trucks rumbling by, and in my mind, always, that little grey ball, bouncing and bouncing and bouncing . . .

At daybreak, I came abruptly fully awake with the sound of crashing echoing in my ears, a battering sound that seemed to come from the basement. I grabbed my coat and pants, rushed out of the room, almost knocked over Farnsworth, who was struggling to get his shoes on out in the hall, and we scrambled down the two flights of stairs together.

The place was a chaos, battered and bashed equipment everywhere, and on the floor, overturned against the far wall, the table that the ball had been clamped to. The ball itself was gone.

I had not been fully asleep all night, and the sight of that mess, and what it meant, jolted me immediately awake. Something, probably a heavy truck, had started a tiny oscillation in that ball. And the ball had been heavy enough to start the table bouncing with it until, by dancing that table around the room, it had literally torn the clamp off and shaken itself free. What had happened afterwards was obvious, with the ball building up velocity with every successive bounce.

But where was the ball now?

Suddenly Farnsworth cried out hoarsely, 'Look!' and I followed his outstretched, pudgy finger to where, at one side of the basement, a window had been broken open – a small window, but plenty big enough for something the size of a basketball to crash through it.

There was a little weak light coming from outdoors. And then I saw the ball. It was in Farnsworth's back yard, bouncing a little sluggishly on the grass. The grass would damp it, hold it back, until we could get to it. Unless . . .

I took off up the basement step like a streak. Just beyond the back yard, I had caught a glimpse of something that frightened me. A few yards from where I had seen the ball was the edge of the big six-lane highway, a broad ribbon of smooth, hard concrete.

I got through the house to the back porch, rushed out and was in the back yard just in time to see the ball take its first bounce on to the concrete. I watched it, fascinated, when it hit – after the soft, energy absorbing turf, the concrete was like a springboard. Immediately the ball flew high in the air. I was running across the yard towards it, praying under my breath, *Fall on that grass next time.*

172

It hit before I got to it, and right on the concrete again, and this time I saw it go straight up at least fifty feet.

My mind was suddenly full of thoughts of dragging mattresses from the house, or making a net or something to stop that hurtling thirty-five pounds; but I stood where I was, unable to move, and saw it come down again on the highway. It went up a hundred feet. And down again on the concrete, about fifteen feet further down the road. In the direction of the city.

That time it was two hundred feet, and when it hit again, it made a thud that you could have heard for a quarter of a mile. I could practically see it flatten out on the road before it took off upwards again, at twice the speed it had hit at.

Suddenly, generating an idea, I whirled and ran back to Farnsworth's house. He was standing in the yard now, shivering from the morning air, looking at me like a little lost and badly scared child.

'Where are your car keys?' I almost shouted at him.

'In my pocket.'

'Come on!'

I took him by the arms and half dragged him to the carport. I got the keys from him, started the car, and by mangling about seven traffic laws and three prize rose-bushes, managed to get on the highway, facing in the direction that the ball was heading.

'Look,' I said, trying to drive down the road and search for the ball at the same time. 'It's risky, but if I can get the car under it and we can hop out in time, it should crash through the roof. That ought to slow it down enough for us to nab it.'

'But – what about my car?' Farnsworth bleated.

'What about that first building – or first person – it hits in San Francisco?'

'Oh,' he said. 'Hadn't thought of that.'

I slowed the car and stuck my head out the window. It was lighter now, but no sign of the ball. 'If it happens to get to town – any town, for that matter – it'll be falling from about ten or twenty miles. Or forty.'

'Maybe it'll go high enough first so that it'll burn. Like a meteor.'

'No chance,' I said. 'Built-in cooling system, remember?'

Farnsworth formed his mouth into an 'Oh' and exactly at that moment there was a resounding thump and I saw the ball hit in a field, maybe twenty yards from the edge of the road, and take off again. This time it didn't seem to double its velocity, and I figured the ground was soft enough to hold it back – but it wasn't slowing down either, not with a bounce factor of better than two to one.

Without watching for it to go up, I drove as quickly as I could off the road and over – carrying part of a wire fence with me – to where it had hit. There was no mistaking it; there was a depression about three feet deep, like a small crater.

I jumped out of the car and stared up. It took me a few seconds to spot it, over my head. One side caught by the pale and slanting morning sunlight, it was only a bright diminishing speck.

The car motor was running and I waited until the ball disappeared for a moment and then reappeared. I watched for another couple of seconds until I felt I could make a decent guess on its direction, hollered at Farnsworth to get out of the car – it had just occurred to me that there was no use risking his life, too– dived in and drove a hundred yards or so to the spot I had anticipated.

I stuck my head out the window and up. The ball was the size of an egg now. I adjusted the car's position, jumped out and ran for my life.

It hit instantly after – about sixty feet from the car. And at the same time, it occurred to me that what I was trying to do was completely impossible. Better to hope that the ball hit a pond, or bounced out to sea, or landed in a sand dune. All we could do would be to follow, and if it ever was damped down enough, grab it.

It had hit soft ground and didn't double its height that time, but it had still gone higher. It was out of sight for almost a lifelong minute.

And then – incredibly rotten luck – it came down, with an ear-shattering thwack, on the concrete highway again. I had seen it hit, and instantly afterwards I saw a crack as wide as a finger open along the entire width of the road. And the ball had flown back up like a rocket.

My God, I was thinking, *now it means business. And on the next bounce* ...

It seemed like an incredibly long time that we craned our necks, Farnsworth and I, watching for it to reappear in the sky. And when it finally did, we could hardly follow it. It whistled like a bomb and we saw the grey streak come plummeting to earth almost a quarter of a mile away from where we were standing.

But we didn't see it go back up again.

For a moment, we stared at each other silently. Then Farnsworth almost whispered, 'Perhaps it's landed in a pond.'

'Or in the world's biggest cowpile,' I said. 'Come on!'

We could have met our deaths by rock salt and buck-shot that day, if the farmer who owned that field had been home. We tore up everything we came to getting across it – including cabbages and rhubarb. But we had to search for ten minutes, and even then we didn't find the ball.

What we found was a hole in the ground that could have been a small-scale meteor crater. It was a good twenty feet deep. But at the bottom, no ball.

I stared wildly at it for a full minute before I focused my eyes enough to see, at the bottom, a thousand little grey fragments.

And immediately it came to both of us at the same time. A poor conductor, the ball had used up all its available heat on that final impact. Like a golfball that has been dipped in liquid air and dropped, it had smashed into thin splinters.

The hole had sloping sides and I scrambled down in it and picked up one of the pieces, using my handker-chief, folded – there was no telling just how cold it would be.

It was the stuff, all right. And colder than an icicle.

I climbed out. 'Let's go home,' I said.

Farnsworth looked at me thoughtfully. Then he sort of cocked his head to one side and asked, 'What do you suppose will happen when those pieces thaw?'

I stared at him. I began to think of a thousand tiny slivers whizzing around erratically, ricocheting off buildings, in downtown San Francisco and in twenty counties, and no matter what they hit, moving and accelerating as long as there was any heat in the air to give them energy.

And then I saw a tool shed, on the other side of the pasture from us.

But Farnsworth was ahead of me, waddling alone, puffing. He got the shovels out and handed one to me.

We didn't say a word, neither of us, for hours. It takes a long time to fill a hole twenty feet deep – especially when you're shovelling very, very carefully and packing down the dirt very, very hard.

THE BIG BOUNCE

Among the basic rules that seem to govern the workings of the universe are the first and second laws of thermodynamics. (There is also a third law of thermodynamics but it doesn't involve everyday life.)

Thermodynamics is the science involving the interchange of work and energy. The first law of thermodynamics can be stated as: 'Energy can neither be created nor destroyed, but can be changed from one form to another.' Another way of putting it is: 'The total amount of energy in the universe is constant.' Sometimes the first law of thermodynamics is called 'The law of conservation of energy' and it is probably *the* most basic and important scientific generalization.

The second law of thermodynamics is a lot harder to define clearly, but the simplest way of putting it is that: 'In every spontaneous change, the total amount of *usable* energy decreases.' Thus, there is a steady vast loss of usable energy in the universe even though the total quantity doesn't change, so that the universe is steadily running down.

Another way of phrasing the second law is to say that: 'The amount of disorder in the universe is constantly increasing.' Since the most disorderly form of energy is heat, there is a constant increase of heat at the expense of other forms of energy. To make it worse there is a constant levelling-out of the intensity of heat; that is, the temperature of the universe generally is steadily

176

becoming 'medium' at the expense of the very hot and very cold.

In *The Big Bounce*, we have a ball that moves higher with every bounce. It gains kinetic energy steadily, and kinetic energy is usable. Since usable energy is increasing with each bounce, the ball is defying the second law of thermodynamics.

This is impossible, of course. No ball, of whatever composition, can gain energy and velocity and height with every bounce. We can be quite sure that Tevis knew it, too, but deliberately introduced this impossibility to start off his story and to demonstrate what an odd world we would live in if the second law could be violated.

Interestingly enough, he escapes from catastrophe by making use of the first law of thermodynamics, which he does *not* violate. If the ball gains energy with each bounce, where does that energy come from? If it came from nowhere, that would be a violation of the first law, so Tevis has it come from the heat content of the ball. The more energy of motion the ball gains, the colder it gets.

That, too, is a violation of the second law for the only way to convert heat into motion is to have two volumes of matter, one much hotter than the other, and allow them to come to intermediate temperature. In this way, some of the heat energy can be put to useful work at the expense of much more of the heat energy becoming more disorderly by evening out in temperature.

Questions and Suggestions

1. What is the stand of the U.S. Patent Office on 'perpetual motion' machines. All of these, incidentally, break either the first or the second laws of thermodynamics. Why?

2. The ocean has vast quantities of heat in it. Even a polar ocean does. Why do ocean vessels have to burn fuel? Why can't they just use the heat of the ocean water over which they pass?

3. In view of the first law of thermodynamics, where does the tremendous energy radiated by the Sun and all the other stars come from?

4. Look up the history of some perpetual motion machines designed in the past. What was the 'catch' in

each case? Why wouldn't they work? Were some of them outright hoaxes?

5. The laws of thermodynamics are based on the general experience of scientists. They have never observed the laws to be broken. Scientists, however, merely observe their own section of the universe and their own general type of environment. What about outer space ten billion light-years away? What about the centre of the Sun? How sure can we be that scientific laws are the same everywhere under all conditions?

6. Suppose a scientist discovered some easily produced phenomenon which seemed to defy either the first or second law of thermodynamics? Should he assume at once there was some mistake and forget the whole thing? Should he instantly proclaim the phenomenon and declare the laws broken? What would *you* do?

9. NEUTRON STAR

Larry Niven

I

The Skydiver dropped out of hyperspace an even million miles above the neutron star. I needed a minute to place myself against the stellar background and another to find the distortion Sonya Laskin had mentioned before she died. It was to my left, an area the apparent size of the Earth's moon. I swung the ship around to face it.

Curdled stars, muddled stars, stars that had been stirred with a spoon.

The neutron star was in the centre, of course, though I couldn't see it and hadn't expected to. It was only eleven miles across, and cool. A billion years has passed since BVS-1 burned by fusion fire. Millions of years, at least, since the cataclysmic two weeks during which BVS-1 was an X-ray star, burning at a temperature of five billion degree Kelvin. Now it showed only by its mass.

The ship began to turn by itself. I felt the pressure of the fusion drive. Without help from me, my faithful metal watchdog was putting me in hyperbolic orbit that would take me within one mile of the neutron star's surface. Twenty-four hours to fall, twenty-fours hours to rise . . . and during that time, something would try to kill me. As something had killed the Laskins.

The same type of autopilot, with the same programme, had chosen the Laskin's orbit. It had not caused their ship to collide with the star. I could trust the autopilot. I could even change its programme.

I really ought to.

How did I get myself into this hole?

The drive went off after ten minutes of manoeuvring. My orbit was established, in more ways than one. I knew what would happen if I tried to back out now.

All I'd done was walk into a drugstore to get a new battery for my lighter!

Right in the middle of the store, surrounded by three floors of sales counters, was the new 2603 Sinclair intra-system yacht, I'd come for a battery, but I stayed to admire. It was a beautiful job, small and sleek and streamlined and blatantly different from anything that's ever been built. I wouldn't have flown it for anything, but I had to admit it was pretty. I ducked my head through the door to look at the control panel. You never saw so many dials. When I pulled my head out, all the customers were looking in the same direction. The place had gone startlingly quiet.

I can't blame them for staring. A number of aliens were in the store, mainly shopping for souvenirs, but they were staring too. A puppeteer is unique. Imagine a headless, three-legged centaur wearing two Cecil the Seasick Sea Serpent puppets on his arms, and you'll have something like the right picture. But the arms are weaving necks, and the puppets are real heads, flat and brainless, with wide flexible lips. The brain is under a bony hump set between the bases of the necks. This puppeteer wore only its own coat of brown hair, with a mane that extended all the way up its spine to form a thick mat over the brain. I'm told that the way they wear the mane indicates their status in society, but to me it could have been anything from a dock worker to a jeweller to the president of General Products.

I watched with the rest as it came across the floor, not

because I'd never seen a puppeteer, but because there is something beautiful about the dainty way they move on those slender legs and tiny hooves. I watched it come straight towards me, closer and closer. It stopped a foot away, looked me over and said, 'You are Beowulf Shaeffer, former chief pilot for Nakamura Lines.'

Its voice was a beautiful contralto with not a trace of accent. A puppeteer's mouths are not only the most flexible speech organs around, but also the most sensitive hands. The tongues are forked and pointed, the wide, thick lips have little fingerlike knobs along the rims. Imagine a watchmaker with a sense of taste in his fingertips . . .

I cleared my throat. 'That's right.'

It considered me from two directions. 'You would be interested in a high-paying job?'

'I'd be fascinated in a high-paying job.'

'I am our equivalent of the regional president of General Products. Please come with me, and we will discuss this elsewhere.'

I followed it into a displacement booth. Eyes followed me all the way. It was embarrassing, being accosted in a public drugstore by a two-headed monster. Maybe the puppeteer knew it. Maybe it was testing me to see how badly I needed money.

My need was great. Eight months had passed since Nakamura Lines folded. For some time before that, I had been living very high on the hog, knowing that my back pay would cover my debts. I never saw that back pay. It was quite a crash, Nakamura Lines. Respectable middle-aged businessmen took to leaving their hotel windows without their left belts. Me, I kept spending. If I'd started living frugally, my creditors would have done some checking . . . and I'd have ended in debtor's prison.

The puppeteer dialled thirteen fast digits with its tongue. A moment later we were elsewhere. Air puffed out when I opened the booth door, and I swallowed to pop my ears.

'We are on the roof of the General Products building.' The rich contralto voice thrilled along my nerves, and I had to remind myself that it was an alien speaking,

180

not a lovely woman. 'You must examine this spacecraft while we discuss your assignment.'

I stepped outside a little cautiously, but it wasn't the windy season. The roof was at ground level. That's the way we build on We Made It. Maybe it has something to do with the fifteen-hundred-mile-an-hour winds we get in summer and winter, when the planet's axis of rotation runs through its primary, Procyon. The winds are our planet's only tourist attraction, and it would be a shame to slow them down by planting skyscrapers in their path. The bare, square concrete roof was surrounded by endless square miles of desert, not like the deserts of other inhabited worlds, but an utterly lifeless expanse of fine sand just crying to be planted with ornamental cactus. We've tried that. The wind blows the plants away.

The ship lay on the sand beyond the roof. It was a No. 2 General Products Hull: a cylinder three hundred feet long and twenty feet through, pointed at both ends and with a slight wasp-waist constriction near the tail. For some reason it was lying on its side, with the landing shocks still folded in at the tail.

Ever notice how all ships have begun to look the same? A good ninety-five per cent of today's spacecrafts are built around one of the four General Products hulls. It's easier and safer to build that way, but somehow all ships end as they began: mass-produced look-alikes.

The hulls are delivered fully transparent, and you use paint where you feel like it. Most of this particular hull had been left transparent. Only the nose had been painted, around the lifesystem. There was no major reaction drive. A series of retractable altitude jets had been mounted in the sides, and the hull was pierced with smaller holes, square and round – for observational instruments. I could see them gleaming through the hull.

The puppeteer was moving towards the nose, but something made me turn towards the stern for a closer look at the landing shocks.

They were bent. Behind the curved, transparent hull panels, some tremendous pressure had forced the metal to flow like warm wax, back and into the pointed stern.

'What did this?' I asked.

'We do not know. We wish strenuously to find out.'

'What do you mean?'

'Have you heard of the neutron star BVS-1?'

I had to think a moment. 'First neutron star ever found, and so far the only. Someone located it two years ago by stellar displacement.'

'BVS-1 was found by the Institute of Knowledge on Jinx. We learned through a go-between that the Institute wished to explore the star. They needed a ship to do it. They had not yet sufficient money. We offered to supply them with a ship's hull, with the usual guarantees, if they would turn over to us all data they acquired through using our ship.'

'Sounds fair enough.' I didn't ask why they hadn't done their own exploring. Like most sentient vegetarians, puppeteers find discretion to be the *only* part of valour.

'Two humans named Peter Laskin and Sonya Laskin wished to use the ship. They intended to come within one mile of the surface in a hyperbolic orbit. At some point during their trip, an unknown force apparently reached through the hull to do this to the landing shocks. The unknown force also seems to have killed the pilots.'

'But that's impossible. Isn't it?'

'You see the point. Come with me.' The puppeteer trotted towards the bow.

I saw the point, all right. Nothing, but nothing can get through a General Products hull. No kind of electromagnetic energy except visible light. No kind of matter, from the smallest subatomic particle to the fastest meteor. That's what the company's advertisements claim, and the guarantee backs them up. I've never doubted it, and I've never heard of a General Products hull damaged by a weapon or by anything else.

On the other hand, a General Products hull is as ugly as it is functional. The puppeteer-owned company could be badly hurt if it got around that something *could* get through a company hull. But I didn't see where I came in.

We rode an escalladder into the nose.

The lifesystem was in two compartments. Here the Laskins had used heat-reflective paint. In the conical control cabin the hull had been divided into windows. The relaxation room behind it was a windowless reflective silver. From the back wall of the relaxation room an access tube ran aft, opening on various instruments and the hyperdrive motors.

There were two acceleration couches in the control cabin. Both had been torn loose from their mountings and wadded into the nose like so much tissue paper, crushing the instrument panel. The backs of the crumpled couches were splashed with rust brown. Flecks of the same colour were all over everything, the walls, the windows, the viewscreens. It was as if something had hit the couches from behind: something like a dozen paint-filled toy balloons, striking with tremendous force.

'That's blood,' I said.

'That is correct. Human circulatory fluid.'

II

Twenty-four hours to fall.

I spent most of the first twelve hours in the relaxation room, trying to read. Nothing significant was happening, except that a few times I saw the phenomenon Sonya Laskin had mentioned in her last report. When a star went directly behind the invisible BVS-1, a halo formed. BVS-1 was heavy enough to bend light around it, displacing most stars to the sides; but when a star went directly behind the neutron star, its light was displaced to all sides at once. Result: a tiny circle which flashed once and was gone almost before the eye could catch it.

I'd known next to nothing about neutron stars the day the puppeteer picked me up. Now I was an expert. But I still had no idea what was waiting for me when I got down there.

All the matter you're ever likely to meet will be normal matter, composed of a nucleus of protons and neutrons surrounded by electrons in quantum energy states. In the heart of any star there is a second kind of matter: for there, the tremendous pressure is enough to smash the electron shells. The result is degenerate matter: nuclei forced together by pressure and gravity, but held apart by the mutual repulsion of the more or less continuous electron 'gas' around them. The right circumstances may create a third type of matter.

Given: a burnt-out white dwarf with a mass greater than 1.44 times the mass of the Sun – Chandrasekhar's Limit, named for an Indian-American astronomer of the nineteen hundreds. In such a mass the electron pressure alone would not be able to hold the electrons back from the nuclei. Electrons would be forced against protons – to make neutrons. In one blazing explosion most of the star would change from a compressed mass of degenerate matter to a closely packed lump of neutrons: neutronium, theoretically the densest matter possible in this universe. Most of the remaining normal and degenerate matter would be blown away by the liberated heat.

For two weeks the star would give off X-rays, as its core temperature dropped from five billion degrees Kelvin to five hundred million. After that it would be a light-emitting body perhaps ten to twelve miles across: the next best thing to invisible. It was not strange that BVS-1 was the first neutron star ever found.

Neither is it strange that the Institute of Knowledge on Jinx would have spent a good deal of time and trouble looking. Until BVS-1 was found, neutronium and neutron stars were only theories. The examination of an actual neutron star could be of tremendous importance. Neutron stars could give us the key to true gravity control.

Mass of BVS-1: 1-3 times the mass of Sol, approximately.

Diameter of BVS-1 (estimated): eleven miles of neutronium, covered by half a mile of degenerate matter, covered by maybe twelve feet of ordinary matter.

Escape velocity: 130,000 mps, approximately.

Nothing else was known of the tiny black star until the Laskins went in to look. Now the Institute knew one thing more. The star's spin.

'A mass that large can distort space by its rotation,' said the puppeteer. 'The Institute ship's projected hyperbola was twisted across itself in such a way that we can deduce the star's period of rotation to be two minutes, twenty-seven seconds.'

The bar was somewhere in the General Products building. I don't know just where, and with the transfer booths it doesn't matter. I kept staring at the puppeteer bartender. Naturally only a puppeteer would be served by a puppeteer bartender, since any biped would resent knowing that somebody made his drink with his mouth. I had already decided to get dinner somewhere else.

'I see your problem,' I said. 'Your sales will suffer if it gets out that something can reach through one of your hulls and smash a crew to bloody smears. But where do I fit in?'

'We wish to repeat the experiment of Sonya Laskin and Peter Laskin. We must find—'

'With me?'

'Yes, We must find out what it is that our hulls cannot stop. Naturally you may—'

'But I won't.'

'We are prepared to offer one million stars.'

I was tempted, but only for a moment. 'Forget it.'

'Naturally you will be allowed to build your own ship, starting with a No. 2 General Products hull.'

'Thanks, but I'd like to go on living.'

'You would dislike being confined. I find that We Made It has re-established the debtor's prison. If General Products made public your accounts . . .'

'Now, *just* a—'

'You owe money in the close order of five hundred thousand stars. We will pay your creditors before you leave. If you return' – I had to admire the creature's honesty in not saying *when* – 'we will pay you the remainder. You may be asked to speak to news commentators concerning the voyage, in which case there will be more stars.'

'You say I can build my own ship?'

'Naturally. This is not a voyage of exploration. We want you to return safely.'

'It's a deal,' I said.

After all, the puppeteer had tried to blackmail me. What happened next would be its own fault.

They built my ship in two weeks flat. They started with a No. 2 General Products hull, just like the one around the Institute of Knowledge ship, and the life-system was practically a duplicate of the Laskins', but there the resemblance ended. There were no instruments to observe neutron stars. Instead, there was a fusion motor big enough for a Jinx warliner. In my ship, which I now called Skydiver, the drive would produce thirty gees at the safety limit. There was a laser cannon big enough to punch a hole through We Made It's moon. The puppeteer wanted me to feel safe and now I did, for I could fight and I could run. Especially I could run.

I heard the Laskins' last broadcast through half a dozen times. Their unnamed ship had dropped out of hyperspace a million miles above BVS-1. Gravity warp would have prevented their getting closer in hyperspace. While her husband was crawling through the access tube for an instrument check, Sonya Laskin had called the Institute of Knowledge. '. . . we can't see it yet, not with the naked eye. But we can see where it is. Every time some star or other goes behind it, there's a little ring of light. Just a minute. Peter's ready to use the telescope . . .'

Then the star's mass had cut the hyperspacial link. It was expected and nobody had worried – then. Later, the same effect must have stopped them from escaping whatever attacked them, into hyperspace.

When would-be rescuers found the ship, only the radar and the cameras were still running. They didn't tell us much. There had been no camera in the cabin. But the forward camera gave us, for one instant, a speed-blurred view of the neutron star. It was a featureless disc the orange colour of perfect barbecue coals, if you know someone who can afford to burn wood. This object has been a neutron star a long time.

'There'll be no need to paint the ship,' I told the president.

'You should not make such a trip with the walls transparent. You would go insane.'

'I'm no flatlander. The mind-wrenching sight of naked space fills me with mild, but waning interest. I want to know nothing's sneaking up behind me.'

The day before I left, I sat alone in the General Products bar letting the puppeteer bartender make me drinks with his mouth. He did it well. Puppeteers were scattered around the bar in twos and threes, with a couple of men for variety; but the drinking hour had not yet arrived. The place felt empty.

I was pleased with myself. My debts were all paid, not that that would matter where I was going. I would leave with not a mini-credit to my name; with nothing but the ship . . .

186

All told, I was well out of a sticky situation. I hoped I'd like being a rich exile.

I jumped when the newcomer sat down across from me. He was a foreigner, a middle-aged man wearing an expensive night-black business suit and a snow-white asymmetric beard. I let my face freeze and started to get up.

'Sit down, Mr. Shaeffer.'

'Why?'

He told me by showing me a blue disc. An Earth-government ident. I looked it over to show I was alert, not because I'd know an ersatz from the real thing.

'My name is Sigmund Ausfaller,' said the government man. 'I wish to say a few words concerning your assignment on behalf of General Products.'

I nodded, not saying anything.

'A record of your verbal contract was sent to us as a matter of course. I noticed some peculiar things about it. Mr. Shaeffer, will you really take such a risk for only five hundred thousand stars?'

'I'm getting twice that.'

'But you only keep half of it. The rest goes to pay debts. Then there are taxes. But never mind. What occurred to me was that a spaceship is a spaceship, and yours is very well armed and has powerful legs. An admirable fighting ship, if you were moved to sell it.'

'But it isn't mine.'

'There are those who would not ask. On Canyon, for example, or the Isolationist party of Wonderland.'

I said nothing.

'Or, you might be planning a career of piracy. A risky business, piracy, and I don't take the notion seriously.'

I hadn't even thought about piracy. But I'd have to give up on Wonderland . . .

'What I would like to say is this, Mr. Shaeffer. A single entrepreneur, if he were sufficiently dishonest, could do terrible damage to the reputation of all human beings everywhere. Most species find it necessary to police the ethics of their own members, and we are no exception. It occurred to me that you might not take your ship to neutron star at all; that you would take it elsewhere and sell it. The puppeteers do not make invulnerable war vessels. They are pacifists. Your Skydiver is unique.

'Hence I have asked General Products to allow me to

187

install a remote control bomb in the Skydiver. Since it is inside the hull, the hull cannot protect you. I had it installed this afternoon.

'Now, notice! If you have not reported within a week I will set off the bomb. There are several worlds within a week's hyperspace flight of here, but all recognize the dominion of Earth. If you flee, you must leave your ship within a week, so I hardly think you will land on a non-habitable world. Clear?'

'Clear.'

'If I am wrong, you may take a lie-detector test and prove it. Then you may punch me in the nose, and I will apologize handsomely.'

I shook my head. He stood up, bowed and left me sitting there cold sober.

Four films had been taken from the Laskins' cameras. In the time left to me, I ran through them several times, without seeing anything out of the way. If the ship had run through a gas cloud, the impact could have killed the Laskins. At perihelion they were moving at better than half the speed of light. But there would have been friction, and I saw no sign of heating in the films. If something alive had attacked them, the beast was invisible to radar and to an enormous range of light frequencies. If the attitude jets had fired accidentally – I was clutching at straws – the light showed on none of the films.

There would be savage magnetic forces near BVS-1, but that couldn't have done any damage. No such force could penetrate a General Products hull. Neither could heat, except in special bands of radiated light, bands visible to at least one of the puppeteers' alien customers. I hold adverse opinions on the General Products hull, but they all concern the dull anonymity of the design. Or maybe I resent the fact that General Products holds a near-monopoly on spacecraft hulls and isn't owned by human beings. But if I'd had to trust my life to, say, the Sinclair yacht I'd seen in the drugstore, I'd have chosen jail.

Jail was one of my three choices. But I'd be there for life. Ausfaller would see to that.

Or I could run for it in the Skydiver. But no world within reach would have me, that is. Of course if I could find an undiscovered Earthlike world within a week of We Made It . . .

Fat chance. I preferred BVS-1 to that any day.

III

I thought that flashing circle of light was getting bigger, but it flashed so seldom I couldn't be sure. BVS-1 wouldn't show even in my telescope. I gave that up and settled for just waiting.

Waiting, I remembered a long-ago summer I spent on Jinx. There were days when, unable to go outside because a dearth of clouds had spread the land with raw blue-white sunlight, we amused ourselves by filling party balloons with tap water and dropping them on the sidewalk from three stories up. They made lovely splash patterns — which dried out too fast. So we put a little ink in each balloon before filling it. Then the patterns stayed.

Sonya Laskin had been in her chair when the chairs collapsed. Blood samples showed that it was Peter who had struck them from behind, like a water balloon from a great height.

What could get through a General Products hull?

Ten hours to fall.

I unfastened the safety net and went for an inspection tour. The access tunnel was three feet wide, just right to push through in free fall. Below me was the length of the fusion tube; to the left, the laser cannon; to the right, a set of curved side tubes leading to inspection points for the gyros, the batteries and generator, the air plant, the hyperspace shunt motors. All was in order — except me. I was clumsy. My jumps were always too short or too long. There was no room to turn at the stern end, so I had to back fifty feet to a side tube.

Six hours to go, and still I couldn't find the neutron star. Probably I would see it only for an instant, passing at better than half the speed of light. Already my speed must be enormous.

Were the stars turning blue?

Two hours to go, I was sure they were turning blue. Was my speed that high? Then the stars behind should be red. Machinery blocked the view behind me, so I used

189

the gyros. The ship turned with peculiar sluggishness. And the stars behind were blue, not red. All around me were blue-white stars.

Imagine light falling into a savagely steep gravitational well. It won't accelerate. Light can't move faster than light. But it can gain in energy, in frequency. The light was falling on me, harder and harder as I dropped.

I told the dictaphone about it. That dictaphone was probably the best protected item on the ship. I had already decided to earn my money by using it, just as if I expected to collect. Privately I wondered just how intense the light would get.

Skydiver had drifted back to vertical, with its axis through the neutron star, but now it faced outward. I'd thought I had the ship stopped horizontally. More clumsiness. I used the gyros. Again the ship moved mushily, until it was halfway through the swing. Then it seemed to fall automatically into place. It was as if the Skydiver preferred to have its axis through the neutron star.

I didn't like that in the least.

I tried the manoeuvre again, and again the Skydiver fought back. But this time there was something else. Something was pulling at me.

So I unfastened my safety net and fell headfirst into the nose.

The pull was light, about a tenth of a gee. It felt more like sinking through honey than falling. I climbed back into my chair, tied myself in with the net, now hanging face down, turned on the dictaphone. I told my story in such nit-picking detail that my hypothetical listeners could not but doubt my hypothetical sanity. 'I think this is what happened to the Laskins,' I finished. 'If the pull increases, I'll call back.'

Think? I never doubted it. This strange, gentle pull was inexplicable. Something inexplicable had killed Peter and Sonya Laskin. *Q.E.D.*

Around the point where the neutron star must be, the stars were like smeared dots of oilpaint, smeared radially. They glared with an angry, painful light. I hung face down in the net and tried to think.

It was an hour before I was sure. The pull was increasing. And I still had an hour to fall.

Something was pulling on me, but not on the ship.

No, that was nonsense. What could reach out to me through a General Products hull? It must be the other way around. Something was pushing on the ship, pushing it off course.

If it got worse I could use the drive to compensate. Meanwhile, the ship was being pushed *away* from BVS-1, which was fine by me.

But if I was wrong, if the ship were not somehow being pushed away from BVS-1, the rocket motor would send the Skydiver crashing into eleven miles of neutronium.

And why wasn't the rocket already firing? If the ship was being pushed off course, the autopilot should be fighting back. The accelerometer was in good order. It had looked fine when I made my inspection tour down the access tube.

Could something be pushing on the ship *and* on the accelerometer but not on me?

It came down to the same impossibility. Something that could reach through a General Products hull.

To hell with theory, said I to myself, said I. I'm getting out of here. To the dictaphone I said, 'The push has increased dangerously. I'm going to try to alter my orbit.'

Of course, once I turned the ship outward and used the rocket, I'd be adding my own acceleration to the X force. It would be a strain, but I could stand it for a while. If I came within a mile of BVS-1, I'd end like Sonya Laskin.

She must have waited face down in a net like mine, waited without a drive unit, waited while the pressure rose and the net cut into her flesh, waited until the net snapped and dropped her into the nose, to lie crushed and broken until the X force tore the very chairs loose and dropped them on her.

I hit the gyros.

The gyros weren't strong enough to turn me. I tried it three times. Each time the ship rotated about fifty degrees and hung there, motionless, while the whine of the gyros went up and up. Released, the ship immediately swung back to position. I was nose down to the neutron star, and I was going to stay that way.

Half an hour to fall, and the X force was over a gee. My sinuses were in agony. My eyes were ripe and ready to fall out. I don't know if I could have stood a cigarette, but I didn't get the chance. My pack of Fortunados had fallen out of my pocket, when I dropped into the nose. There it was, four feet beyond my fingers, proof that the X force acted on other objects besides me. Fascinating.

I couldn't take any more. If it dropped me shrieking into the neutron star, I had to use the drive. And I did. I ran the thrust up until I was approximately in free fall. The blood which had pooled in my extremities went back where it belonged. The gee dial registered one point two gee. I cursed it for a lying robot.

The soft-pack was bobbing around in the nose, and it occurred to me that a little extra nudge on the throttle would bring it to me. I tried it. The pack drifted towards me, and I reached, and like a sentient thing it speeded up to avoid my clutching hand. I snatched at it again as it went past my ear, but again it was moving too fast. That pack was going at a hell of a clip, considering that here I was, practically in free fall. It dropped through the door to the relaxation room, still picking up speed, blurred and vanished as it entered the access tube. Seconds later I heard a solid Thump.

But that was *crazy*. Already the X force was pulling blood into my face. I pulled my lighter out, held it at arms' length and let go. It fell into the nose. But the pack of Fortunados had hit like I'd dropped it from a *building*.

Well.

I nudged the throttle again. The mutter of fusing hydrogen reminded me that if I tried to keep this up all the way, I might well put the General Products hull to its toughest test yet: smashing it into a neutron star at half lightspeed. I could see it now: a transparent hull containing only a few cubic inches of dwarf star matter wedged into the tip of the nose.

At one point four gee, according to that lying gee dial, the lighter came loose and drifted towards me. I let it go. It was clearly falling when it reached the doorway. I pulled the throttle back. The loss of power jerked me violently forward, but I kept my face turned. The lighter slowed and hesitated at the entrance to the access tube. Decided to go through. I cocked my ears for the sound, then jumped as the whole ship rang like a gong.

And the accelerometer was right at the ship's centre of mass. Otherwise the ship's mass would have thrown the needle off. The puppeteers were fiends for ten-decimal-point accuracy.

I favoured the dictaphone with a few fast comments, then got to work reprogramming the autopilot. Luckily what I wanted was simple. The X force was but an X force to me, but now I knew how it behaved. I might actually live through this.

The stars were fiercely blue, warped to streaked lines near that special point. I thought I could see it now, very small and dim and red; but it might have been imagination. In twenty minutes, I'd be rounding the neutron star. The drive grumbled behind me. In effective free fall, I unfastened the safety net and pushed myself out of the chair.

A gentle push aft – and ghostly hands grasped my legs. Ten pounds of weight hung by my fingers from the back of the chair. The pressure should drop fast. I'd programmed the autopilot to reduce the thrust from two gees to zero during the next two minutes. All I had to do was be at the centre of mass, in the access tube, when the thrust went to zero.

Something gripped the ship through a General Products hull. A psychokinetic life form stranded on a sun twelve miles in diameter? But how could anything alive stand such gravity?

Something might be stranded in orbit. There is life in space: outsiders and sailseeds and maybe others we haven't found yet. For all I knew or cared, BVS-1 itself might be alive. It didn't matter. I knew what the X force was trying to do. It was trying to pull the ship apart.

There was no pull on my fingers. I pushed aft and landed on the back wall, on bent legs. I knelt over the door, looking aft/down. When free fall came, I pulled myself through and was in the relaxation room looking down/forward into the nose.

Gravity was changing faster than I liked. The X force was growing as zero hour approached, while the compensating rocket thrust dropped. The X force tended to pull the ship apart; it was two gee forward at the nose, two gee backward at the tail and diminished to zero at the centre of mass. Or so I hoped. The pack and lighter had behaved as if the force pulling them had increased for every inch they moved sternward.

The dictaphone was fifty feet below, utterly unreachable. If I had anything more to say to General Products, I'd have to say it in person. Maybe I'd get the chance. Because I knew what force was trying to tear the ship apart.

It was the tide.

The motor was off, and I was at the ship's midpoint. My spread-eagled position was getting uncomfortable. It was four minutes to perihelion.

Something creaked in the cabin below me. I couldn't see what it was, but I could clearly see a red point glaring among blue radial lines, like a lantern at the bottom of a well. To the sides, between the fusion tube and the tanks and other equipment, the blue stars glared at me with a light that was almost violet. I was afraid to look too long. I actually thought they might blind me.

There must have been hundreds of gravities in the cabin. I could even feel the pressure change. The air was thin at this height, one hundred and fifty feet above the control room.

And now, almost suddenly, the red dot was more than a dot. My time was up. A red disc leapt up at me; the ship swung around me; and I gasped and shut my eyes tight. Giants' hands gripped my arms and legs and head, gently but with great firmness, and tried to pull me in two. In that moment it came to me that Peter Laskin had died like this. He'd made the same guesses I had, and he'd tried to hide in the access tube. But he'd slipped. As I was slipping....

When I got my eyes open the red dot was shrinking into nothing.

IV

The puppeteer president insisted I be put in hospital for observation. I didn't fight the idea. My face and hands were flaming red, with blisters rising, and I ached like I'd been beaten. Rest and tender loving care, that's what I wanted.

I was floating between a pair of sleeping plates, hideously uncomfortable, when the nurse came to announce

194

a visitor. I knew who it was from her peculiar expression.

'What can get through a General Products hull?' I asked it.

'I hope you would tell me.' The president rested on its single back leg, holding a stick that gave off green, incense-smelling smoke.

'And so I will. Gravity.'

'Do not play with me, Beowulf Shaeffer. This matter is vital.'

'I'm not playing. Does your world have a moon?'

'That information is classified.' The puppeteers are cowards. Nobody knows where they come from, and nobody is likely to find out.

'Do you know what happens when a moon gets too close to its primary?'

'It falls apart.'

'Why?'

'I do not know.'

'Tides.'

'What is a tide?'

Oho, said I to myself, said I. 'I'm going to try to tell you. The Earth's moon is almost two thousand miles in diameter and does not rotate with respect to Earth. I want you to pick two rocks on the Moon, one at the point nearest the Earth, one at the point furthest away.'

'Very well.'

'Now, isn't it obvious that if those rocks were left to themselves they'd fall away from each other? They're in two different orbits, mind you, concentric orbits, one almost two thousand miles outside the other. Yet these rocks are forced to move at the same orbital speed.'

'The one outside is moving faster.'

'Good point. So there *is* a force trying to pull the moon apart. Gravity holds it together. Bring the Moon close enough to Earth, and those two rocks would simply float away.'

'I see. Then this *tide* tried to pull your ship apart. It was powerful enough in the lifesystem of the Institute ship to pull the acceleration chairs out of their mounts.'

'And to crush a human being. Picture it. The ship's nose was just seven miles from the centre of BVS-1. The tail was three hundred feet further out. Left to themselves they'd have gone in completely different orbits.

195

My head and feet tried to do the same thing, when I got close enough.'

'I see. Are you moulting?'

'What?'

'I noticed your are losing your outer integument in spots.'

'Oh, *that*. I got a bad sunburn from exposure to starlight.'

Two heads stared at each other for an eyeblink. A shrug? The puppeteer said. 'We have deposited the remainder of your pay with the Bank of We Made It. One Sigmund Ausfaller, human, has frozen the account until your taxes are computed.'

'Figures.'

'If you will talk to reporters now, explaining what happened to the Institute ship, we will pay you ten thousand stars. We will pay cash so that you may use it immediately. It is urgent. There have been rumours.'

'Bring 'em in.' As an afterthought I added, 'I can also tell them that your world is moonless. That should be good for a footnote somewhere.'

'I do not understand.' But two long necks had drawn back, and the puppeteer was watching me like a pair of pythons.

'Would you be interested in . . .'

'. . . a million stars? I'd be fascinated. I'll even sign a contract if it includes what we're hiding. How do you like being blackmailed?'

NEUTRON STAR

In 1962, astronomers discovered that there were X-rays coming from certain points in the sky. (These were absorbed by our atmosphere and it was only when rockets with appropriate instruments could be sent beyond the atmosphere that these X-rays could be detected.)

The problem was to work out what could possibly serve as a source for those X-rays. To send out so many X-rays that they were still detectable after spreading out over many, many lightyears, the source would have to be the size of a star at least and very, very hot. Ordinary stars could not be that hot, and astronomers began to suspect the existence of very tiny stars with unusual properties.

The Sun has very dense matter at its centre, where atomic nuclei are pushed unusually close together; much closer than in normal matter. Some stars, like the tiny companion of Sirius, are made up mostly of this crushed matter. What if, in some stars, the atomic nuclei are crushed together till they touch, so that they become solid 'neutronium'. Such a 'neutron star' would contain all the mass of the Sun compressed into a sphere just under ten miles across. These might produce vast quantities of X-rays.

Scientists didn't expect to be able to see tiny stars, but they studied the X-rays carefully, hoping to deduce from them whether neutron stars definitely existed or not. For a variety of reasons, hope waned and by 1966, when *Neutron Star* was published, a good deal of the earlier enthusiasm had vanished. Nevertheless, Niven was still justified in basing a story upon the existence of such an object – it had not been ruled out altogether.

Then in 1968, two years after the story was published, astronomers discovered a new phenomenon – radio-wave pulses in the sky that came and went very regularly, in some cases as quickly as thirty times a second, in other cases as slowly as once in three seconds. The new phenomenon was referred to as 'pulsars'.

Something in space had to be pulsing, revolving, or rotating fast enough to account for this and the best suggestion seemed to be that of a rotating neutron star. A neutron star would be small enough to rotate in seconds or fractions of a second and the results of such a rotation seemed to fit the observed facts. At the moment neutron stars are big again and Niven seems to have been right to have held on to his notion.

Questions and Suggestions

1. What observations in connection with 'X-ray stars' made it seem less likely that they represented neutron stars. How were pulsars discovered? What other suggestions were made, in addition to neutron stars, concerning their nature?

2. Suppose the Sun's mass were condensed into a ball of matter ten miles across. How much would a cubic inch of its matter weigh?

3. If the Sun suddenly became a neutron star without loss of mass, would that affect its gravitational pull on us? What changes would take place on Earth?

4. What would be the gravitational pull on the surface of a neutron star as compared with that on the surface of the Earth?

5. What causes tides? The moon's tidal effect on Earth is greater than the Sun's, even though the Sun's gravitational pull on Earth is greater than the Moon's. Explain that. Calculate the tidal effect of the neutron star on the man in the spaceship in the story as compared with the tidal effect of the Moon on the Earth.

APPENDIX

Further Reading

1. A MARTIAN ODYSSEY by Stanley G. Weinbaum
   Is There Life on Other Worlds? by Paul Anderson (Macmillan, 1963)
   We Are Not Alone by Walter Sullivan (Hodder, 1965)

2. NIGHT by Don A. Stuart
   Frontiers of Astronomy by Fred Hoyle (Heinemann, 1955)
   Great Ideas and Theories of Modern Cosmology by Jagjit Singh (Constable, 1963)

3. THE DAY IS DONE by Lester del Rey
   Mankind in the Making by William Howells (Secker and Warburg, 1961)
   Man, Time & Fossils by Ruth Moore (Jonathan Cape, 1962)

4. HEAVY PLANET by Lee Gregor
   Weather on the Planets by George Ohring (Doubleday, 1966)
   Earth, Moon, and Planets by Fred L. Whipple (Oxford University Press, 1968)

5. '—AND HE BUILT A CROOKED HOUSE—' by Robert A. Heinlein
   A New Look at Geometry by Irving Adler (Dobson, 1967)
   Introduction to Geometry by H. S. M. Coxeter (2nd ed., Wiley, 1969)

6. PROOF by Hal Clement
   The Sun by Giorgio Abetti (Faber and Faber, 1957)
   The Stars by W. Kruse and W. Dieckvoss (Mayflower, 1960)

7. A SUBWAY NAMED MÖBIUS by A. J. Deutsch
   Intuitive Concepts in Elementary Topology by B. H. Arnold (Prentice-Hall, 1962)
   Experiments in Topology by Stephen Barr (John Murray, 1965)

8. SURFACE TENSION by James Blish
   Cells and Cell Structure by E. H. Mercer (Hutchinson Educational, 1961)

    The Procession of Life by Alfred S. Romer (Weiden-
    feld and Nicolson, 1968)

9. COUNTRY DOCTOR by William Morrison
    Life on the Planets by Robert Tocquet (Grove,
    1962)
    Life in the Universe by Michael W. Ovenden
    (Heinemann, 1964)

10. THE HOLES AROUND MARS by Jerome Bixby
    Celestial Mechanics by Y. Riabov (Dover, 1961)
    Astronautics for Science Teachers by John G.
    Meitner (Wiley, 1965)

11. THE DEEP RANGE by Arthur C. Clarke
    The Sea by Leonard Engel (Time, Inc., 1961)
    Whales by E. J. Slijper (Hutchinson, 1962)

12. THE CAVE OF NIGHT by James E. Gunn
    Appointment on the Moon by Richard S. Lewis
    (Viking, 1968) (revised edition, Ballantine, 1969)
    We Reach the Moon by John Noble Wilford
    (Bantam, 1969)

13. DUST RAG by Hal Clement
    Pictorial Guide to the Moon by Dinsmore Alter
    (Thomas Y. Crowell, 1967)
    The Case for Going to the Moon by Neil P. Ruzic
    (Putnam, 1965)

14. PÂTÉ DE FOIE GRAS by Isaac Asimov
    Isotopic Tracers in Biology by Martin David Kamen
    (3rd ed., Academic Press, 1957)
    Isotopes by J. L. Putnam (Pelican, 1960)

15. OMNILINGUAL by H. Beam Piper
    Lost Worlds by Leonard Cottrell (Elek Books, 1964)
    *To the Rock of Darius: The Story of Henry Raw-
    linson* by Robert Silverberg (Holt, Rinehart and
    Winston, 1966)

16. THE BIG BOUNCE by Walter S. Tevis
    The Laws of Physics by Milton A. Rothman (Basic
    Books, 1963)
    Understanding Physics by Isaac Asimov (Volume I,
    Allen and Unwin, 1967)

17. NEUTRON STAR by Larry Niven
    The Tides by Edward P. Clancy (McCorquodale,
    1968)
    The Astounding Pulsars, Science Year, 1969, page
    37 (Field Enterprises, 1969)